D0609163

# E.GODZ

**ALSO BY ROBERT ASPRIN**
**The Time Scout series with Linda Evans**
*Time Scout*
*Wagers of Sin*
*Ripping Time*
*The House That Jack Built*

*For King and Country* (with Linda Evans)

*License Invoked* (with Jody Lynn Nye)


**ALSO BY ESTHER FRIESNER**
**Editor, Chicks in Chainmail series**
*Chicks in Chainmail*
*Did You Say Chicks?!*
*Chicks and Chained Males*
*The Chick is in the Mail*

# E.GODZ

## ROBERT ASPRIN
## ESTHER FRIESNER

E.Godz

This is a work of fiction. All the characters and events portrayed in this book are fictional, and any resemblance to real people or incidents is purely coincidental.

Copyright © 2003 by Bill Fawcett & Associates

All rights reserved, including the right to reproduce this book or portions thereof in any form.

A Baen Books Original

Baen Publishing Enterprises
P.O. Box 1403
Riverdale, NY 10471
www.baen.com

ISBN: 0-7434-3605-9

Cover art by Gary Ruddell

First printing, May 2003

Library of Congress Cataloging-in-Publication Data

Asprin, Robert.
    E. Godz / by Robert Asprin & Esther Friesner.
       p. cm.
    ISBN 0-7434-3605-9 (hc)
       1. Family-owned business enterprises—Fiction. 2. Inheritance and succession—Fiction. 3. Brothers and sisters—Fiction. 4. Wizards—Fiction. I. Friesner, Esther M. II. Title.

    PS3551.S6E155 2003
    813'.54—dc21

                                                             2003041677

Distributed by Simon & Schuster
1230 Avenue of the Americas
New York, NY 10020

Production by Windhaven Press, Auburn, NH
Printed in the United States of America

10   9   8   7   6   5   4   3   2   1

# E.GODZ

# ⇒ CHAPTER ONE ⇐

ON A LOVELY SPRING MORNING in the hyperborean wilderness of Poughkeepsie, New York, Edwina Godz decided that she had better die. She did not make that decision lightly, but in exactly the manner that such a (literally) life-altering choice should, ought, and must be made. That is to say, after a nice cup of tea.

It wasn't as if she was about to kill herself. Just die.

She reached the aforementioned decision almost by accident, while pondering the sorry state of her domestic situation and seeking a cure for the combination of headache, tummy trouble, and spiritual upheaval she always experienced every time she thought about her family. Under similar circumstances, most women would head right for the medicine cabinet, but Edwina Godz was a firm believer in the healing power of herbs. Better living through chemistry was all very well and good, yet when it came down to cases that involved the aches,

1

pains, and collywobbles of day-to-day living, you couldn't beat natural remedies with a stick.

Especially if the stick in question was a willow branch. Surprising how few people realized that good old reliable aspirin was derived from willow bark.

Edwina realized this, all right. In fact, she was a walking encyclopedia of herbal therapy lore. It was partly a hobby, partly a survival mechanism. You didn't get to be the head of a multicultural conglomerate like E. Godz, Inc. without making a few very . . . *creative* enemies. When you grew your own medicines, you didn't have to worry about the FDA falling down on the job when it came to safeguarding the purity of whatever remedy the ailment of the moment demanded. Perhaps it was a holdover from her chosen self-reliant life-style all the way back in the dinosaur days of the '60s, but Edwina Godz was willing to live by the wisdom that if you wanted to live life to the fullest, without the pesky interference of the Man, you should definitely grow your own.

No question about it, Edwina had grown her own, and it didn't stop at herbs for all occasions. However, at the moment, herbs were the subject under consideration.

Specifically: which one to take to fix Edwina's present malaise? It wasn't going to be an easy choice, not by a long shot. Peppermint tea was good for an upset tummy, though ginger was better, but valerian was calming and chamomile was the ticket if you were having trouble getting to sleep. Then again, green tea was rich in antioxidants, which were simply unsurpassed when it came to maintaining one's overall health, and ginseng was a marvelous source of all sorts of energy, while gingko biloba—

Edwina sighed and stared at the multicolored array of boxes in the little closet sacred to her tea things. It was built into the wall beside the fireplace in her office, though "office" wasn't quite the right word to describe the room Edwina used for transacting most of her business. "Office" conjured up visions of sleek, sterile twenty-first century furnishings, pricey pieces with surfaces made of wood, stainless steel, brushed aluminum, and name-brand plastics, garnished with a liberal sprinkling of high-tech trappings.

While Edwina did command enough bells-and-whistles machinery to satisfy even the nerdiest of technogeeks, she chose not to show them off. Discretion was her watchword, in both her personal life and her business dealings. It was enough for her to rejoice privately in the fact that she owned a *very special* kind of fax machine (to put it mildly); she didn't need to put it out on a marble pedestal so that visitors might ooh and ah over it in green-eyed envy.

Like so much else in her life—from technotoys to tea—the fax machine was tucked away, out of sight but never out of mind, in one of the many hidey-holes that riddled her office: either behind the dark wood paneling that flanked the fireplace, the *faux*-Oriental papered walls, or within one of the many unique items of furniture so tastefully taking up floor space. Let others more insecure than she flaunt their desktops, laptops, and palmtops: Edwina Godz's office looked like nothing more than the plush, snug, and inviting parlor of a Victorian mansion.

Which it was.

None of which self-congratulatory knowledge did a thing to help her in the matter of deciding which herbal tea to take right now.

If she brewed herself a cup of comfort incorporating every last one of the herbal essences she needed to cure everything that ailed her, there wouldn't be any room left in the teapot for the boiling water. She shrugged and closed the tea-closet door, and instead ambled over to the other side of the fireplace where the liquor cabinet reposed. Gingko biloba was all very well and good when you were confronting the ordinary headaches of day-to-day life, but when it came to dealing with one's children there was no substitute for single malt scotch.

Grain was an herb, when you got down to it, and so was malt, she told herself. As for the peat that was involved somewhere in the manufacturing process of a decent single malt, well, you couldn't get any more back-to-Mother-Earth than that unless you got down on all fours and sucked topsoil. Edwina was still rationalizing in top form as she downed the first shot and poured the second, all while standing in front of the liquor cabinet with a grim expression on her face that would have stopped a charging wildebeest.

Not that there were many wildebeest running loose in the greater Poughkeepsie area (unless you went by appearances alone, in which case some of the individuals to be found roaming the vast bureaucratic savannahs of nearby Vassar College might be considered as—ah, but that was strictly a matter of personal opinion). Edwina Godz's palatial home stood in splendid semi-isolation on the banks of the mighty Hudson River with a breathtaking view of some of the loveliest countryside on the whole Eastern Seaboard. Her back yard was refuge to vast nations of squirrels, chipmunks, raccoons, opossums, deer, and the occasional fox. A fabulous assortment of birds also called Edwina's estate home, but the only winged wildlife that made it through the great oak and Tiffany-stained-glass front doors was the dusty bottle of Wild Turkey shoved into the rear right corner of the liquor cabinet.

Edwina polished off the second shot and considered taking a third. She was not a hard drinker, as a rule, but there were some situations that drove her to it and kept the motor running.

"Bah," said Edwina, gazing at the empty shot glass in her hand. "Who's to be master here?" She knew the answer to that one well enough, and slammed down the glass to prove it. Shoulders squared, she closed the liquor cabinet, returned to the tea things, and brewed herself up a steaming pot full of the ginseng-ginger blend. The present situation had given her a bellyache that screamed for ginger, but it would take the energizing powers of ginseng to give her the mental and physical oomph she'd need to deal with the cause of it all.

The causes. Plural.

Edwina settled herself on the sofa, sipped her tea, and stared stonily at the framed family photograph on the small marble-topped table at her elbow. Of all her attempts to evoke the American ideal of domestic harmony, this photo was the best and only thing she had to show for her efforts.

"Smiling," she said, regarding the three faces in the picture. "We were all smiling. I know that *I* meant it, but how on earth did I ever manage to persuade Peez and Dov to do it? Was it bribery or just good old-fashioned threats?"

She set down her teacup and picked up the framed photo for closer study. It had been taken some ten years ago, maybe a little farther back than that, certainly long before Dov and Peez had left the nest to pursue their own fortunes.

"And mine," Edwina muttered.

Her children had gone through the usual period of adolescent rebellion, loudly declaring that no one understood them and that they would show Edwina how things ought to be done as soon as they were out of the house and running their lives their way. They didn't need her to tell them what to do, or to do anything for them. By heaven, they didn't need *anybody*, if it came to that! Just let them hit the legal age of adulthood and then, look out! They'd make their own marks in the world, and they'd do it widescreen, big time, and Broadway style.

So what had happened when that day of dear-won independence finally dawned?

They went to work in the family business. Dov manned the Miami office, Peez held down the fort in New York City, and both of them still looked to Edwina to handle all the really big management decisions for E. Godz, Inc. Not since they'd nursed at Edwina's ample bosom had her two children been so dependent on her for their daily sustenance. She called the shots and they hastened to implement every word of her orders. They trusted her business sense implicitly, and so far, that trust had paid off for all concerned. Edwina couldn't have asked for more attentive corporate lieutenants, to say nothing of more biddable children, even if solely in this aspect of their lives together. It was all so very sweet, so drenched in the heady musk of family traditions, solidarity, and mutual support that they might as well have belonged to the Mafia.

"Ha!" Edwina remarked to the air. "At least a Mafia family knows enough to fight its *real* enemies."

As embittered as she felt at the moment, she couldn't help but smile when she regarded the image of herself in the family photo. It was, of course, the likeness of a much younger Edwina Godz, made back in the days before all of her hair had gone from a rich auburn to a sparkling silver-gray. There were plenty of white streaks lacing the younger Edwina's tawny mane, but the effect was both charming and attractive.

"You had it then, woman, and you've still got it now," Edwina told herself complacently. She looked up from the photo in her hands to a trio of larger pictures hanging on the wall just above the parlor fireplace. The one in the middle was the largest of the three: an old-fashioned, sepia-toned example of turn-of-the-century photographic art. A walrus-mustached man in what was clearly a very uncomfortable suit stood behind a seated lady with her hair done up in the fashion popularized by the Gibson Girl. She wore a high-necked lace dress with a small cameo brooch at her throat and she held a large bouquet of orange blossoms on her lap. She wasn't a beauty, by common cultural standards, but despite her wedding-day air of socially acceptable unease she still managed to project confidence and self-possession that was somehow . . . sexy.

There was an unmistakable resemblance between Edwina and the woman in the sepia picture. "I'll bet if *you'd* been the one who came through Ellis Island instead of *him*"—her eyes flicked to the walrus-moustached gentleman in the photo—"you'd never have stood for it when the Customs officer got your name wrong. What's so hard about spelling 'Goetz' anyway? You'd have made him change it back in short order, and no arguments about it! On the other hand, I suppose I ought to be grateful that Grandpapa was such a don't-make-waves wuss about how the Customs man changed his family name. Having a name like 'Godz' is *so* much more effective in this business, from a marketing standpoint."

Edwina gazed fondly at this relic of her ancestors' wedding day. Marriage was such a quaint, dated concept. Still, some of the attendant trappings were alluring—on a purely aesthetic level—even for a product of the '60s like Edwina, who had come of age in the full flowering of the Sexual Revolution. She then let her eyes drift from the big photo above the mantelpiece to the pair of smaller ones flanking it. They too were framed with gold-leafed wood, but color photos and streamlined, minimalist frames alike spoke of more modern provenance than the sepia centerpiece.

The resemblance between Edwina and the people in the two companion photos was even more pronounced. The man in the photo on the left had supplied most of the genetic input evident in Edwina's appearance, while the woman in the photo on the right had provided a good deal of much-appreciated editorial tweaking. Thus the keen, gung-ho go-getter looks of Edwina's father were nicely softened by her mother's influence, leaving their daughter looking less like a hawk and more like a lamb. For this, Edwina was thankful.

"Not that I'm not deeply grateful to you, Daddy," Edwina told the photo. "After all, looks aren't everything. Especially at the bank."

*You know it, kiddo,* the photograph seemed to reply, and Edwina liked to believe she could see the long-gone yet still beloved twinkle in her father's eye when he said that.

It was the same sort of twinkle that had lit up his face when he was about to make a fresh "kill" in his

ongoing role as a highly paid, extremely effective corporate lawyer. Litigation was his lifeblood, but investment savvy was his vocation. He took his income and
sank it into a portfolio that fairly gushed profits. His
dream had been to make enough money to buy one
of the smaller Hawaiian islands and set himself up as
an independently wealthy writer of science fiction, his
first true love.

Alas, the dream was not to be. (And a good thing,
too. Edwina had found some of her father's old note-
books with ideas for his Great American Sci-Fi novel.
Nothing good could come of a book that began "Cap-
tain Studs Poleworthy arose from the bed of the sated
Bazinga slave-girl, dabbed lime-flavored eroto-gel from
his magnificent chest, and said, 'Sorry to come and go,
my dear, but the starfields beckon.'") While visiting
Hawaii to scope out potential real estate buys, both of
Edwina's parents had died in a tragic accident. They
were touring a poi factory when one of the holding
tanks broke and they drowned in the glutinous flood.

Their untimely deaths came just at the dawning of
the Age of Aquarius, when their daughter was first
beginning to scent the cultural changes in the air, to
hear the distant beat of a different drum, and to
inhale . . . her destiny. An only child with no living close
relatives, Edwina had mourned the loss of her small
family—for family had always been important to her—
but then had dealt with her grief in what seemed to
be the best available manner, at the time. Having been
rendered an orphan, she performed a series of reverse
adoptions, for want of a better way to describe matters. Independently wealthy, thanks to her late father's
savvy for high finance, and just plain independent on
account of the Great Poi Flood of '64, Edwina Godz

set out to replace the family she had lost by making herself a part of every ragtag tribe, clan, commune or gaggle of rock band groupies that took her fancy.

Now, settled into comfortable middle age, a rich and respectable businesswoman, Edwina looked back over her wild, freewheeling youth without so much as a blush. And why should she be embarrassed to recall her counterculture odyssey and the many lovers she'd enjoyed en route to Enlightenment? She'd hurt no one by her amorous escapades, and even in the pre-AIDS era she'd had the foresight to take certain precautions that had preserved the robust health of her girlhood from pesky STDs.

Besides, it was thanks to the Summer of Love—which had somehow slipped into the Autumn of Eros and the Winter of Whoopee—that Edwina had obtained not only her darling children, but a method of earning more money than her dear, departed Daddy had ever imagined, even had he lived long enough to invest in Microsoft.

Her darling children . . .

Edwina turned her back on the family portraits above the fireplace and returned her full attention to the framed photograph in her hands. She shook her head sadly. The smiles frozen in the instant of a camera's shutter click meant nothing. A photograph was a moment's illusion artificially preserved. The reality of the situation concerning her precious offspring had nothing at all to do with smiles.

"Why can't the two of you just get along?" she inquired peevishly of the glossy faces. "I'm not asking you to adore one another. I'm not even asking you to remember each other's birthdays. All I want is just one itsy-bitsy little indication that you can work *together*.

And I don't mean simultaneously plotting each other's professional destruction. Good gods, I *hope* it would be limited to professional destruction only, but the way you two have been going for each other's throats lately, who knows? A little cooperation for your mutual benefit, to say nothing of cooperation for the benefit of the company: Is that so much to ask?"

Something behind one of the parlor walls went *ding!* This was followed by the sound rather like a passel of cats scratching madly in their litterboxes, but when Edwina went to the wall whence issued these noises and touched the spring catch that opened the desired panel, she revealed their true source, a flock of fountain pens rapidly scribbling away as if guided by unseen hands. There were twelve of them in all, though only two of them were working at the moment, transcribing a telephone conversation between Dov Godz and his older sister, Peez. Each one of the dozen pens was linked by suitably arcane spells to a piece of office equipment—be it telephone, fax machine, or any item of computer wizardry from desktop to day planner—in either the Miami or New York City offices of E. Godz, Inc.

Which was to say that the items themselves—all gifts from Edwina to her offspring—were enspelled eavesdropping devices, clandestine portals that permitted her to keep constant, magically enabled tabs on the children's every move.

Wouldn't it be silly to own and run America's only family-operated clearinghouse for magical power and not put some of that power to work spying on your kids?

For that, in a nutshell, was E. Godz, Inc.'s stock-in-trade: magic.

It was not a career path that Edwina had consciously

sought out, at first. Rather, it was a by-product of all those years back in the '60s that she'd spent crisscrossing the country in flower-splashed vans, salvaged schoolbuses, or, in a pinch, VW Bugs painted to look like Peter Max's worst nightmare. Like so many of her hippie brethren, Edwina discovered that life on the nation's back roads and byways led a person to consider whether there were also spiritual roads-less-traveled that might bear exploration. The faith of her forebears wasn't a good fit for her new lifestyle: Peyote and Presbyterians didn't mix worth a damn.

She was not alone in this quest for new ways of getting in touch with her mystic side. The '60s were famous for having driven hordes of young people out of their families' churches and into the arms of the "earthy" religions out there. Chanting mantras was in, catechisms were out, and the incessant beating of drums was much more desirable than any silly old Bach mass for organ. It was part of the whole tribal-is-cooler/ethnic-is-in package. And in some cases it was a pretty good excuse to get high, in the name of seeking the One True Path, though heaven help anyone uncool enough to mention that the end-justifies-the-means trip had its roots in the writings of Saint Jerome.

It was here that Edwina's One True Path took a sharp right off the spiritual interstate and left the rest of her contemporaries far behind. Whereas they only nosed around the borderline belief systems, she jumped in feet first, with eyes and mind wide open. While her tribemates picked up this or that back-to-the-Earth faith, only to put it down again when the glitter of the new toy wore off (or when it failed to piss off their parents sufficiently), Edwina actually spent serious study time on every non-suburbia-standard religion she encountered.

And when Moonbeam Suntoucher (née Greta Bradford-Smythe) announced that she was a shaman because she had bought a genuine dreamcatcher and a boatload of dried sage, or when Frodo Freelove (Mr. and Mrs. Kaplan's firstborn son, Sammy) insisted he'd achieved *samsara* because the check he'd written out to the Happy Times Ashram and Salad Bar had finally cleared, Edwina calmly went about the business of improving her grasp on the true powers that underlie the more Gaia-centric beliefs, if you sought them out with enough application and sincerity.

Either that or she just got lucky. But whatever the case, the fact remained that Edwina Godz came away from all of her spiritual quests with a command of magic and something more: the realization that the people who were following the many separate paths of some *really* Old Time Religions didn't have the business sense of bread mold.

It was sad. There they sat—be they tribe or coven or council or conglomeration of congregants—able to raise the might of the great earth-powers but helpless to do more than take it in the unmentionables every year when Income Tax Day rolled around.

Edwina had fixed all that. Edwina was good at fixing things. Perhaps it was her personal muse at work, perhaps it was thanks to her father's legal-eagle spirit, raised during one of the many assorted ceremonies in which Edwina had participated over the years, perhaps it was simply out-of-the-blue inspiration, but whatever the source, the result was the same: Edwina Godz saw a way to help both the old earth-religion followers, by whatever name they chose to call themselves, and herself. Retracing the steps of her spiritual journey, she approached them one by one with her modest proposal:

that she show them the ropes of fund-raising, the benefits of obtaining tax-exempt status as registered, organized religions, and the basics of bookkeeping to safeguard their continued economic health.

Could she help it if the best, most efficient way for them to do this was by her founding her own corporation and taking all of them on board as her subsidiaries? Was she to blame if they were so grateful to lay hold of the advantages she offered that they never uttered so much as a whisper of objection when she collected a nice, fat piece of the action in exchange for services rendered? Did anyone protest when she used the magic powers she'd mastered during her years of Searching to help run E. Godz, Inc. so smoothly?

Of course not. There was more than enough butter to go around so that everyone's bread was fully covered. The boat wasn't rocking, nothing was broken, and all was roses.

Except for a couple of thorns named Dov and Peez. In a perfect world, Edwina's children would have appreciated the goldmine that their mother had created for them. Instead they seemed to spend their free time trying to give each other the shaft. Didn't they understand that if their bickering over personal differences got out of control it could adversely affect E. Godz, Inc.? And *then* where would they be? Were they even fit for any other sort of employment?

That annoying *ding!* sounded again, signaling the end of a transmission. The pair of pens softly laid themselves down, their jobs done. Still clutching the family photo in her left hand, Edwina reached in with her right to remove the sheets bearing the transcribed conversation. It was a miracle that the papers didn't spontaneously combust in her hand, given the level of volcanic vituperation zipping back and forth between the siblings. As with every intercepted communication Edwina had ever seen, Dov and Peez each managed to let the other know that:

A.  He/she did not *like* her/him.
B.  He/she did not *trust* her/him.
C.  He/she knew how to run the family business far better than her/him.
D.  If there were any justice in the universe, the day would come when he/she would have the power to push her/him the hell out of her/his cushy, undeserved position and then all would be right with the world.
E.  So there.

"I blame myself," Edwina muttered, crumpling up the papers and tossing them away. The parlor wastebasket sprouted cherub wings and zoomed in to catch the discarded transcriptions before they hit the floor, then fluttered back to its place, only pausing long enough to trade high-fives with the fireplace-ash broom. "A little. On second thought, no, I don't blame myself at all. Why should I? I always did what was best for them. I sent them away from home as soon as I could manage it, legally and financially. So I'm the Great Earth Manager, not the Great Earth Mother: So sue me. Which is worse, raising your kids yourself, come hell or high water, when you darn well know that it's not your scene, or sending them to the finest daycare centers and boarding schools and colleges that money can buy? Money which, might I add, we never would have had in the first place if I'd been tied down wiping runny noses and kissing boo-boos and baking cupcakes instead of being free to build up the business. I think I did damn well by those kids. If it's anyone's fault that they can't get along, it's theirs."

She put the family photo back on the table and made herself a fresh pot of tea, but despite a brew containing enough St. John's wort to turn Attila the Hun into a tree sloth, Edwina found herself unable to release her troubles and go with the cosmic flow.

The cosmic flow didn't have children.

She made an impatient sound with her tongue and sat up straight on the sofa. She had reached a decision:

"It may not be my problem if Dov and Peez want to wear each other's guts for garters, but if I don't want E. Godz, Inc. to go down the corporate tubes, I'd better be the one to fix it," she said. "The question is—how?"

She settled back among the cushions, took a deep draught of tea, and closed her eyes while she brought all the powers of a mind Machiavelli might envy to bear upon the present sticky wicket. Music from an unseen source wafted gently through the parlor, a medley of New Age hits that she had conjured up to help her think. At last, when it seemed as though she would burst out of her house stark naked and foaming at the mouth if she had to listen to one more meandering flute trill, Edwina's eyes popped open, the light of inspiration shining bright within.

"Of course," she said aloud. "It's the perfect plan: simple, elegant and practical. Excellent." A sharklike grin—her father's corporate lawyer heritage at work— spread itself across her face as she told the air: "Take a letter."

Three more ensorcelled fountain pens floated up from the green baize-lined leather box atop Edwina's desk. The left-hand top drawer opened of its own accord and three sheets of blank paper like three white miniature flying carpets arose to take their places beneath the waiting nibs. The top right-hand drawer opened and two envelopes slithered out to await developments. A ghostly file cabinet hovered on the edge of materialization, pending the completion of the letter under composition. Ever the consummate businesswoman, Edwina never failed to make a copy of all correspondence for her personal records.

"My dearest children," she began her dictation, to the accompanying scritch-scritch-scratch of the three animate pens. "It is with a heavy heart that I write this from what will be, in the inevitable course of time, my death bed. There is no cure for the ailment that has so suddenly come over me and my doctor tells me that I have, at most, a few months more to live. I admit that I've been toying with the idea of retirement for a while now, but this news has forced my hand.

"Thus I find myself compelled to make a decision which I have been putting off, namely determining who shall succeed me as the new chairperson of E. Godz, Inc. My deepest desire has always been to be able to turn over cooperative control of the business to the two of you, but I realize that this is impossible. You two couldn't find *cooperative* in the dictionary even if I cast a spell on it and had it bite you in the butt. How to describe your relationship? Cats versus dogs? Hatfields versus McCoys? Pepsi versus Coke? Trekkies versus Trekkers?

"If I gave you joint control of E. Godz, Inc., it would only be a matter of time before your bickering, sniping, and outright attacks on one another distracted you from the business of running my company well and profitably. I didn't work so hard all these years to have my creation torn to shreds after I'm gone.

"Therefore I am resolved: Only one of you will inherit control of the company, together with the bulk of my estate. Which one? I'm still thinking it over. To be frank, though I love you both for the totality of your person-hoods and embrace your unique younesses with the wholehearted, nonjudgmental attitude of our Mother Earth, as far as your business smarts go, neither of you has impressed me worth a dog fart. As for leadership ability, if either one of you encountered a horde of midair lemmings who had already gone headfirst over the cliff's edge, I sincerely doubt whether you could persuade them to complete the plunge.

"I may be telling you something you already know. Perhaps you have been working for E. Godz, Inc. solely out of family loyalty rather than real vocation. If you've spent the last few years just pushing papers without a thought for the people behind them, this is your chance to bow out gracefully and seek your true world-path. If one or the other of you wishes to withdraw from the running, voluntarily, do so, and do it quickly. Lift the burden of decision from my shoulders.

"Please.

"Love, Edwina."

The three pens capped themselves and retreated to their box. One copy of the letter flew across the room to pop itself neatly into the phantom file cabinet, which promptly vanished. Only the copies of the letter intended for Dov and Peez remained, along with the two envelopes.

"On second thought," Edwina told the loitering sta-tionery, "I believe I'll fax this." The superfluous copy of the letter let out a low moan of despair and tore itself into a shower of still-grieving confetti. The two envelopes slunk back into their desk drawer, mutter-ing darkly through their gummed flaps.

As the lone page fluttered away to run itself through the fax machine, Edwina headed upstairs. If she was going to pose as the victim of a mysterious-but-fatal illness, it wouldn't hurt to get into the spirit of things by taking to her bed. In fact, it might be more than just a melodramatic necessity. Dov and Peez weren't exactly newly hatched chicks when it came to matters of magic. Though Edwina had spied on them diligently ever since they'd taken up their posts in the New York and Miami offices, she knew that even the tightest espionage net could still let a fishie or two slip through the meshes.

For all she knew, someday *they* might try spying on *her*. The nerve!

Edwina's bedroom was as luxuriously Victorian as the rest of the mansion, its centerpiece being a four-poster with creamy white brocade curtains, an avalanche of plump pillows, and mattresses soft yet firm enough to demand a 911 call to the Paradox Police. A big-screen TV with built-in DVD player was hidden in the armoire opposite, with two large, well-stocked bookcases flanking it. A satisfactory selection of drinks and snack foods were stowed in the refrigerator disguised as a hope chest that stood at the foot of Edwina's bed. If she required anything more, she had only to invoke her powers and it would be brought to her by invisible hands.

"Not a bad way to wait for Death," Edwina said, changing into an Egyptian cotton nightgown. "A nice, *long* wait, but the kids won't need to know that."

She grabbed a pleasantly tawdry romance novel to keep her company, slipped under the bedcovers, and settled comfortably back among her pillows to await developments.

# ⇒ CHAPTER TWO ⇐

THE PHONE IN PEEZ GODZ'S OFFICE rang while she was in the middle of giving dictation. Her secretary, the formidable Wilma Pilut, answered it with the warm, welcoming tones of a testy Doberman. One bark, two snarls, and a protracted growl into the mouthpiece later, she turned to her employer and reported: "Chicago on line two, Ms. Godz."

"Not those idiots again," Peez grumbled, finagling a particularly tricky paper clip into the chain she'd been working on since eight that morning. She looked up from her mindless, endless task and gave the secretary her most engaging smile. "Tell them I'm not in, please, Wilma."

Wilma refused to be engaged. "That would be a lie, Ms. Godz," she said brusquely. "The Great Mother doesn't like lies."

"The Great Mother doesn't need to know," Peez

replied, doing her best not to sound like she was wheedling. "Besides, it's not like *you're* lying; you're just
relaying a teensy, weensy, miniscule li'l ol' fib of *mine*."

Wilma shook her blocky head ponderously. "The Great
Mother would know. And She wouldn't like it." When
Edwina first had set up Peez in the New York City office
of E. Godz, Inc., she'd provided her daughter with everything needed to run the business smoothly, including
this short, stocky, monolithic secretary. There was something so very, well, not earth-*y* so much as earth-*en*
about the woman that Peez had spent most of her first
week at work on the phone to her mother making
Edwina swear again and again, on a stack of talismans,
that Wilma was not actually a golem in disguise.

Now Peez stared at the impassive face of her recal-
citrant secretary and gritted her teeth in silent frustra-
tion. *Too bad she's* not *a golem*, she thought. *At least
a golem obeys orders.* With the sigh of the much put-
upon she replied, "If it weren't for *me*, Wilma dear,
you'd never have discovered the Way of the Great
Mother and you'd still be doing those dreary covered-
dish suppers at that former church of yours. I'm sure
that if you do me this one itsy-bitsy favor, She'll forgive you. She's good that way."

"She's not *good*, She's just *Great*." Again that slow,
weighty, side-to-side turning of Wilma's almost cubic
head on her nigh-nonexistent neck. Peez found herself
marveling at the fact that her secretary's terra-cotta-
colored hair shed real dandruff and not flakes of dried
clay. "You can't *guarantee* that She'll forgive me," Wilma
intoned in a voice so husky it spoke of a three-box-
a-day cigar habit begun some time in kindergarten. "She
might even get angry. You know what happens when
the Great Mother gets angry."

Peez sighed again, bringing this one all the way up from the soles of her plain black ballet flats. Of *course* she knew what happened when the Great Mother got angry. So did Wilma, having just achieved the rank of Junior High Priestess of the Sacred Grove, *cum laude.* However, Peez reasoned, if she took the time to enumerate the various afflictions that could ensue from the Great Mother's anger, perhaps her off-the-cuff filibustering would take up so much time that those pests on the line from Chicago would get tired of waiting for her to answer and would hang up.

One by one she uncurled her fingers, reckoning up the sum of divine displeasure: "Floods, droughts, crop blights, cattle murrain, slowed download times, failure of the cacao crop, plagues of feral hamsters, skyrocketing movie ticket prices—"

She could have gone on for a much longer time, ticking off all the ways that the Great Mother had on tap to let mortals know that they'd pissed Her off, but Wilma cut in with the last item on the list.

"—zits," Wilma said in a no-nonsense tone of voice that let Peez know that further disaster-listing was unnecessary and would be punished to the full extent of a secretary's considerable powers. "I know about all the rest and I can handle them just fine, but I'm *not* going to risk zits. Not this weekend. I've got a date."

"*You've* . . . got . . . a . . . *what?*"

A little while later, after she had sent Wilma off to do some filing and had dealt with the call from Chicago (more whining about the whole human sacrifice squabble, which somehow had managed to slip out of committee and turn into a full-blown flamewar on the Net), Peez leaned back in her butter-soft leather desk chair with built-in footrest, CD player, aromatherapy dispenser, heating and massage capabilities, and wished she were dead.

"Brilliant," she told the ceiling. "I am just *so* brilliant. If I were any more brilliant, I'd be a black hole. What was I *thinking?*"

"You were thinking that Wilma Pilut, the girl voted Most Likely to Date Mount Rushmore, has romantic plans for this weekend and you don't."

The voice that responded to Peez's self-deprecating declaration was a little too thin and a lot too sweet to be anything human. The sweetness, however, was all inherent in the false-as-a-padded-bra tone of voice, not in the cold, cruel words it spoke.

"*Then* you thought that Wilma didn't notice how shocked you were to hear about her upcoming date. But you know that she *did* notice; she's only *built* thick." The voice skirled up into a trill of nerve-grating giggles. It was coming from one of Peez's desk drawers and it showed no signs of shutting up any time soon. "Then you thought you covered *that* little faux pas by pretending that you'd misheard her, that you thought she'd said she had some *bait* this weekend, so you asked her where she was going fishing. Oh, *that* was a brave effort! Remember how you never got cast in any of your school plays? Ever wonder why? Well, if you can't figure it out after having given *that* lousy performance for an audience of one very ticked-off secretary, maybe *you're* the one with clay between your ears! And *then* do you want to know what you thought?" The desk drawer rattled loudly. Something inside was trying to get out. "Do you? Do you? Huh, huh, do you?"

Peez closed her eyes and tucked a limp strand of her long, dull black hair behind one ear. "Tell me," she said wearily.

"Take me out first," said the thing in the desk.

"Why should I? I know you can let yourself out any time you like. And I also know what I was thinking, and just how stupid it was, so I don't really need you to tell me that."

"But it's not the same unless you hear it from *me*, is it Peezie-pie?" The drawer shook with a new attack of those high-pitched giggles.

"No." This time Peez's sigh seemed to come from somewhere beneath the continental shelf. "It's not the same when I don't hear it from you, Teddy Tumtum." She bent over and slid the desk drawer open.

The little stuffed bear grinned up at her, malice shining in his green glass eyes.

"And *then*," he said, picking up where he'd left off. "And then, last but not least, you thought: 'Why me?' Or should I say: 'Why *not* me?' I couldn't say for sure. It all depends on whether you were pondering the fact that you are so very, very, *very* much alone, the undisputed queen of the Dateless Wonders, Wallflowers, and Social Rejects Chowder and Marching Society, or whether you were instead dealing with the fact that even Pavement-Puss Pilut has got herself a date this weekend while all *you've* got is *me*!" The unholy bear ended his speech on a nasty note of triumph, then broke into a fresh batch of giggles.

Peez's hand shot out and seized the demonic toy by his pink-beribboned neck. "Give me one good reason not to run you through the shredder," she snarled.

"I'll go you one better and give you two," the bear replied, not even mildly flustered by her threat. "One: Because the shredder only does paper. Two: Because if you *could* shred me, who would you have left to talk to?" The bear's black-stitched mouth squirmed into a horrible parody of a sincerely affectionate smile. "I is your ittoo Teddy Tumtum an' I jes' *wuuvs* oo all to pieces, Peezie-pie."

"Well, I don't love *you*," Peez snapped, shaking the toy roughly.

"No fooling. Wow. Big surprise." The bear's smile was a sneer once more, and it looked much more credible. "You might not love me, lady, but you do *need* me. A lot. Any dumb floppy-eared beagle puppy with four paws too big for his body can be loved. I'll settle for being indispensable."

"I don't need you," Peez shot back. "I've got plenty of—"

"—friends?" the bear finished for her. Then it laughed in her face—not giggles, full-out guffaws of the purest scorn. "Yeah, sure, all of those wonderful, close friends you made back in your hometown of— What was it called again? Oh right, I remember now: *Loserville*. Brother, when you were in high school, you couldn't even get the chess club nerds to hang out with you!"

Peez didn't deny Teddy Tumtum's words. She couldn't. She'd had the uncanny little bear for as long as she could remember, a present from her mother. What Edwina hadn't bothered to mention to her firstborn when she'd given her the bear was that there was something . . . *special* about Teddy Tumtum. She'd had only the best intentions, of course—didn't she always?—when she'd enspelled the toy so that it would be more than a simple, inanimate source of comfort for her lonely daughter. Using the powers she'd acquired in her spiritual scavenger-hunt past, Edwina Godz had attached Teddy Tumtum to Peez by an unbreakable (albeit glacially slow-acting) homing hex, plus she'd empowered it with more than an ordinary teddy bear's ability merely to listen to a little girl's private wishes, dreams, and sorrows.

Edwina thought she'd done a bang-up job of guaranteeing that her daughter need never feel truly alone, but as far as Peez was concerned, Edwina's good intentions had backfired beyond belief. Ordinary teddy bears might not be more than glorified throw pillows, but at least they could *keep* all the secrets that their owners poured into their raggedy fake fur ears. Teddy Tumtum not only listened to Peez's secrets, he remembered them and could blab them to the whole wide world. Too bad Edwina hadn't stuck a discretion spell on the bear while she was at it.

"Never mind what my social life was like in high school," she told him, making a weak stab at rebuttal. "That was then." She set Teddy Tumtum down on her desk blotter.

"And this is now? Oooh, *deep*," said the bear. "I've got news for you, sugarpants, this *is* now and as far as your social life goes, *now* sucks even worse than *then*. At least in the olden days you had a few playmates who'd actually talk to you after class or even come by the house during school breaks sometimes. So what if they only did it 'cause their parents were trying to kiss up to your mother and her money?"

"My mother . . ." In Peez's mouth the word did not reek of apple pie and chocolate chip cookies, but of ice and gall. "Maybe if my dear *mother* hadn't been so damn wrapped up in establishing the corporation, I could've had the chance to have a *real* childhood and make some *real* friends. But no. Instead I was dragged along like an oversized piece of baggage while she spent all those years knocking around the country with those dumb hippie pals of hers. And then, as soon as she could, she dumped me on one nanny after another. Where did she find them? Is there an employment agency that specializes in placing the poster children for substance abuse?"

"Tsk. So ungrateful," Teddy Tumtum said, enjoying himself. "Your dear mamma got rid of the nannies as soon as she saw that they weren't working out and found a much better way to guarantee you'd get a good education. Think of all the money she spent on sending you to the best day-care centers, the top prep schools! Nothing was too good for her little Peez."

"Nothing," Peez repeated sourly. "That's the word for what she gave me. I had no roots, no stability, no fixed abode, no permanent mailing address, no one to care what I did with myself as long as it wasn't fatal or didn't impact the precious family business. The one thing I *did* have was a name that was so bloody ridiculous that the regular school bullies didn't even bother making fun of it. Too much like shooting fish in a barrel. But there were plenty of juvenile improv sadists who weren't above dragging me into the girls' room, dunking my head in the toilet, flushing, and telling me to visualize whirled Peez. Good gods, it's just a wonder that I turned out as well as I did."

The teddy bear snickered spitefully. "Yeah, those were the days. Remember back in the pre-nanny years, just before Edwina decided she'd better get you dear little tykes off the road and settle down? Remember that town you stayed in for, what, four whole months where your teacher told everyone to draw a picture of a house and you drew a Volkswagon van? Boy, did the kids in your class laugh at you or what?"

Peez's pale, heart-shaped face turned bright red all

the way up to her hairline. "At least it was better than what happened in the town we moved to after that."

"Right, I remember," said Teddy Tumtum, who remembered much too much of everything. "That was where you scored so badly on the standardized tests for your age group that they stuck you back a year and you had to be in the same class with your little brother."

"That was also the place where the teacher asked our class to draw a picture of our daddies for Father's Day." Peez was bitter. It had all happened a long time ago, but the sound of her classmates' rude laughter and ruder name-calling was still loud and clear in her ears. It didn't take a rocket scientist to tell that the drawings produced by Peez and her brother were of two radically different men.

"It wasn't so bad when the other kids just called us stupid," Peez said. "But then the teacher stepped in and tried to make things aaall better. Better! She went into that big song-and-dance about how some brothers and sisters from the same family can have different daddies."

"Sometimes two at once," Teddy Tumtum put in.

"This was a *little* too close to the Pleistocene for a public school teacher to talk about alternative life-style families," Peez reminded him. "Hell, she didn't even want to open the whole widowhood can o' worms in front of the kiddies—death was a big no-no—but she *did* mention divorce. That was when my genius baby brother had to go and ask, 'What's a divorce?' "

Teddy Tumtum nodded wisely. "And she told him it's what happened when mommies and daddies decided they didn't want to be married to each other any more. And that was when he told her that *your* mommy would never get a divorce because *your* mommy never bothered to get married to either one of your daddies in the first place."

Peez blushed a deeper shade of scarlet. Even after so many years, she was still sensitive about her mother's Olympic-grade amorous shenanigans. When most children learn where babies come from, the first thing they do with the information is to search for exceptions, escape clauses, loopholes, *anything* to keep them from thinking of their parents doing something like *that*. Gross. Peez not only had to contend with the image of her mother "doing it," but also with the inescapable knowledge that Edwina had "done it" with enough men to stock a small road company of *The Mikado*, chorus included.

All of which probably accounted for Peez's own scrupulously preserved virginity, although her official excuse was that staying a virgin meant she could have direct access to and participation in some of the more esoteric rites for the pickier sorts of gods. And if some of her clients chose to believe that she stood ready to offer herself up as an emergency virgin sacrifice— Do Not Use Except in Case of Imminent Volcano Eruption—there was no harm in letting them do so. Not while she also had access to a wide variety of speedy getaway vehicles, anyhow. Peez was all for building customer confidence, but she wasn't about to die for it.

Teddy Tumtum made a clucking sound of commiseration. It was about as authentic as a beauty queen's I-want-to-work-with-orphans-and-small-animals speech. "Po' ittoo Peezie-pie," he said sadly. "No friends then, nothing but business acquaintances now. No one you can really talk to but me."

"You are *not* the only one I can talk to," Peez insisted

angrily, rising partway out of her chair. "My life is made up of more than just business acquaintances."

"Of course it is." Teddy Tumtum couldn't blink, lacking eyelids, but he still managed to project the effect of a Southern belle coyly batting her lashes at some helpless beau. "There's always your family."

Peez sat down. Hard. Her mouth became a hyphen. Teddy Tumtum smiled. "And how *is* your beloved baby brother these days?" he asked, letting syrup drip over every syllable.

"How would I know?" Peez shot back. "The only time I see him or hear from him is when we need to discuss the business. And that's the only time I *want* to see or hear from him, the self-satisfied, smug, egotistical, unbearable little jerk!"

The bear looked bemused. " 'Little'? The last time I saw him, he was taller than you by a head."

"An empty head," Peez gritted. "Not that it's doing him any harm in the Miami office. He could have a double lobotomy and still be sharper than half the population of South Beach." In spite of herself, Peez felt tears rising in her pale blue eyes. Furiously she tried to fight them back by shouting, "It's not *fair*, Teddy Tumtum!"

"What's not fair? The fact that Dov's tall and blond, tanned and toned, charming and handsome? The fact that he's only got to whistle once if he wants to find himself covered with starlets and supermodels? The fact that from the time you were both kids he always managed to have friends—*real* friends—and you couldn't do it to save your life?"

"The hell with all of that." Peez spat. "What fries *my* tail is the way that bubble-brained son of a bitch wouldn't recognize what real work looks like if it spat in his silly face, but Edwina *still* put him in charge of the Miami office!"

"Is that all you care about?" Teddy Tumtum gave Peez a curious look. "The business?"

"Why not?" she replied. "The business is all I've got to care about. You just proved that yourself. And it's the only reason anyone on earth ever cares about me. A kiss is just a kiss, but if all I can hope to get are kiss-ups, I'm willing to settle for that."

The bear pretended to wipe a tear from its green glass eye. "Ah, my child, you have learned your lesson well. You can leave the monastery. Do not pass Go, do not collect two hundred dollars, do not let the doorknob hit you in the butt on your way out."

"Would you just shut the hell—?"

Peez's exasperation was cut short by the hum of the fax machine in the corner. The silver amulet affixed to the front of the machine added its two cents to the interruption by announcing: "Personal message from Edwina Godz for your immediate attention and reply, Ms. Peez."

Peez cast a jaded glance at the fax machine. "Isn't that just like Mother? Probably just some stupid little nitpicky reminder for me to update the client database when she knows that I do it automatically twice a week without being told. I'll bet she never bothers Dov with this kind of garbage, even though he's the one who *could* use the nudge. Well, this time she can wait." She sounded as sulky as a two-year-old on a naptime strike.

"No, she can't," said the fax machine amulet.

Peez leveled a warning finger at it. "Don't you start with me. I'm not in the mood."

"Who's starting?" the amulet argued. "I'm just doing my job."

"By enforcing my mother's bidding? By making sure I jump high enough when she says 'frog'?"

"By making sure you don't get turned into one," the amulet snapped back. "There's a whole lot of things your brother could do with all that power."

A suspicious look crossed Peez's face. "All *what* power?"

"Oh, so *now* you're interested? Well, you'll find out soon enough." The amulet was gloating. "That is, you'll find out the hard way if you don't get off your ass and read this message right now, before I invoke a self-destruct spell on it. Hmmm, how did that go again? Rama-lama-double-slamma . . ."

Peez was out of her chair and across the room so fast that the force of her takeoff knocked Teddy Tumtum backwards off the desk and into the wastepaper basket. Grabbing the fax from the machine, Peez skimmed her mother's message quickly. With every line she read her face grew paler, her eyes grew wider, and her brows rose high enough to apply for membership in her bangs.

At last she was done. The hand holding the message dropped to her side and slowly began crinkling the paper into a tight little ball. Without thinking, she crammed the wad of fax paper into the pocket of her dowdy ankle-length skirt. It was made of wrinkly black cotton, like her blouse, and the whole ensemble made her look like a much-abused umbrella, but if she'd ever cared about being a fashion plate before this moment, she certainly didn't care now. She was too angry to care about anything but the obnoxious possibility of her brother Dov taking over the entire company and most of their inheritance. The knuckles of both fists turned a livid white and there was a tiny vein just under her jaw on the right side of her face that was twitching in flamenco tempo.

"No."

That was all she said. She didn't shout it, or shriek it, or moan, groan, or whine it: She merely *said* it. She sounded perfectly calm when she said it, too, and yet Teddy Tumtum, who had almost succeeded in hauling himself out of the wastepaper basket, took one look at her and promptly dropped back down to safety. He had been with her a long time, long enough to recognize all the signs that pointed to storms on the horizon. He didn't need the Weather Channel to tell him that when this one broke, it was going to be a doozy.

Peez Godz strode out of her office and confronted her secretary. Wilma had finished the filing and was now working diligently at her terminal.

"Wilma, I'm leaving," Peez announced. "Now. I'll be going on an extended business trip and I don't know when I'll be back. I'd like you to call my place and have Delilah pack my bags. Tell her to allow for a minimum of one month's absence, to provide clothing for a wide variety of climates, and to have everything ready to go within fifteen minutes. Also, tell Frederick that I'll expect him here with the luggage within the half hour, and that he's to use the town car to take me to the airport."

"Yes, Ms. Godz," Wilma said, her square hands poised just above the keyboard. "Which airport?"

"Um . . ." Peez's air of stone-cold efficiency abruptly deserted her. She looked a little confused.

"Maybe if you told me where you're going?" Wilma suggested. "I have to order your tickets, after all."

"Uhhh . . ." Peez gnawed her lower lip in thought, then brightened. "Call up the company records. Make me a list of our top ten power bases derived from cross-referencing income, population, and demographic impact."

"Impact?" Wilma echoed, puzzled.

"Loudness. Boldness. In-your-faceness. Annual amount of media coverage. It doesn't matter if a client unit has ten thousand members if they don't *do* anything, or if they do it so quietly that hardly anyone knows they're there. Drama counts. Flash works. That's the sort of thing that attracts new custo—seekers. If the ancient Romans would've left the early Christians alone, would so many people have become aware of their existence so fast? A few, sure, but without the Imperial persecutions to keep them in the spotlight, they probably would've gone the way of the Yellow Turbans in China."

"The what?"

"My point exactly. Instead of ignoring the Christians, those fool Roman emperors set them on fire, gave them to the gladiators, tossed them to the lions. You can't *buy* that kind of publicity! And any fool knows that showmanship always equals money." As usual, when she spoke about the family business, Peez was transformed from a droopy, rather nondescript young woman to a soul possessed. There was a fire in her eye that didn't come from any martyr's pyre: It was all her own inner flame.

Wilma Pilut was the sort of person who knew where all the fire extinguishers were kept and who had the ability to take them out and use them calmly, where and when needed. Peez might be swept away by the power of her own oratory, but Wilma wasn't going anywhere.

"Uh-huh," was all she said in response to her boss's impassioned speech. There was a momentary blur of flying fingers over the terminal keyboard. "Done," she stated. "You're booked for a six-stop itinerary that will cover all major power bases within the company."

"Only six? I asked for ten."

Wilma tried to shrug and couldn't. It was a gesture that required having a visible neck. "That's all there are, according to the search parameters you gave me. I could attach the next four hits, but as far as income and impact go, they'd just be time-wasters. However, if you insist . . ."

"Hmmm. No, no, don't bother. I guess six will have to be enough."

"Enough?" Wilma repeated. "Enough for what, may I ask, Ms. Godz?"

"Enough for me to put my darling baby brother right where he belongs: out of the Miami office, out of the company, out of my hair. Plus, if I'm lucky, out of my life." Her smile was amazingly like Teddy Tumtum's most gut-chilling grin.

Wilma remained indifferent to her employer's diabolical expression. No doubt if Peez had burst into a melodrama villain's *Mwahahahahahaha!* the stoic secretary would have likewise maintained her composure.

"Very good, Ms. Godz," she said. "I've downloaded all the pertinent information to your laptop and palmtop. Have a nice trip."

Peez snapped her fingers. There was a papery rustling from the inner office as Teddy Tumtum came floating out to her hand, a few scraps of torn-up phone memo slips and a used tissue clinging to his fur. He was followed closely by Peez's laptop and palmtop, both of them among the most recent influx of up-to-the-minute cutting-edge office equipment that Edwina had given her daughter.

With teddy bear and electronic arsenal in her grasp, Peez turned to leave, then paused at the door. "If those idiots from Chicago call again, tell them I'm gone and you don't know when I'll be back."

"That would be lying, Ms. Godz," Wilma reminded her quite needlessly. "The Great Mother doesn't like—"

"Then just tell them I'm gone. That'll be true enough to suit the Great Mother."

"You can tell them yourself," Wilma said. "They're on the list."

"They're *what*? But they can't possibly represent more than a handful of—"

"You didn't ask for a search based on numbers alone. Some of the items on the list are actually individuals. As far as impact goes, the members of the Chicago group are very good at drawing a crowd, when it suits their purposes. As for income, I checked their books: They're loaded."

Peez stared, taken aback by this revelation and the manner in which her secretary had chosen to voice it. Wilma Pilut used slang sparingly, the way some people used profanity, so that when she did employ it at all, it made a much bigger impression. For Wilma to say "loaded" rather than "rich" was a red flag of the first order. Attention must be paid.

"Are they now?" Peez said slowly, one eyebrow raised in speculation. "Are they indeed?" She left E. Godz, Inc.'s New York City office still pondering this information *sotto voce* to herself.

The office itself was not located in any of the commercially zoned skyscrapers that formed the Manhattan skyline, but rather in a residential high-rise on the Upper West Side. Edwina didn't believe in zoning laws— or any other laws that told her she couldn't have things her own way—and she had used her magic to establish the two subsidiary offices of E. Godz, Inc. wherever the hell she wanted them to be. The authorities never caught wise, and an A.R.S. or Automatic Rationalization Spell kept the residents of the buildings comfortably clueless.

Thus when Peez stepped onto the elevator, juggling her laptop, her palmtop, and Teddy Tumtum, the nice little old lady already riding down to the ground floor took one look and said, "Oh, isn't that nice! You must be going to pick up your child at school and taking his favorite teddy bear along as a surprise. It's such a joy to see one of you young women who cares more about your family than some silly little career. I think family is *so* important, don't you?"

Peez smiled pleasantly and replied: "Ma'am, you are a dinosaur. I refuse to accommodate your outdated prejudices by spending my life barefoot, pregnant and in the kitchen, even if you could somehow guarantee me one that comes with its own Iron Chef. I have no children, this teddy bear is possessed by the devil, I despise my baby brother with an intensity that could liquefy diamonds, and my mother is dying."

"You don't say? Four of them, and all boys! My dear, I don't know whether to congratulate you or pray for you." She smiled serenely, for as soon as Peez's words left her lips, the A.R.S. had kicked in, causing the old lady's mind to do an immediate slash-and-burn editorial job on every syllable. She only heard what her mind told her she *ought* to be hearing.

It was a wonderful spell. It let the New York City office of E. Godz, Inc. exist unmolested and it gave Peez the freedom to say anything that popped into her head to anyone she wished. As long as she restricted uttering her rants to the confines of the building proper, she could vent to her heart's content. Who needed a therapist when you could unload all your peeves and problems on whoever happened to be sharing the elevator, doing laundry, or getting the mail?

Unfortunately, there were times when you needed a therapist to do more than listen. The Automatic Rationalization Spell wasn't equipped to make its subjects give Peez any kind of feedback, and as for handling breakthrough moments of realization . . .

"My mother . . . is dying," Peez repeated dully as the full import of the fax from Edwina sank in. She stared at the illuminated display above the closed elevator doors and saw it not as simply the passing floors counting themselves off but as the passing days of Edwina's final months of life falling inexorably away, one by one.

Peez dropped everything she was carrying except Teddy Tumtum and, hugging him fiercely, burst into tears.

"There, there, dear," said the little old lady, solicitously patting Peez's shoulder. "I know just how you feel. Men really are all sex-crazed pigs, but maybe *this* time you'll have a girl."

# ⇒CHAPTER THREE⇐

DOV GODZ WAS ENJOYING HIS DAILY massage-and-aromatherapy treatment when the fax from Edwina arrived. His long, limber, beautifully bronzed torso was stretched out full length on the masseuse's portable table, his muscles almost purring under the ministrations of her gifted hands, his eyelids growing heavy, and his consciousness drifting blissfully off to the edge of slumber.

Then that blasted watchdog amulet on the fax machine let out a Rebel yell shrill enough to raise General Robert E. Lee himself from the grave and Dov's gilded barge to dreamland was torpedoed by a single *yeeeeehaaaaw* amidships. He jumped straight up off the towel-covered massage table so high that he nearly left an oily imprint of his body on the white acoustic tiles overhead.

It was a mercy that Solange hadn't set up her table under the ceiling fan.

"Damn it, I'm going to have to fix that thing," Dov announced as he strode across the room to retrieve the incoming message. With one hand he nabbed the fax, with the other he tore the amulet from the front of the machine and held it at eye level. "Okay, sport," he told it. "Either tone it down, change it entirely, or get ready for an unguided tour of the Greater Miami sewer system."

"I'm afraid I can't let you do that, Dov," the amulet replied in a level voice that reeked of rationality. It was cast of the purest silver in the shape of a human face with the full, pouting lips, curly hair, and classically beautiful features found on ancient statues of Greek youths. There was, of course, one salient difference: The faces of the old, old statues were as lifeless as the marble from which they were carved; the amulet's features were animated.

"I don't think you understand the situation, friend," Dov said. "You're the one working for me."

"I am not," the amulet replied. "I am working for the corporation."

This was true; Dov knew it. His mother had furnished his office and his bank account with a liberal hand, but with enough strings attached for Dov to start his own marionette theater. One such string was decked out with tags reading *If Thou Touchest Any Item of Thine Office Equipment, O Heedless Chump, Verily Thine Ass Belongeth Unto Me*. The tags were all in Edwina's handwriting and were attached to Dov's life by strings of solid carborundum. Mom was very protective of the family business, and since she allowed Dov the freedom and the money to do whatever he fancied in all other aspects of his life, he found it convenient to bow to her inclinations in this small matter.

Unfortunately, her inclinations included a fax amulet that screamed like a horde of Johnny Rebs on bad acid whenever a message came in. He'd spoken to her several times before about changing it, but she'd always replied that as his mother she knew him better than he knew himself.

"You're a good boy, Dov, and a good worker when you want to be, but as the old joke about the camel goes, first I've got to get your attention."

Dov winced every time he recalled those words. The joke in question concerned the best way to make a camel obey commands and involved two bricks and the beast's testicles. He disagreed with his mother's assessment of his work ethic. Oh sure, when he was a teenager he'd slacked off at boarding school and college on a regular basis. So did lots of kids. It was all part of growing up, testing the limits, seeing how far you could go before you wound up with egg on your face. He'd never actually flunked any courses; he'd even managed to get some grades that were better than he deserved thanks to his seemingly inborn talent for charming the pants off most people.

But that had been then. He knew better now. He was a grown man with an adult sense of responsibility, though he still cultivated the roguish image of a devil-may-care playboy. It tended to lull his rivals and opponents into a false sense of security, never expecting the happy-go-lucky hedonist to be concealing a killer business instinct worthy of his corporate lawyer grandpa. (He'd gotten the idea from reading Batman comics and even had a T-shirt printed up with the question: What Would Bruce Wayne Do?)

Edwina had told him not to tamper with the office equipment, but there was no maternal ruling to prevent him from trying to persuade the office equipment to tamper with itself.

"You know, I'm not asking for the world," he told the amulet.

He was wearing Smile #297-A, the one he reserved for uncooperative clients who hunkered down behind barricades of blind, stubborn resistance. Logical arguments and all the tools of rational persuasion couldn't reach them there and Dov knew better than to waste his time trying. That was when he whipped out Smile #297-A, which offered its unsuspecting targets a devastating combination of fifty percent charm, fifty percent intimacy, and one hundred thirty-eight percent good old American bullshit.

The amulet wrinkled up its perfect Greek nose and uttered words of dread: "And what if you were? It wouldn't matter any more than you do."

The verbal barb flew true and speared Dov straight through the heart. He felt a stab of pain as vivid and agonizing as if the amulet's words had really taken the form of a physical weapon. But this exchange between Edwina Godz's pampered baby boy and his least-favorite piece of office equipment was nothing new. He had been on the receiving end of the amulet's sniping countless times before, whenever he'd expressed a desire to change the way things were run in the Miami office. Somehow the little lump of exquisitely crafted metal always knew just the right thing to say to leave Dov's monolithic ego shattered into rubble and dust. There was only one way for Dov to come out of these clashes with some shred of self-esteem intact, and that was to act as if the inevitable surrender had been all his own idea from the start.

"Attaboy," he told the amulet, switching to Smile #15,

one of the basic models employed when buttering up
maître d's prior to wheedling his way around the waiting
list at exclusive restaurants. "Just testing. You know how
most office equipment starts to show wear and tear,
doesn't work up to snuff, inches its way towards
becoming obsolete and needing to be replaced?" He
stressed that last word just enough to zing the amulet. (It worked: He saw the perfect lips contract just
a hair and mentally high-fived himself for scoring hurt
points on the tiny silver tyrant.) "That's why I like to
run these periodic checks, make sure that you're still
functioning in top form. I'll be telling Mother that you
passed with flying colors."

"How kind," the amulet said coldly. "Will that be
before or after the funeral?"

"What funeral?"

The silver lips grinned. "You know, most people *read*
the faxes they receive."

Dov stared at the ensorcelled trinket, his smooth brow
momentarily creasing with uncharacteristic worry
wrinkles. He read the fax as he replaced the amulet
on the machine. It was a simple task, one he'd done
so many times before that he could do it blindfolded,
by touch alone.

This time was different.

This time he dropped the amulet into the little wastepaper basket next to the fax machine. It was sheer luck
that the trash receptacle's automatic shredding spell was
temporarily disabled.

"HEY! What the hell do you think you're trying to
pull?" the enraged amulet demanded from the depths.

Dov acted as though he had heard nothing. This was
more or less true. The news from Edwina was so stun-
ning, so shocking, so earthshaking that it threw Dov

for a loop the size of Halley's comet's trajectory. He didn't notice that he'd dropped the amulet, and the only reason he finally snapped out of his daze was the reaction he got when the towel around his waist slipped its moorings and fell in a terry cloth puddle at his feet.

Solange squealed like a teenybopper at a Generic Boy Band concert.

"Wha—?" Dov looked up suddenly at the mortified masseuse, then down at his nakedness. "Oops." He retrieved the towel. "Uh, why don't you come back later, honey?" he told Solange.

She didn't wait for a second invitation: She fled the premises, leaving her portable massage table and other equipment behind. The amulet in the wastepaper basket was still snickering when he fished it out.

"Not very professional, is she?" it remarked.

"She's new to the business," Dov muttered. "Plus, she went to Yale—not the best place to learn what a naked man's really supposed to look like."

Still somewhat distracted, he paced across the floor to the panoramic windows of his office and gazed down at the street scene of Miami's smart South Beach section. Buildings that were all the colors of Easter eggs stood like graveyard monuments to the Art Deco movement. Palm trees swayed like topless waitresses with overloaded trays. Swarms of people at least as bronzed, blond, and beautiful as Dov Godz went sailing along their carefree life-paths. Their gleaming golden tresses streamed out behind them as they were whisked along via every form of transportation known to man—from rollerblades to red convertibles—so long as that form of transportation was guaranteed to show off their perfect bodies to the max.

"Bubble-heads," Dov growled.

"Wow," the amulet said. "You want to be them so bad it hurts, doesn't it?"

"Like an abscessed tooth." Dov saw no point in denying it.

"Well, I've got news for you, fella: You *are* them," the amulet stated. "Or hadn't you noticed?"

"I used to be," Dov said. He sounded world-weary enough for a whole platoon of French novelists. "Once. But not any more."

The amulet raised one silver eyebrow and looked truly concerned. "Uh-oh. You're *thinking* again, aren't you? I warned you not to try that. You're not used to the strain. What's the matter, fella? You need help? You want me to fax your guru, your personal trainer, your dietician, your *feng shui* consultant, what?"

"My mother is dying."

Dov dropped the words without prelude or fanfare, like a stick of bombs from the belly of an old warplane. He turned away from the window, leaned his spine against the cool glass, tilted his head back, and closed his eyes.

"Oh." The amulet was abashed. "Gosh. I—I—I'm real sorry to hear that."

"What do you mean, you're sorry to hear that?" Dov snapped, his eyes wide open again and shooting sparks at the amulet. "You knew about this before I did, the minute the fax came in! *You're* the one who was talking about funerals!"

"Yeah, but—but—" The amulet groped for the right thing to say. "Look, when the messages come in, they're just words to me, okay? What do I know about any power they might contain until I see how they affect *you*? What do I look like, a human being?"

"Hardly." Dov's lips curled as he studied the amulet.

"Although you're obnoxious enough to join the club. Maybe that's what makes me forget, sometimes, that you're nothing more than a glorified interactive gewgaw."

"Maybe you wouldn't forget that so much if you spent as much time talking to other human beings as you spend talking to me."

Dov stared at the amulet, stunned. "What did you say?"

"You heard me." The amulet was smug, knowing it had scored another hit off its master. "And you know it's true."

That was the worst of it: The trinket was right. Dov frowned, trying to drum up some evidence to the contrary, but he was a truthful man at heart and he couldn't honestly say that there was any mortal soul with whom he'd traded as many words as he had with Ammi.

He blushed to realize that he'd actually given the thing a name.

"This is all *her* fault," he snarled under his breath. His bitter words did not escape Ammi's silvery ears.

"Oh, come on, now! You can't blame your mother for dying!"

"I'm not talking about her: I'm talking about my sister, Peez." The look in Dov's eyes was grim and brimming with years' worth of anger.

Peez, his dowdy, depressing, hangdog big sister. Peez, who didn't have the socialization skills of a squashed spider; Peez, who couldn't make a friend if Dr. Frankenstein himself gave her the raw materials, the how-to instructions, and a spare needle and thread; Peez, who lacked the affable, easygoing charm that seemed to have come to Dov naturally.

Peez, who had envied Dov's personal magnetism from

the day that they were both placed in the same class at school, and who decided that if she couldn't have her baby brother's boundless charisma and all the good things it brought him, at least she could enjoy playing the harpy and tainting everything before he had a hope of enjoying it himself.

*Friends?* Dov could still hear her dry, mocking laughter in his head. It was Valentine's Day and while his construction paper mailbox was stuffed full to bursting with flocks of little white envelopes from their classmates, hers was almost as flat as when she'd finished making it. *You think they're your friends? Why? Just because they gave you valentines? Stupid! They only did it because their parents* forced *them to! And you know why? Because the only reason anyone* ever *does anything nice for us is because they want something from Mother!*

He remembered fighting back against the ugly words, arguing that if what she said were true, then wouldn't the kids have given *her* a bunch of valentines too?

She only laughed again. She didn't even try to answer his question, she just gave him the same look she'd given him when he'd found out the truth about Santa Claus. It was a horribly *knowing* look that said: *Have it your way. They're all your dear, dear friends. Sure they are. Trust them. Only when they make a fool of you, don't come crying to me. I* tried *to warn you. I tried to tell you the truth.*

"It's all her fault," Dov repeated. "She's the reason I never let anyone get too close, the reason I've got hundreds of acquaintances, associates, social contacts, but not one single, solitary friend. She's why I've got no one I can really talk to except—except a refugee from a charm bracelet!"

"Thanks a lot," the amulet said dryly. "You think I

like her any better than you do?" The chain that usually suspended Ammi from the front of the fax machine made a tinkling sound when the amulet trembled with rage in Dov's hand. "I can't stand it when I've got to announce a fax from *that* one. The bile positively oozes from every syllable in her transmissions! Mind you, big guy, you give her back as good as you get, but being forced to listen in on your exchanges is like playing go-between for a pair of rabid hyenas. It's starting to wear on my nerves."

Dov's mouth quirked up at one corner. "You don't *have* nerves."

"I've got sorcery-generated circuitry," Ammi replied peevishly. "It's practically the same thing."

"Well, in that case, I've got some good news for you: You won't be troubled by faxes between my sister and me for much longer. You know what the rest of Mother's message said, don't you? She's going to leave the family business to just one of us." His mouth tightened. "That one's going to be me."

He strode over to his desk and snapped his fingers. The polished glass top glowed. Rainbow-hued swirls of energy swam across the surface, transforming it into a seer's pool. Most mere mortals owned desktop computers that they hoped would meet all their needs, but Dov Godz was master of a *real* desktop that actually could do that and more.

"Research all available data and compile a list of key players in the E. Godz corporation. Include prospective as well as active clients if their potential influence is comparable. Make all necessary travel arrangements enabling me to visit each of these in the most efficient manner possible, allowing for M.E.S.T."

"M.E.S.T.?" Ammi the amulet echoed.

"Minimum Essential Schmooze Time," Dov replied. "I want to depart today by—" He consulted his wristwatch. Then he noticed that it wasn't there. He'd taken it off for his aromatherapy-massage session. "Oh, hell, I'll leave at six. Make New Orleans my first stop and get a really *good* dinner before getting down to business. No way New Orleans won't make the list." He glanced at the still-swirling desktop. "Stream the appropriate documents to my palmtop. Copy that?"

The desk uttered a soft, almost voluptuous sigh and in the voice of the divine Diana Rigg replied, "Anything you say, Dov."

Dov grinned. "I never get tired of that."

"I do," Ammi said petulantly.

"Jealous?" Dov's grin widened. "Too bad. And now it's back to the fax for you." He headed for the machine, intent on replacing the moody amulet.

"Wait a minute!" Ammi protested. "Don't put me back there! Take me with you!"

"Why?"

"I can provide remote access for all fax messages that might arrive in your absence."

"My palmtop already has that capability."

"I'm a portable firewall. You can stick me on your hotel phone and I'll screen all your calls."

"Nothing a discretionary shielding spell can't do."

By now the little amulet was grasping at straws. "Take me into any jewelry store and have them chip off as many bits of me as you want. Drop them off on the clients and you'll be able to eavesdrop on everything they're up to even after you're long gone!"

Dov clicked his tongue and shook his head. "No sale. You think these people are rubes? They've got their own resources for detecting bugs, even magical ones." He hung the amulet back on the fax machine and brushed invisible dust from his hands. As he turned to go he said, "Sorry, Ammi, but there's really no good reason for me to take you with me."

He was almost to the door when a very small, very shaky voice behind him said, "But I'll miss you."

Dov stopped in his tracks and looked back. "Say what?"

"I said I'll miss you," the amulet repeated, almost reluctantly. "A lot. There. I said it. Happy?"

Dov snatched the little trinket up again and confronted it with the impossible. "You're an *appliance*. How could you miss me? Or anyone, for the matter? It's like someone claiming he can't program his VCR because he once said something to hurt its feelings."

"Look, I can't *explain* it; I just know it," the amulet said, getting defensive. "And that crack about VCRs was uncalled for: They happen to be very sensitive. It comes from all the soppy chick flicks people make them play. Hey, take me with you or leave me behind, see if I care. But I'll tell you this much: It's going to get mighty lonely out there on the road, and one of those cold, solitary nights you're going to wish you had a sympathetic ear to listen to your troubles, even if it's only one that's made out of silver."

Dov stared at the amulet, taken aback by its outburst. The trouble was, its words made sense and he knew it. Only an idiot kept fighting when it was past time to surrender.

"Oh, *fine*," he growled. "You'll probably do something nasty to the fax machine if I leave you here alone. Might as well take you with me." He thrust the amulet into his pocket.

There was only one problem: He was still wearing nothing but a towel.

"Put on some pants, Einstein," said Ammi from the floor where he'd fallen. "Then let's get this show on the road."

# ⇒ CHAPTER FOUR ⇐

"AH, SALEM!" SAID TEDDY TUMTUM, pressing his fuzzy nose to the glass of the passenger's side window as Peez's rental car glided up Lafayette Street, heading north for the center of town. "Lovely, notorious Salem, infamous and immortal for fostering the mass hysteria that reached its bloody conclusion in the seventeenth-century witchcraft trials . . . *not!*" He giggled.

Peez pulled the car over. "What do you mean, '*not*'?" she demanded. "Everyone who knows even a crumb of American history has heard of the Salem witchcraft trials!"

"Sure," said the diabolical bear, enjoying himself. "The way they've heard of George Washington's wooden teeth and Pocahontas being a total supermodel babe with the hots for John Smith and Betsy Ross making the first United States flag . . . *not!*"

"I wish you'd stop saying that," Peez muttered. "You sound like a refugee from a no-brainer teen flick."

"Flick? Did you say *flick?*" The bear could not open his mouth, but he gestured at it with his paw and made choking noises. "Even your vocabulary is dowdy, and your lack of cool is immeasurable. Gag me with a spoon full of honey!"

"I would, if it'd shut you up. I may not be 'cool,' but I'm sure I know more about American history than you do, you glorified wad of dryer lint!"

"This is the thanks I get for trying to educate you," Teddy Tumtum said. He sounded worse than hurt: He sounded Stereotype Jewish Mother hurt, the kind of hurt that packs a load of payback. "You only *think* you know American history when all you really know is a grab bag full of popular anecdotes, sound bites, and shaggy dog stories that are about as historically accurate as saying that the French invented French fries!"

"They didn't?" Peez was genuinely taken aback.

"Nope. That was the Belgians."

"Oh." Suddenly she realized she'd given the bear the upper hand. She quickly affected a fake air of indifference, trying to regain lost ground. "I mean, oh, who cares, anyway? History is irrelevant."

"Not here in Salem, it's not," the bear replied. "Here it's business. *Big* business. And if you think big business is irrelevant, don't call yourself an American!"

Peez made a face and started the car up again. Teddy Tumtum had been making himself unbearable—pun intended or not, she didn't really give a hoot—ever since they'd picked up the rental car at Logan Airport. Somehow or other he'd reached the unilateral decision that being Peez's traveling companion wasn't enough of a challenge for him. No, he had to be her self-appointed mentor, strategic advisor, and back-pocket Machiavelli too. He'd filled their driving time with an unending stream of chatter, alternately briefing her on what awaited them in Salem and telling her exactly how to handle it once they arrived.

He sounded just like her mother.

"Fine, ignore me," the little bear declared. "See where it gets you. More to the point, see where it gets your brother!"

Peez took a hard right, heading the car east. She tried to focus on the traffic and the driving directions that the ever-thorough and reliable Wilma Pilut had provided for her, not so much out of the fear of getting lost but the better to shut out Teddy Tumtum's nittering.

"Ooooh, nice Beethoven imitation there," the bear sneered. "A regular Meryl Streep, no less. You could almost make me believe you're deaf . . . *not*! You don't have to pay attention to anything I say, but by Teddy Roosevelt's overstuffed ghost, you are going to *hear* it! It's not just your future you're risking here; it's mine. I've been thinking it over and I've decided that I don't want to spend the rest of my unnatural life as the only close companion of a total failure. Because that's what you'll be if your brother gets the corporation and you get the shaft. What'll become of you then? Wilma's got a better resumé. You might find a job somewhere, something that pays crap per hour and has benefits too small to be seen with the naked eye. If you're lucky, you'll be able to scrimp and save and manage your pitiful finances well enough to get yourself a dinky little apartment somewhere so far from New York City that your neighbors think a bagel is a kind of dog like Snoopy! Remember how you always used to tell Dov that the only reason people were nice to him was because they wanted to get close to Edwina? Well, that was true enough and let me tell you, it wasn't because she made the best chocolate chip cookies on the block. No sir, it was because she had the *power*. Power's got the pull of a million magnets, and it's more of an aphrodisiac than oysters, perfume, trips to Maui, lace lingerie, Super Bowl tickets, Swiss bank accounts—"

"All right, all right!" Peez threw in the towel, though it was about the size of a bath sheet. "I'll listen to you, you furry-assed pest! Even a history lesson has to be better than this. So go ahead and educate me."

"Sorry, that's too big an assignment, Peezie-pie," Teddy Tumtum replied. "But I will give you a few tidbits that might help you out when we call on Queen Fiorella. First of all . . ."

Peez Godz stood on the sidewalk outside Ye Cat and Cauldron Booke Shoppe and took a deep breath, steeling herself for the interview to come. She never had been much good with face-to-face business meetings, preferring the anonymity of e-mails, faxes, phone calls and, in a pinch, the old-fashioned letter. She suffered from selective shyness: She never had any problems when it came to giving orders to her employees, because in that situation she held all the aces and she knew it. But a client was by no means an employee, and when that client was the head of one of E. Godz, Inc.'s most influential subscriber groups, the playing field became so incredibly tilted in that client's favor that it resembled the down-at-the-bow Titanic just before it slipped beneath the waves.

Could the situation possibly be any worse? What a silly question! Peez knew that most situations could *always* be worse, and were only awaiting the opportunity to do so, especially if she was involved. It wasn't a question of *if* the manure would hit the whirlwind, it was a matter of how much, what kind, and when it would ever stop raining cosmic cowpats.

In this case, the manure had taken a form whose best description was seldom associated with manure: beauty. Fiorella, undisputed queen of the largest chain of wiccan covens in America, was beautiful.

Peez stared at the life-size photographic cutout of herself that Fiorella had placed dead center in the window of Ye Cat and Cauldron Booke Shoppe. The witch-queen (as she always styled herself whenever she appeared on talk shows, usually right around Halloween) had a body that would not quit, the perfect combination of curves and concavities, slender but not skinny, voluptuous yet without a single excess ounce of warm, welcoming flesh. Her summery blond hair fell in a silky cascade down to her hips, her full, red lips curved upward in a *very* knowing smile, and her slightly slanted green eyes seemed to burn with their own inner fire. If you believed in such a thing as body language, then Fiorella's body was playing an endless loop tape of that great old hit, "I Can Get Anything I Want From Anyone I Please Because I Look Like This And You Don't."

To which Teddy Tumtum would probably add the chorus: *Neener, neener, neener.*

Teddy Tumtum wasn't there to add anything. Peez had opted to lock him in the trunk of her rental car. He'd served his purpose, giving her a crash course in the true history of Salem and how best to apply that knowledge during her upcoming interview with the witch-queen. She had to admit, he did have a devious mind, for a stuffed animal, full of practical insights on human nature. On the other hand, Peez didn't need anyone to tell her that the person who showed up at a business meeting packing a loaded teddy bear—even a magically articulate one—had already lost the first through fifteenth rounds of negotiations.

*She's beautiful*, Peez told herself. *But I've got something that's better than beauty: I've got brains. I'm smart, and I'm only going to get smarter as time goes on. Meanwhile, she's just going to get old and wrinkled and saggy. There's just so much that plastic surgery can do. She's not going to flummox me. I can take her.*

She drew another centering breath and went into the bookstore.

A small brass bell above the door chimed sweetly as Peez entered. The shop appeared to be deserted, which was strange. Peez checked the sign on the front door, but it said OPEN.

*Maybe she's doing something in the storeroom*, Peez thought, glancing at the red and black bead curtain veiling the doorway behind the counter. She opened her mouth to call out, but changed her mind. She'd never been very good at knowing what to say under such circumstances. *Yoo-hoo? Helloooo? Hi, it's me?* All lame, all guaranteed to make her feel like a fool. Fools did not win the support of influential clients for a pending corporate takeover. Not unless they were highly-placed government officials. She decided to say nothing and simply await Fiorella's inevitable appearance. Meanwhile, she looked around her.

The interior of Ye Cat and Cauldron was a comforting blend of dim light and musty smells. The shelves were laden with a fine selection of books, hardcover and paperback both, dealing with matters of the occult, though there was an entire section marked off as Love Spells. A thread of patchouli incense wove its way through the displays of plaster skulls, crystal balls, and mass-produced Egyptian statuettes of gods, goddesses, cats and hippos. There was a real cat present—black, of course. He lay stretched out full length across the top of a glass display case that was crammed with enough silvery ankh pendants to outfit half the population of suburban Goth wannabees on the Eastern Seaboard. There was also a cauldron in one corner. It was full of umbrellas.

"Loaners, in case of a sudden cloudburst," said Fiorella. She had passed through the bead curtain without calling forth so much as a click-click. The black cat let out a *wowowowwwwwlllll* of ecstatic greeting and leaped onto her shoulder where he perched like an owl. "They're for the tourists."

"Isn't everything?" Peez said, letting her eyes sweep across the shop. Her smile mirrored Fiorella's. It was a stratagem that Teddy Tumtum had suggested to her. She wished he were there to see how well she had begun this interview. Amazing how coolly she could comport herself on the outside when her gut felt like a blender set on puree. "Very kind of you to help them out, but doesn't it run into money when they don't return them?"

"Not at all." The witch-queen's little pink tongue ran lightly across her upper lip as if she were relishing the taste of something very toothsome indeed. "Please note the sign."

Peez looked at the wall above the cauldron. There hung a sheet of yellowed parchment, slightly charred at the edges, with the calligraphed words:

*Welcome Ye Be to Borrow Mee in Tyme of Neede,*
*Yet Hearken Ye: A Witche's Curse Doth Follow Fast*
*on Hee Who Keepeth Mee.*

"That," said Peez, "is false advertising. There's no curse on those umbrellas. I'd be able to feel it."

"Nothing but the curse of truly awful poetry," said Fiorella complacently. "But it works like a charm, and it's much cheaper than imbuing the umbrellas with a homing spell. The tourists come here because they believe, or because they want to. The first rule of successful retail is to give the public what the public wants, or thinks they do. I'm in the business of meeting popular expectations. Just between the two of us, black isn't my best color, incense makes me sneeze, and I'm frightfully allergic to my darling Pyewacket, here." She reached up and scratched the black cat's fluffy chest. He purred mightily. "But the tourists expect Ye Cat and Cauldron to have both, and I have a reputation as a witch-queen to uphold. You can buy an awful lot of antihistamines on what this store clears in a week."

"I know. I've reviewed your records."

"Thorough," Fiorella murmured. "But I'd expect no less of Edwina Godz's daughter." She stepped back, gesturing at the bead curtain. "Would you care for some tea? I've just been making preparations in the back— my Lilith Lair, as I like to call it. The two of us have much to discuss."

The area behind the bead curtain was a miniature jewel of a room, all ruby glass, burgundy velvet, and gold silk tassels. The tea things were already set out on a low mahogany table with ball-and-claw feet. Fiorella waved Peez to a place at one end of the settee before settling herself at the other. "Two sugars and a squeeze of lemon for you," she said, filling Peez's cup.

*How does she know that's what I always put in my tea?* Peez fought to keep her self-possession. Fiorella had meant to astonish her, to throw her off-stride and gain the initial advantage in this interview. I-know-something-about-you-that-you-didn't-know-I-knew was a business ploy that had been old when Babylon was young. The witch-queen was up to something. Peez felt a fleeting urge to rush out to the car and fetch Teddy Tumtum, but she knew that was impossible. Instead she sat up a little straighter and launched a silvery laugh.

"How very kind of you to find out how I take my tea," she said smoothly. "But I'm afraid your information is sadly out of date. I no longer care for lemon. Just cream." She arched one eyebrow and peered critically into the tiny porcelain pitcher on the tea tray. "That *is* cream, isn't it? *Real* cream?"

Fiorella's perfect cheekbones flushed red. She muttered a few arcane words and wiggled her fingers over the little pitcher. The level of liquid went down slightly and the color deepened from the bluish-white of skim milk to the more buttery-white of full dairy cream.

"It is now," she said, somewhat testily.

Peez sipped her tea and looked demure. Inside she was gloating and doing a victory dance, even if it was just to honor a small victory. *That wasn't so hard,* she thought. *That was even . . . fun! Fiorella already sees that I'm smart, that I can think on my feet—or on her settee—and that I've got to be the only worthy successor to my mother's empire. Besides, I'm a woman. That's got to count for something with this country's number one wiccan! It's a Goddess thing.*

She set down her teacup and said, "Fiorella, under normal circumstances I would enjoy a long chat with you, but since we're both businesswomen, we know that sometimes one must sacrifice nicety to necessity. I hope you won't mind my cutting to the chase, but you do understand that I'm—that I'm working under a terrible deadline."

"Of course." Fiorella removed a cobwebby lace handkerchief from one long, black sleeve and dabbed at her eyes. "Your poor mother, my dear friend Edwina. So sad. So sudden. So—so strange. When I first heard about her condition I rather wondered why— It just wasn't *like* her to—to—" Fiorella's voice trailed off and a distracted look came into her face that had nothing to do with sorrow.

Peez didn't know why or whither the witch-queen's attention had wandered, but she determined to recapture it forthwith. There were other places for her to be, other people to meet. She was doing all right so far, mastering her innate awe of beautiful people, handling a face-to-face meeting, but she didn't know if she could keep it up indefinitely.

"I don't think any of us would be our usual selves if our doctors had just handed us that sort of news," she said. "We owe it to Mother to help her get all of her affairs in order while we can, if only to unburden her spirit."

"Is there really no hope?"

Peez shook her head. "Mother would have told me if there were. You know what an optimist she is. A visionary, really. Your organization was one of our first clients." Peez was pleased with herself for that *our*. "You saw how she built up E. Godz bit by bit, channeling the power, giving back far more than she ever got, making it all run smoothly for everyone involved. E. Godz meant—*means* everything to her. She gave her life for the dream. She worked too long, too hard for it to all go to pieces. If the company is to continue to succeed, we've got to make a commitment to

excellence, dedicate ourselves to the future, to fresh leadership that's devoted to maintaining the same high standards that—"

"How do you do that?" Fiorella asked.

"Do what?" Peez was brought up short by the
interruption.

"Talk for so long without stopping for a breath *and*
without saying much of anything. It's half empty sen-
timent, half corporate claptrap, and all pure piffle." She
helped herself to more tea. "Look, Peez, I know why
you're here. As you said yourself, we're both businesswomen who know how to cut to the chase. You want
to take over as the head of E. Godz, Inc. after Edwina's
gone, right?"

"And why shouldn't I?" It was Peez's turn to sound
testy.

"No, the proper question is why *should* you? Your
mother always gave my people value for money—"

"I'll do that, too," Peez cut in.

"Easy enough for you to say. But *how* do you propose to do it? I don't know you, Peez; not the way I
know your mother. I can't tell what your management
style is or if it's what I want for my organization or
even if you have a style worthy of the name. Are you
going to let things coast, playing the 'If It Ain't Broke,
Don't Fix It' card, or are you going to be so hands-
on that you don't leave one corporate brick standing
on top of another? And why should I assume that whatever your style, I won't like your brother's better?"

Peez's face hardened at the mention of Dov. "When
did you talk to him?" she demanded coldly.

Fiorella shrugged her beautiful shoulders. "Does it
matter? We both know he's out there. And since I was
the one who had to mention him in the first place, I

don't think that the two of you have any plans for a joint directorship."

"Do you seriously believe that Dov could steer this company by himself?" Peez snapped. "That mama's boy? He never had to take an independent step in his life! He's only a figurehead in the Miami office. How can he do something for the American wiccan population when he's got absolutely no experience doing anything for himself?"

"You seem to think that you know what American wiccans need," Fiorella remarked calmly. "But do you? Do you really?"

"I know that you represent more than talk-show fodder," Peez shot back. "I've followed your career, Fiorella. Every Halloween, just like clockwork, there you are on TV, in the newspapers, sometimes in those slick-and-sleazy gossip magazines: Fiorella, a so-called 'real' witch, fashions by Morticia Addams, props straight out of Stereotypes-R-Us, something for the rubes to gawk at and imagine they've glimpsed the Dark Side. And it doesn't hurt that the Dark Side shows a lot of cleavage. Am I wrong?"

Fiorella smiled and shook her head.

"But the reality is that you're just about as 'real' as this whole town. Salem, Massachusetts, home of the infamous witchcraft trials! There's a joke."

Fiorella stood up, no longer smiling. "Have a care what you say, woman," she intoned, her voice going deep and menacing. "Have a care, lest you summon up the shadows of vengeance! This ground is sanctified with the blood of our venerable ancestors, those women who gave their all, America's first wiccan martyrs who—"

"Oh, please." Peez dismissed Fiorella's outburst with

an airy wave of her hand. "In the first place, this ground wasn't sanctified by any bloodshed: They *hanged* all the accused witches, except for that man who died under the *peine forte et dure*, crushed under a load of rocks when he wouldn't confess. You know, Giles Corey, Mr. 'More Weight'?" Teddy Tumtum's impromptu history lesson was coming in handy after all. "Second, none of those poor souls was a witch, and they'd probably look at you funny if you so much as mentioned the word 'wiccan' to them. And finally, Salem isn't even where most of the madness happened. Salem *Village*, now that's more like it! Only there isn't any Salem Village any more. They changed the name to Danvers because they had the good grace to be ashamed of the whole nasty business. Bad publicity and a load of embarrassment are very strong charms. They have the power to transform a place or a person or even a financial empire."

She leaned towards the still-bristling witch-queen and concluded: "Don't make me use them on you."

"Threats?" Fiorella raised one eyebrow. "Didn't take you long to reach that point, did it? Well, and how would your bad PR bugaboo touch me?"

"How hard would it be for me to set up someone else as a rival witch-queen, Fiorella? Some out-of-work model who's at least as pretty as you are, only younger and maybe with some connections to the music industry? I can help her tap into the earth magic just enough to give her that air of authenticity—my equivalent of start-up funds—then get her all of your old Halloween spots in the media. You may be the founder of several dozen covens, but can you hold onto your constituents in the face of some real heavy-duty competition?"

Peez held her hands up in front of her face, palms

outward, thumbs touching, in the classic director-framing-a-shot pose. In the voice of TV hype artists everywhere she declared: "She's beautiful, she's a witch, *and* she's slept with rock stars! You, too, can share the glamour, the power, the six-degrees-of-Kevin-Bacon celebrity! It's not just witchcraft, it's *cool!*" She lowered her hands and gave Fiorella a hard stare. "And it's the same principle behind every cosmetics ad ever run. Rationally, women know that they're not going to look like Cindy or Naomi or Husker-du or whoever's the supermodel *du jour* just because they buy that brand of lipstick. Ah, but somehow, when they look at those ads, reason flies out the window. They're like your precious tourists: They believe because they *want* to believe. I'll just give them something to believe in that's a whole lot trendier than you. They'll flock to her in droves! Or drive to her in flocks! Who cares? Either put your power in my camp or kiss it good-bye."

By this time the fire in Fiorella's green eyes had escalated to the white-hot heat of fresh lava. "If you're trying to woo my support over to your side, you're going about it in quite the wrong way," she hissed.

"I don't woo," Peez said. "I win. And when I win, so do you. Or you can give your support to my baby brother, if you like. It's a free country. Then see where it gets you."

"Because you're packing a stealth witch-queen?" Fiorella pursed her lips. "Maybe I ought to be afraid. Maybe I ought to pledge my support to you right now . . . but I won't. I like to review all of my options. I want to hear what Dov's got to say."

"Think he can protect you?" Peez laughed. It sounded a lot like Teddy Tumtum at his nastiest.

"You know, Peez, I'm still going to wait for Dov, but

I think you just might have the right mix of gall and backbone to be a decent corporate harpy after all," Fiorella mused. "I don't like you, but I respect you."

"I'll settle for that," Peez said, grinning. But in her heart a lonely little girl hung her head and thought: *I always have.*

# ⚡CHAPTER FIVE⚡

IT WAS A WELL-DOCUMENTED FACT, attested to by all the highest authorities among gourmets, gourmands, trenchermen, foodies, and just plain greedy-guts, that the only way to get a really *bad* meal in New Orleans was to search for it with all the fervor of a knight of old upon a holy quest.

But who would want to be fool enough to do that? Certainly not Dov Godz. He had a fondness for all of the best things in life, which included food. New Orleans would always have a special place in his heart, but his stomach infallibly came along for the ride. It was a pleasure undimmed by repetition to visit that storied city at the mouth of the Mississippi on a whim, but when he had the opportunity to justify his self-indulgence by coming to New Orleans on *business*— Ah, that was a thrill divine.

Now, ensconced behind a plate of sugary beignets,

his third cup of chicory coffee readily to hand, Dov sat under the awnings at the famous Café du Monde and reviewed his game plan. He'd arrived the previous evening and enjoyed a sumptuous dinner, but apart from that, he hadn't accomplished a thing. There was something about New Orleans that told a body not to fret or fluster, because there was time for everything, and everything in its own good time.

*First thing I have to do is go back to the hotel and change my clothes*, he thought, casting a rueful glance at the front of his formerly dapper suit. He had forgotten the first rule of dining in New Orleans, namely: Never eat beignets while wearing black. Those small, pillowy, feather-light, unbelievably delicious squares of fried dough were traditionally served buried beneath avalanches of powdered sugar. During the height of the tourist season, a sweet, white fog hovered immobile over the open-air tables at Café du Monde. It was said that the emergency rooms and walk-in clinics of the Queen City were frequently jammed by periodic influxes of out-of-towners who had unwisely attempted to eat beignets and talk at the same time, almost choking to death in the process.

Rule Two: If you're going to eat beignets, don't inhale.

Dov sipped his coffee and signaled the waiter for his check. When it arrived, he put down a stack of crisp tenners, slapped on his most charming smile, and said, "I beg your pardon, but do you think you could help me out with a small matter of—?"

The waiter gave him the gimlet eye. "Look, friend, I don't know what you've been told about N'Awlins, but even if it were Mardi Gras, which it's not, I wouldn't—"

"Oh, no! Nonononononono," Dov said hastily, blushing

to the eyebrows. "All I want is a little help finding someone. An old friend of mine. You see, he lives in the
French Quarter, and he doesn't—"

"—have a telephone?" the waiter finished the thought
for him. "What about an address? Do you have that
much?" Dov shook his head. "Not very friendly for an
'old friend,' then, is he?"

Dov's smile wobbled just a bit. "I misspoke. He's a
business acquaintance."

"Ah. I see." The waiter eyed the stack of bills wist-
fully. "I'd love to help you, sir, really I would, but you
don't know how it is down here. When a man lives
in the Quarter and doesn't have a phone and a stranger
comes nosing around, asking about him, it's a sure thing
that ain't no one going to be giving that stranger any
information. You might accidentally tread on a man's
toes, doing that. Folks don't appreciate having their toes
trod on. Now you say this man's a . . . business acquaintance?"

Dov nodded and said, "I suppose you want to know
what sort of business."

"Oh no, sir, no, not at all." The waiter raised one
hand, fending off any unwanted information. "Matter
of fact, I'm happier not knowing."

"Why? Afraid I'll lie to you for my own nefarious
purposes?" Dov kicked his boyish smile up a notch.
"I'm flattered."

"I'm not afraid of nothing like that; I just kinda expect
it as a matter of course." The waiter had a pretty high-
intensity grin of his own. He placed two fingers on the
stack of bills and gave them a short push back in Dov's
direction. "A word of advice, friend, and it's free: If
you're bound and determined to find a man in the
Quarter and you don't have a clue about where to start,

wait until dark. Then go there, be there, look around. You'll find him if you're meant to. Otherwise, be smart: Go home."

"You're kidding. You want me to blunder through the French Quarter all night long, trying to find one man?" Dov peeled two bills off the top of the stack and shoved them onto the waiter. "Think again."

The waiter took a step back, away from Dov and his persistent attempts at bribery. His upper lip curled. "You want to know what I think, sir?" His hand swooped in and scooped up the pile of tens still on the table-top. "I think a man like you will only find what he's looking for in St. Louis 1, that's what." He turned on his heel and was gone.

"St. Louis 1? What the hell does *that* mean?" Dov cursed the waiter under his breath, but his snit was interrupted by the sound of muffled laughter coming from inside his shirt. He grabbed the silver chain around his neck and fished Ammi out into the sunlight. The little amulet was giggling.

"Oh, he told *you*, all right!" Ammi said. "You big idiot."

"What did he tell me, if you're so smart?" Dov countered. He had no fear that his fellow breakfasters would think him insane for talking to jewelry: He'd wrapped Ammi in an A.R.S. even before getting into the car that took them to the Miami airport. Any person within range of their conversations would unconsciously come up with self-convincing reasons to account for everything seen and overheard. Thus, instead of the panicky realization *That lunatic is talking to his necklace. And it's talking back!* the innocent bystander would instead calmly reflect *Gee, I wish I had a cell phone as small as the one* that *guy's got. And it's silver. Classy. Cool.*

"Weren't you listening?" The amulet enjoyed taunt-ing Dov. "He told you to go to St. Louis 1, which is the same thing as saying— Well, I'd rather not lower myself to using that kind of language, if you don't mind."

"I don't get get it. What's St. Louis 1?"

"A cemetery. Very historic, very quaint, very famous, and very likely a good place to get the snot kicked out of you during a mugging. *Not* the place a person sends someone he likes."

Dov glared in the direction the waiter had gone. "He sends me to get mugged and he's got the nerve to take my money. Bastard."

"Oh, please, you did everything but stuff that bankroll in his pocket! You're going to have to learn how to take 'No' for an answer, Dov."

"I don't think so. That's more my sister's style." Dov stood up from the table. He left no payment and no tip. The waiter had more than enough in the stack of tens he'd taken to cover both.

"Where are we going now?" Ammi asked.

"Back to the hotel. I need a change of clothes and a nap."

"Kind of early for that, isn't it?"

"Not for what I've got to do. I paid for information and all I got was advice, but I paid plenty and I'm going to take it!" He popped Ammi back down inside his shirt and declared: "I'll find Mr. Bones tonight, or know the reason why."

"You'd think that someone with a name like Mr. Bones would be easy to find," Ammi said as he and Dov walked around Jackson Square for the third time that night. "But noooo."

"Quit your bitching," Dov snapped. They had spent the better part of the night crisscrossing the streets of the Vieux Carré, with Dov making only the most discreet enquiries of the natives as to the whereabouts of his prey. He had not repeated his attempts at buying information, figuring that a flash of cash was more likely to buy him trouble. Still, despite a powerful combination of diplomacy, tact, and charm, his queries turned up nothing but blank stares at best, hostile looks and muttered curses at worst. "I'm the one who's been doing all the legwork. You're just along for the ride."

"And a damn bumpy one," the amulet's voice arose from the depth's of Dov's shirt. "And dark, damp, and *scratchy*. You know, many men have discovered that they feel a lot more liberated when they shave their chests."

"I am not going to shave my chest to accommodate you."

"You don't love me any more!" Ammi whined.

"What are you, nuts? I never loved you to start with! You're not a person, you're not a dog, you're not even a pet gecko: You're freakin' *jewelry*! What's there to love?"

"Isn't that just like a man? The sort who kisses World Series tickets and pledges his heart to a DVD player, but can't for the life of him see how someone could love a beautiful piece of art like me."

"Oh, shut up," Dov told the amulet. "You're not convincing anyone."

"And you're not finding anyone," Ammi countered. "I'll bet your sister's made three business calls by now! In fact, I'll bet that she gets here and finds this Mr. Bones bozo before you ever—"

A gaunt, dark hand seemed to thrust itself out of thin

air and thudded against Dov's chest with the force of a crossbow bolt, smothering the amulet's words.

"Little silver one, I would not be calling me a bozo. It is not polite, *hein*? Also it is not prudent."

Dov found himself gazing into the aged, ebony face of one of the most extraordinary individuals he had ever seen. "Mr. Bones, I presume?" he inquired. There was no need to waste the question: *How did you know it was the amulet talking?* Mr. Bones' various "talents" were a matter of record in the E. Godz, Inc. databanks.

"At your service, sir." The tall, skeletal gentleman doffed his shiny black top hat and made a bow that an eighteenth-century dancing master might envy, capping it with a flourish of the brightly painted wooden staff he carried. This courtly gesture set the staff's eclectic collection of bird and animal bones rattling eerily. A whole flock of feathers, tethered to the staff's head by satin ribbons, fluttered on the night air.

"You know, you're not an easy man to find," Dov said with a boyish grin.

"I don't intend to be." Mr. Bones returned the smile with interest. His teeth were a dazzling white, almost as brilliant as his impeccably starched and ironed shirt. He was clad like a clownish version of a bridegroom from another time: purple morning coat, pinstriped pants in black and red, shiny yellow spats over pointy-toed shoes of bottle-green patent leather. "As I reckon it, *mon vieux*, the only ones who find me are the ones by whom I wish to be found. Not a bad way to live, eh?"

"You could persuade me to join you," Dov replied. "But then, who'd there be to look after your best interests? Your financial interests, that is."

Mr. Bones shrugged and scraped his feet along the sidewalk in a halfhearted shuffle-shuffle-tap-kick. "Oh, friend, I am a silly, simple old man. My needs are few. I wander the streets of the Vieux Carré and greet the visitors to our fair city. For some reason, they find me a most interesting individual, and offer me money if I will pose with them for photographs. Thus I manage to scrape together a few coins, more than enough to keep body and soul together. Not that there is much body here to feed." He gestured modestly at his own gangly, scrawny frame.

Dov's mouth turned up at one corner. *What a performance!* he thought. His admiration was sincere. *The old fellow's a showman from the get-go. I like him. Here's hoping he likes me. It's always easier to close a deal when you can make them like you. But that's something Mr. Bones knows too.*

"Come now, Mr. Bones, sir," he said. "You know you're not fooling me with such talk. I'm Edwina Godz's son, remember?"

"Ah, yes, the fair Edwina!" Mr. Bones kissed the tips of his fingers in tribute to the absent lady's charms. Then he removed his top hat and bowed his head. "My dear boy, I cannot tell you how devastated I was to hear the news about her. I was *desolé, completment desolé*! I summoned the people to the dancing ground to see if perhaps we could not raise a cure for her, but the signs were all against it, the *loa* sounded quite . . . cross over having been bothered with such a thing. For my life, I could not tell why. Perhaps we did not make them a rich enough sacrifice—"

"Well, that's how it goes in this country," Ammi piped up. "One *loa* for the rich and another for the poor."

This time it was Dov who smothered him.

Mr. Bones leaned towards him and in a confidential tone of voice said: "You know, *mon vieux*, we are near enough to the river. If it would be your pleasure to drop that creature in?"

Dov chuckled. "No, thanks. He's got his uses."

"Ah. Suit yourself, then." The old man donned his top hat at a rakish angle and set off up St. Ann Street with Dov trailing after.

They went a few blocks and turned onto Bourbon Street. Walking with Mr. Bones down the most famous thoroughfare in the French Quarter was like being in your own miniature Mardi Gras parade. The old man didn't so much walk as strut down the street, his every move a loud, proud *Here I am! Admire what you see and can never be!* Dov took in the reactions of the passers-by with the eye of a diligent scholar. There was much about the old man that would bear imitating. He found himself walking more proudly, giving every step he took a subtle dramatic undertone. The lovely women of the French Quarter saw him and appreciated what they saw. He returned their alluring looks with his own unspoken *Perhaps later, my dears.* He had always been charismatic with the ladies, but as soon as he aped Mr. Bones' style he realized that he hadn't taken it far enough.

"Not bad, *hein*?" his venerable guide murmured. "You have the spark, the warmth that can never be taught, the charm that goes beyond any magic. And I see that you are not afraid to use it. This is good. Most boys fear their power while hungering to use it, and so they starve for love."

"Who are you calling a boy?" Dov replied, half-joking.

"To me, all men are boys," Mr. Bones said solemnly. "It happens when a body turns one hundred and twenty-three."

"Really? I wouldn't have pegged you for a day over

one hundred and five." Two grins flashed across the darkness and Mr. Bones laughed.

"*Petit*, we will get along fine, you and I," he said. By this time they had left Bourbon for one of its many side streets. Mr. Bones stopped outside a building that looked as old as the city itself, a little worn, a little shabby, but comfortable, like a respectable old maiden aunt who had enjoyed more than a few exciting indiscretions in her girlhood. A wooden sign on a wrought iron frame swung back and forth over the battered blue door proclaiming that this was Aux Roi Gris-Gris: Voodoo Supplies, Tarot Readings, Cold Drinks and Postcards.

The woman behind the counter was young, plump and beautiful, clad in a low-cut yellow blouse, a flounced skirt, and a tignon headwrap, the whole ensemble clearly worn to fulfill tourist expectations, the better to attract tourist dollars. She looked up from a tarot layout with a practiced saleswoman's smile on her face until she saw who it was had just come into the shop. At once her smile became heartfelt and, with a happy cry of recognition, she flew into Mr. Bones' arms, hugging him to her ample bosom so hard that Dov thought there was a good chance she'd break him in two.

There were worse ways to die.

"Please, Aurore, a little restraint, if you please. We have a guest." Mr. Bones tipped his hat in Dov's direction.

Dov stepped forward and raised the woman's hand to his lips. *When in Rome . . .* he thought. *But this looks like* much *more fun than Rome!* The lovely Aurore gave him a devastating smile in payment for his gallantry and Mr. Bones observed everything with a contented look.

"My dear, Mr. Godz and I will have brandy and coffee in my office," the old man said as he led the way around the counter into the rooms behind the store. As Dov followed, he took in the stock of Aux Roi Gris-Gris. As advertised there were plenty of postcards and a cooler full of cold drinks. There were also piles and piles of mass produced bric-a-brac for the tourist trade: overpriced feathered masks, plastic krewe doubloons from Mardi Gras past, rubber crawfish keyrings, suitably primitive-looking voodoo dolls that came with pins included.

"See anything you like?" Mr. Bones teased, glancing back over one shoulder.

Dov picked up one of the so-called voodoo dolls. Its body was made of sticks swathed in a couple of scraps of brightly colored cloth and its skull-like head was molded on white clay with the features daubed on in black ink.

"Now, Barbie, what did I tell you?" Dov addressed the doll. "Anorexia is *not* a laughing matter."

"The real ones are not sold here," Mr. Bones said. "They are made to order."

"I expected no less." Dov pulled Ammi out of his shirt and draped the amulet's chain around the fake voodoo doll's neck. "What do you think would happen if I stuck a pin into this thing now?" he asked lightly. He reached for one and was about to test his hypothesis when Mr. Bones' hand fell over his in a surprisingly strong grip.

"You may laugh freely, but laughter and mockery are two different things." There was a dangerous look in his eyes, a look that conjured up graveyard midnights and forces that were old when the world was young.

Dov set the doll down carefully and reclaimed his

amulet. "I didn't mean any disrespect. Not to anything but him, that is." He tapped Ammi's silver face.

"Hey! Watch it, you big boob," Ammi protested. "You've got thumbs fatter than a Bronx butcher's!"

"I believe you," said Mr. Bones. "And belief is everything." He took Dov into a small, snug room in back of the store, a place decked out with fine antique furnishings, most of them heavy, ornate pieces reflecting the on-and-off influence of forty-odd years of Spanish occupation. As Dov settled into the purple velvet seat of a high-backed oak chair, Aurore came gliding in with a tray bearing a demitasse service, a crystal brandy decanter, and two big-bellied snifters.

Mr. Bones did the honors, keeping his staff cradled in the crook of one elbow even while he poured brandy and coffee. Seeing Dov's curious look, he said, "There are many hands that would be eager to lay hold of my little beauty here." He gave the staff an awkward jiggle, making the bones click together. "The price of power is high—vigilance, courage, calculation, insight—but I find the rewards outweigh the inconveniences."

"I couldn't agree with you more." Dov accepted a demitasse and sipped the hot, strong brew. "That's why I've come here, to speak with you about—"

"I know." Mr. Bones saw no rudeness in interrupting his guest. "It is the dearest wish of my heart that your mother may yet surprise us all and make a full recovery. However, if she must instead go off with my good friend the Baron, I think she would do so less reluctantly if she knew that all her good works were being continued, and that the transition of power was to be accomplished as smoothly as possible."

"The Baron?" Dov asked.

"Baron Samedi." Mr. Bones pointed at a painting that

hung on one wall of his backroom retreat. It was oil on a large slab of cedarwood, and it showed a gentleman who very much resembled Mr. Bones, except for the fact that his face was painted so that he looked even closer kin to an animate skeleton. "He is . . . a friend of mine, a personage of great honor who takes a kindly interest in those whose lives have reached their close."

Dov studied the painting and mulled over Mr. Bones' rather evasive words. *Probably one of his deities,* he thought. *I should know this. Well, I can learn. Yes, and I will learn everything I must, once I'm head of the company!*

"I would like to hope," he said slowly, "that perhaps some day I may count on the Baron as a friend of mine as well."

Mr. Bones was visibly pleased by Dov's reply. "My friend, you commend yourself to me more with every word from your mouth. You show us respect, even though you have not got a baby's comprehension of what it is we do or how we worship. I would be honored to bring you to the temple where I serve as priest and my dear Aurore as priestess, but I fear your time with us is short. Is this not so?"

Dov bowed his head. "I'm afraid so, Mr. Bones. I deeply regret—"

"We've got to catch a plane to Arizona tomorrow," Ammi horned in. "We'd've had a lot more time to visit with you, maybe visit that temple of yours, if only you'd been a little easier to find in the first place. It's all very *spoooky,* you drifting through the French Quarter, no one knows where to find you, come and go like the wind, like a shadow, blah, blah, blah, but come on, Bones! Is that really any good for business?"

"*That* does it." Dov pulled the amulet from his neck so sharply that he snapped the chain. "You're going in the Mississippi. Now. That or down the toilet. Mr. Bones, where's the bathroom?"

The old man leaned forward and laid one hand on Dov's arm. "Let the creature be. Only the weak fear those who censure them. Only the truly poor cannot afford to laugh at themselves. I am neither weak nor poor. This garish shop is not my only source of income any more than the few pitiful coins I gather by posing for photographs with the tourists. My true power, in many senses, lies elsewhere."

Dov nodded. "The temple. Your followers. You also run a second shop, a botánica. Very thoughtful of you to provide your followers with a handy place to shop for all their voodoo needs. And not just your followers: This city shelters many different practitioners of the old ways, and you can't buy skulls or images of the gods or *those* kind of herbs at Winn-Dixie. I've done my research, Mr. Bones."

"So have I, Mr. Godz." The old man clapped his hands, summoning the beauteous Aurore. This time she had put off her gaudy tourist-trapping clothes and the tignon, wearing instead a smartly cut designer ensemble, her hair secured by elegant silver clips that whispered: *Tiffany's, of course.* She was carrying a leather portfolio stuffed to the bursting point with papers.

She smiled when she saw how Dov was staring at her. "You preferred me as I was?" she asked lightly.

"No, ma'am," he said, recovering himself. "Your other outfit was just fine for bringing down the pigeons, but I can see you prefer to stalk big game. I suppose those are the latest financial reports on the corporation?"

She nodded and she laid the portfolio in Mr. Bones' lap. The old man opened it to a random spot and ran one finger down the outer margin. "Compiled by a reliable and trustworthy research firm."

"Is that so." Dov bristled inwardly. "Do you think it's quite wise to have outsiders investigating E. Godz, Inc.? All it takes is one moron on their staff whose idea of a good time is an old-fashioned book burning and we won't be talking *small* can of worms; we'll be up to our eyeballs in nightcrawlers."

"A fate that will be ours soon enough, when our time comes," Mr. Bones replied. "But I agree: Why rush it? Rest easy, Mr. Godz. This research firm harbors only those who wish us well, and even though the payment for their services is . . . unconventional, I have the resources to meet it." He closed the folder and Dov caught sight of the image of Baron Samedi impressed on the cover in gold. "Now, let us discuss the reasons behind the corporate portfolio's continuing refusal to invest in the futures market."

"Say what?" said Ammi.

"Shut up, wart," Dov muttered. He rested his hands on his knees and leaned forward eagerly. "I'm glad you asked that question, Mr. Bones. After all, it's your group's future that's at stake. And I don't mean pork bellies! I've been following Mother's investment strategies for years, even if she doesn't know it, and the way I see things going is—"

Two hours later a sleek black Bentley pulled up to the blue door of Aux Roi Gris-Gris and a uniformed driver stood by at attention while Dov got in. He sank back against the sumptuously soft leather interior and closed his eyes. "Next stop, Arizona," he murmured.

"Without your underwear?" Ammi demanded. "This is not the way to the hotel!"

"No, it's the way to the airport. Mr. Bones took care of getting my things packed and loaded into the trunk. He's got his ways."

"He's also got a killer instinct for finance."

"Yes, well, so do I. I'm glad he saw that. I think it's what clinched the deal. One of the most influential members of the E. Godz, Inc. corporate family and I've got his support in my pocket. Yesss!" He punched the air in triumph before settling back down into the seat again and drifting off into wonderful dreams. They all featured himself tossing his sister Peez out into the cold, cruel world and a script consisting entirely of the words *Neener, neener, neener.*

Teddy Tumtum would have appreciated it.

# ⇒ CHAPTER SIX ⇐

"WHO ARE WE LOOKING FOR?" asked Teddy Tumtum from deep within Peez's carry-on bag. They had just arrived at Chicago's O'Hare airport following a flight out of Boston that had been severely delayed by bad weather. Peez was convinced that the springtime storm that had kept her from her second appointment was all her sneaky baby brother's doing. It would be just like him to phone up one of his minions and order a tempest or two, just to thwart her. "How are you going to recognize the guy they sent to meet you?"

"Simple. He'll be holding up a placard with my name on it," Peez replied. Like her brother, she had slapped a portable A.R.S. over herself and Teddy Tumtum so that she could converse with the insidious toy in public and in peace for the duration of her travels. Even in the crowded airport, no one seemed to be at all puzzled by a grown woman talking to her carry-on bag, and when she'd taken Teddy Tumtum out on the plane to distract herself from the worst of the turbulence (Peez was *not* a good flyer) no one on board had so much as batted an eye. Sometimes Peez wondered what it was they *thought* they were seeing.

"Well, that's mighty obliging of them," Teddy Tumtum remarked. "They must think highly of you."

"Oh, please." Peez tossed her head. "They're only kissing up to Mother through me. I don't matter as much as a squashed cockroach to these people. Probably less. I think they worship cockroaches."

"Dung beetles," Teddy Tumtum corrected her. "Among other things. I offered to brief you on the flight here, but someone I could mention thought she had better things to do."

"Yes, making sure I threw up *into* the barf bag was my top priority," Peez replied mordantly. "What *was* I thinking? Silly me."

"Ha, ha," the bear said, deadpan. "You were thankful enough that I prepped you for the meeting with Fiorella."

"For all the good it did me," Peez said.

"Awwww, izzums Peezie-pie upset 'cause nasty ol' witchy-lady didn't fall right into um's arms? She's a businesswoman! One tough honey, and believe me, I know from honey. Your victory will be all the sweeter once she's had a chance to think things through."

"You sound sure that I'm going to win her over. Aren't you forgetting something?"

"Like what?"

"Like my baby brother. I'm not naïve. I know that Dov's probably doing the exact same thing that I am, right now, zipping around the country, drumming up grassroots support for *his* takeover as head of the corporation. That little moop can charm the pants off anyone. Why not Fiorella?"

"Why assume she thinks with her pants?" Teddy Tumtum countered. "I told you, she's a businesswoman. Emphasis on the *business* part."

"Yes, but—"

"But nothing! You *are* naïve if you believe that the really successful movers and shakers get led around by the hormones. Your problem is you've been ruined by so-called 'entertainment' TV. According to them, it's all about sex when it isn't all about staying young. Sure, you'll hear tell of some high-placed corporate honcho or honchita horndogging after a bit of crumpet, but you can bet your T-bills that they lock up their assets first."

"Then what about that old dead billionaire whatz-isname, the one who married that boob-job bimbo and left her everything in his will? His kids are *still* duking it out with Suzie Skank in court!"

The carry-on bag chuckled. "Ever think that maybe the old guy didn't leave everything to the bimbo because he was stupid in love? Ever wonder if maybe he knew *exactly* what he was doing, and he was doing it pre-cisely because he wanted to aggravate his kids from beyond the grave? Never underestimate a parent, Peezie-pie. They could give sneaky weasel lessons to Machiavelli."

"Whatever." Peez was still feeling cranky and peaked after her bout of airsickness. She was in no mood for another of Teddy Tumtum's lectures. All she wanted was to make contact with the Chicago group, secure their backing, and then go to her hotel and the chaste embrace of a hot, scented bubble bath. "Where the hell *is* that driver?" she muttered, her eyes sweeping the crowd. "I can't stand here forever. I've got to retrieve my luggage. If he doesn't show up—"

That was when she saw him. It was a miracle that she did, considering how thick the crowd around him stood. The little cardboard sign with PEEZ GODZ scrawled on it in conventional Roman lettering wigwagged desperately over the heads of the gawking mob surrounding the short, dumpy little man whose only clothing was a pleated linen kilt, red leather sandals, and a heavy black Cleopatra wig. Peez fought her way through the pack just as the little man flipped the sign over to display the cartouche lovingly drawn on the other side.

*It's either my name or the word HELP done in hiero-glyphics,* Peez thought. "I'm here," she announced, laying one hand on her escort's naked shoulder. "Shall we go get my bags?"

"Oh yes, please," he replied. His moist, doggy eyes brimmed with gratitude. "I'm Gary. It's an honor to meet you."

"Gary . . ." Peez repeated thoughtfully, trying to merge the commonplace name with the bizarrely dressed little man before her.

Somewhere between their initial meeting point and the baggage carousels Gary excused himself, stepped into the men's room, and emerged wearing jeans, work shoes, a Bears T-shirt and a battered denim jacket. He was carrying a small blue gym bag from which protruded a few stray braids of the discarded wig. In answer to Peez's inquiring look he said, "Ray Rah tapped the power just enough to let me greet you in costu—in suitable regalia but with enough shielding to keep airport Security happy."

"An A.R.S.?" Peez asked. Then, noting how badly

bewildered he was, she explained: "Automatic Rationalization Spell. Very popular."

"I guess that must be what he used, then. But your flight was delayed; the spell began to wear off. That's why I was surrounded by all those people. I'm glad you showed up when you did."

"Me, too. You'd have hated to have to explain yourself to Security."

"Tell me about it." He shuddered.

He retrieved Peez's bag from the carousel, then escorted her to his car, a late-model Volvo convertible. The faience image of a hippopotamus dangled from the rearview mirror and the dashboard was a forest of figurines depicting some of the many gods of Ancient Egypt. As soon as they had their seat belts fastened, he pointed to one of the miniature statues and said, "She's my favorite—I mean, the object of my primary veneration: Sekhmet, the lion-headed goddess of war and sickness."

Peez gave the little man a searching look. He appeared to be about as bloodthirsty as a penguin. "Interesting choice," she remarked. "You a lawyer?"

"I sell insurance."

"Oh."

They drove from the airport in silence. Gary took it upon himself to offer Peez a brief guided tour of downtown Chicago. The weather was not cooperating; the city did not show its best face under dingy gray overcast skies. Still, the drive along the lakeshore was inspirational, and the skyline spoke to Peez with its own strange, steel-and-glass poetry.

As they drove, Peez discovered that Gary was about as scintillating and outgoing a conversationalist as she was herself. He only spoke when he had no other choice, on pain of death, and after he had pointed out this or that landmark his store of chitchat was drained dry. There was nothing wrong with silence—Peez rather liked being alone with her thoughts—but the Volvo was filled to bursting with that hideous beast, the nervous silence, the kind that sprang to ugly life when both tongue-tied parties felt the pressing obligation to say something to fill the soundless depths because— because—

*Because I don't really know who the hell this edgy little man is within the Chicago hierarchy,* Peez thought. *He's not the head of the organization—that's Ray Rah— but what if he's second-in-command, or even third? If this visit ends like the last one, without a firm commitment of support, they're going to talk about me after I'm gone. I'd need all the allies I can muster. Might as well start with Gary. No harm in taking a leaf from Dov's slimy little book and trying to chat him up.*

She glanced around for a prop to use in order to break the ice and her eye happened upon the placard with her name cartouche that Gary had dropped onto the passenger-side floor. She picked it up and studied the column of images within the red ovoid frame for a time, then said:

"Well, that's disappointing."

Gary almost jumped over the steering wheel at the sound of her voice. "What is?" he squeaked.

"How my name looks in hieroglyphics. I'd hoped it would require some of the more, well, interesting elements to render Peez Godz. You know: snakes, owls, lions, people. I can't even tell what some of these symbols are supposed to be. This one here looks like a spittoon."

She was trying to be funny. She lacked the practice, and it showed.

Gary didn't laugh. Instead he flashed her a look of such violent alarm that Peez realized she might have overestimated her ability to charm and had instead insulted a potential ally right to the marrow of his soul. She could feel any chance of winning him over slipping away, leaving the Chicago field wide open for an easy conquest by her baby brother.

Her oh-so-poised and charming baby brother. Except sometimes he didn't land on his feet, either. In all the years of their growing up, she could remember more than a score of incidents where Dov had put his foot in it up to the thigh.

*But he saved himself. Every single time. How did he do it? Think, Peez, think! What did he always do to pull his worthless butt out of the meat grinder?*

And she remembered. It was such a straightforward ploy, so basic, and yet proven so very effective almost every time Dov had applied it.

Peez gazed at Gary, gave him a smile, and said, "Oh my, did I say that? I don't know what I was thinking. I certainly didn't mean any disrespect for the ancient ways, it's just that— Gosh, this is so embarrassing, but you see, I always get sooo nervous when I have to talk to handsome men."

"Whuh—?" said Gary, and nearly ran the Volvo up the tailpipe of the car ahead of it.

By the time they reached Ray Rah's self-styled Temple of Seshat-by-the-Shore, Peez was amazed yet gratified to find that her brother's simple stratagem had earned her the utter devotion of Gary, the bloodthirsty penguin.

*So Dov has his uses after all,* she thought as her newly smitten escort raced ahead of her, carrying her suitcase, to hold the temple door open and await her pleasure.

The Temple of Seshat-by-the-Shore was housed in an

old mansion with absolutely no view of Lake Michigan whatsoever. It was by-the-Shore the way Minneapolis was by-the-Sea, yet the house and its master were both so undeniably rich that no one was going to argue semantics as long as the bills got paid. Ray Rah had a bank account fat enough for him to call his self-created house of worship the Temple of Seshat-on-the-Moon if he felt like it.

As soon as Peez stepped over the threshold, she knew that she was in the presence of old money and lots of it. Behind that turn-of-the-previous-century façade was the Egyptian temple of Cecil B. DeMille's dreams, or perhaps his nightmares. The entire first floor and most of the second had been gutted to accommodate a row of lotus-crowned pillars, painted red and gold, blue and green. These led from the former vestibule into what had once been the parlor, only now it was transformed into the sanctuary of the gods. Peez walked between two rows of twelve different images as Gary led her deeper into the temple. Ibis-headed Thoth stared down jackal-headed Anubis. Set the kin-slayer snarled his eternal defiance at Horus the avenger. Ptah and Amon, Osiris and Isis, the cobra goddess Renenutet and the cow-horned goddess Hathor, all these and more besides watched over Peez's passage.

Ray Rah was waiting for her at the end of the alleyway of images, standing before a gauzy painted curtain depicting Osiris in the Underworld, sitting in judgment of the dead. The head of the Chicago group was wearing the same sort of pleated linen kilt that Gary had sported at the airport, only his was fringed with scarlet and gold. If he wore a wig, it was not visible beneath his striped Pharaonic headdress surmounted by the cobra-and-vulture uraeus. The bejeweled gold pectoral covering his shoulders and chest was so heavy that Peez wondered how much longer Ray Rah was going to be able to stay standing. He had the look of a failed high school basketball star, all stringy sinews and long bones but not a heck of a lot of useful muscle.

"Hail, Peez, whose coming is most beautiful," he intoned from atop the low flight of shallow marble steps before the curtain. He stretched out the blue and silver flail he carried in his right hand, his left being occupied by a glittering ankh rather than the pharaoh's traditional shepherd's crook. He kept shifting his grip on it, as if uncertain of exactly how he could display it to best advantage. "Behold thy coming is welcome to us. When we do rise up and when we do lie down, we bid thee—"

At that point, the knobbly fake beard attached to his chin fell off, hit the floor, bounced down the steps, and rolled almost to Peez's feet before one of the temple's ubiquitous cats pounced on it with happy murfing sounds. When Gary tried to recapture the errant beard, the cat clawed his hand and he gave up.

Ray Rah said a word that was more Anglo-Saxon than Ancient Egyptian. Then he looked at Peez and blushed.

"Sorry," he said. "That always happens. I don't usually wear the beard, you know—spirit gum and false eyelash adhesive are way too weak to hold it, and anything stronger is too darn strong for my skin—but seeing as how this was going to be our first visit from a corporate representative, I thought it might be nice to do something special. Won't you come into the inner chamber? The rest of the congregation are expecting you."

Peez dutifully followed him, wending her way around the countless cats, as he conducted her behind the painted curtain and through a little door. Some of the cats attempted to come along, but Ray Rah was having none of it.

"Shoo, O She-who-walks-in-beauty. You can't come in here, Thou-who-art-swifter-than-gazelles. *Scat*, Eternal-glory-of-the-Lady-Bast! Scat, I say!"

Of course the cats, being cats, shot through the door anyway, but as soon as they took one good snort of the air quality on the far side, they turned tail and raced right back out again.

Peez wished she could have joined them. The inner chamber's atmosphere was so thick with the smoke of burning incense (at least she *thought* that was the source of the sickly-sweet aroma) that her eyes flooded with tears and she began to cough uncontrollably.

"Can I get you something, Ms. Godz?" The faithful Gary was at her elbow, his round face barely visible through the roiling smoke. "Some water? Organic fruit nectars? A beer?"

"Whatever," Peez croaked. He vanished into the mist only to return almost immediately with a gold goblet.

"Beer," he said as she raised the cup to her lips. "We have a highly authentic microbrewery on the premises that—"

He got a faceful of microbrew when Peez spritzed out her first taste of Horus Lite. "Dear gods, what *was* that stuff?" she gasped.

From somewhere deep in the heart of the pungent clouds there came a giggle and someone said: "*That is what we like to call an acquired taste.*"

Peez blinked her stinging eyes and little by little was able to distinguish solid shapes amid the whorls of smoke. "I don't suppose there's a window in here?" she asked.

"Yes," said the voice. "But we prefer not to—"

"The Lady Peez has spoken!" Ray Rah thundered. "All power to the words of the Lady Peez! So let it be written, so let it be done! Gary, open the window." There came the sound of much scrabbling, a couple of bumps, a thud, several curses, Gary's mumbled "'Scuse me, sorry," and at long last the squeak of a sash being raised. A cool breeze blew into the room, banishing the worst of the haze and giving Peez a clear view of her surroundings.

Apart from the birdbath-sized incense burner in the center of the rug, the inner chamber of Ray Rah's temple looked like nothing more than a frat house rumpus room. There were several mismatched sofas and chairs, some wobbly-looking tables, a big screen TV complete with DVD player, a middle-of-the-line stereo system and a wet bar.

Peez decided to make the wet bar her number one priority. Striding across the room, ignoring the twenty-odd people lounging around, she went right up to the bar and set down her gold goblet with a mighty thump. "I don't call a practical joke an acquired taste," she informed the woman behind the counter. "And I sure as hell don't call this gunk *beer*."

The woman, like Ray Rah and the rest, was wearing the pleated white linen garb made famous by New Kingdom tomb paintings. She too wore a sparkling assortment of gold jewelry, heavy on the lotus/ankh/eye-of-Horus motifs. However, instead of a wig she had opted to cornrow her mousy brown hair and top the whole ensemble with a Cubs cap.

"Sorry to disillusion you, Princess, but that *is* beer," she said. "Authentic Ancient Egyptian beer. I brewed it myself, after copious research and the proper sacrifices to the gods. It may be a little sweeter than what you're used to—"

"Sweet, hell; it's *chewy!*" After Ray Rah and Gary's subservient behavior, Peez didn't care for this woman's in-your-face attitude at all. "There are pieces of—of— Well, I don't really want to know *what* they're pieces of, and I sure don't want to drink them!"

The woman reached under the bar and slammed a strange metal object down onto the counter between them. "That's because Gary was so hot to fetch you your drink that he forgot to give you the strainer straw. Want to give it a second try?" Her eyes added: *Or do you want to wimp out now, Princess?*

Peez thrust her goblet under the barkeep's nose. "Fill 'er up," she commanded. Using the straw as directed, she sucked up half the beer in one go. It still tasted too sweet, there wasn't any fizz to it worth mentioning, and it had about as much alcoholic kick as a dose of cough syrup, but she got it down.

The other temple members crowded up to the bar to watch. When she drained her goblet dry, they made small sounds of approval and gazed at her with reverence.

"Wow," one of them said. His slack belly lapped over the top of his long kilt. "You're the first person I ever saw who could stomach a whole serving of Meritaten's beer."

"Yeah," another man put in. "Even Ray Rah couldn't do that. You're cool!"

Peez scanned the ring of friendly faces surrounding her. Men and women alike all looked to be in their late forties to early fifties, with physiques that were not displayed to best advantage by a few paltry layers of translucent linen.

"I'm . . . cool?" she repeated. "What is this, a hazing?"

"Oh no, Lady Peez, by no means, none at all!" Ray Rah hastened to say. He shoved his way through the crowd and glowered at Meritaten. "*Some* people seem to think it's all right to sacrifice the holy tenets of hospitality on the altar of historical authenticity, even if what they serve our honored guest tastes like a kitty litter cocktail! *Some* people seem to have forgotten that the gods see all and that a list of their errors will be forever inscribed on their hearts. *Some* people don't seem to care that when they die their hearts will be weighed in the Scales of Justice against the Feather of Ma'at and if they don't measure up, their hearts will be thrown into the jaws of a monster and devoured. *Some* people—"

"—don't care if they get to dwell in blessedness forever in the Field of Reeds, yadda, yadda, yadda." Meritaten leaned one elbow on the bar, chin in hand, and looked bored. "*Some* people are actually capable of reading the Book of the Dead for ourselves, thank you very much." She looked at Peez. "Hey, I'm sorry if you didn't like the beer. I didn't mean it as a practical joke, no matter what you think. I just assumed that since you're Edwina's daughter you'd be just as open to new experiences as she is. No hard feelings?"

"None." Peez summoned up one of her brother's patented ingratiating smiles. "Sorry if I snapped at you. I came here on serious business. I'm not exactly in the mood for initiation hijinks."

"We know," Meritaten said. "We heard." A chorus of sympathetic murmurs ran through the congregation. The news of Edwina's impending death had traveled fast.

"If it's any consolation, Nenufer's been studying the old ways of embalming," Gary said, nodding at another one of the women in the group.

Ray Rah chimed in with: "When the time comes, we promise to give your mother the most sumptuous burial the law allows. A pity we can't have slaves to help out with the arrangements, though. Without them you can't get a whole lot of good, solid tomb construction done at today's prices, and as for providing her with a suitable entourage to serve her in the Afterlife—" He shrugged. "I suppose she'll have to make do with *ushabti* figurines. I know that's what most pharaohs did, but if you ask me, you can't rely on a mere *image* of a servant to provide you with the same quality labor you got back in the good old days."

"Which was when—?" Peez asked, not entirely sure she wanted to hear the answer.

"Which was when the pharaohs had *real* servants sacrificed and put in their tombs with them." Ray Rah didn't seem at all disturbed by this aspect of his chosen spiritual path.

"Ah, come off it, Ray!" one of the men scoffed. "The only reason you're so keen on human sacrifice is 'cause the only way you'll ever get a woman is if she's too dead to run away."

"Shut up, Billy-hotep," Ray Rah said through gritted teeth.

The peculiarly named Billy-hotep giggled. The eyes behind his bifocal wire-rimmed glasses were two blobs of solid black, their pupils dilated to the point of no return.

*That must've been some powerful incense he was inhaling,* Peez thought.

Billy-hotep's inhibitions had gone the way of the

pharaohs. "Well, excuuuse *me*, Your Revered Date-lessness," he said, "but you forget: We've all known you since college. Whenever we did see you with a girl, we always found out later she'd been bought and paid for."

"Like your membership dues in the temple?" Ray Rah countered. "I've been floating you one loan after another, and this is the thanks I get? The first live contact we have with the head office in over twenty-five years and you try to embarrass me in front of her? Maybe I should let you sink or swim on your own. No dues, no membership; no membership—"

"—no parties." The realization yanked Billy-hotep down to earth with a thud. He began to blubber: "You can't do that to me, man! I love our parties! They're just like the ones we used to throw back in college!"

"Everything's just the way it used to be for us back in college," Meritaten muttered. "Except our waistlines, our cars, and our computers."

"Ah, eternal Egypt," Peez commented. She considered this little nest of aging Baby Boomers. They'd grown up in a society that saw them as the center of the universe, they'd indulged one set of whims after the other, they'd amassed great heaping piles of Stuff, and if you didn't think too much about their age-mates who'd been destroyed by the Viet Nam War, as a group they'd had it good. Why let a little thing like death stop the fun?

A remarkably pharaonic outlook, that. All in all, she was surprised that more Boomers hadn't subscribed to Ray Rah's restored stab at that Old Time Religion.

*At least their tombs won't be despoiled*, she thought. *No self-respecting burglar would be interested. All the electronics they stow away with them for eternity will be obsolete before the seal on the sarcophagus dries.*

"You know," she said aloud. "Tradition is a wonderful thing. A sacred thing. I know that of all the different groups that we at E. Godz, Inc. represent, yours is the only one worthy enough to fully appreciate the holiness of continuity. The gods themselves smile upon those who—"

Fifteen minutes later she was sitting in the back seat of Ray Rah's own Lincoln Town Car while his driver whisked her off to her hotel. The first thing she did after fastening her seat belt was to dig Teddy Tumtum out of her carry-on bag and wave a piece of parchment in his furry face.

"Look!" she crowed. "They *loved* me, Teddy Tumtum. They all told me how much they appreciated my coming out to see them in person this way. Sure, their group's nothing more than a bunch of old yuppies trying to keep a death grip on their youth, but why should I care about that? Read this and weep, Dov! Chicago's power—money, numbers, media clout, the whole shebang—and it's all promised to *me*, right there, in black and white!"

"Looks more like black, yellow, and a little red," Teddy Tumtum said, studying the parchment. "This is written in hieroglyphics. Good luck getting it to stand up in court, even if some of these squiggles do look like legs."

Peez jealously snatched the parchment away from the bear. "It won't come to court. Why should it? This is only the first of my victories. I hadn't yet hit my stride while dealing with Fiorella, but now—! Ho, *ho*! Look out, world, here comes Peez."

"Good idea," said Teddy Tumtum. He dove back into the carry-on bag and hid himself beneath a spare pair of Peez's serviceable white underpants. "I think I liked her better when she was shy," he grumbled to himself as Peez's maniacal, triumphant laughter filled the car.

# ⋝ CHAPTER SEVEN ⋜

DOV LEANED ACROSS THE TABLE in one of the Blue Coyote Diner's back booths and played an ongoing game of Twenty Questions with the Native American man opposite. He'd been at it ever since he'd showed up for this agreed-upon meeting with Sam Turkey Feather and he was starting to get sick of it.

"Zuni?" he asked. Sam shook his head. "Hopi? Navajo?" More misses. Dov sighed. "Okay, fine, I give up. What *is* your—nation? Tribe? Look, I don't mean any offense, I'm just not sure which one's okay to say."

"You mean today?" Sam's mouth curved up. The rest of his face—bright eyes, black hair, smooth skin—made him appear to be about the same age as Dov, but his mouth was oddly older. Much older. A fine webbing of wrinkles creased his lips and the surrounding skin, and when he smiled he revealed crooked yellow teeth. It was striking, disconcerting, and fascinating all at the

105

same time, and it made it extremely difficult for a body to look elsewhere when conversing with this man.

In fact, it was as if Sam Turkey Feather's mouth exerted an incredible power over anyone he met, a power he was more than happy to exercise to the fullest, to his own advantage.

*No wonder he insisted on a face-to-face*, Dov thought, his eyes riveted. *Not that I wasn't going to insist on it myself, after coming all this way out here to Arizona to get his support. But I'll bet he gets plenty of other business contacts who try to keep their interactions with him on a long-distance-only basis.*

What was it Ammi had said when they'd first beheld this man out in the diner parking lot? Oh, right: *That mouth gives him a leg up on the competition, a foot in the door, and the upper hand.* Then the amulet had started laughing so raucously, with no sign of ever stopping, that Dov had been forced to stuff the little silver blob into his back pocket and sit on him.

"Is that all the answer you'll give me?" Dov demanded.

Sam shook his head. He wore his jet black hair long, in braids tied with rawhide strips, adorned with silver balls and clusters of tiny animal fetishes carved from semi-precious stone. They clicked and clattered together whenever he moved his head, like the macabre decorations on Mr. Bones' painted staff.

"Why is it always so important for you white men to know the names of everything? What is it, a passion for pigeonholing? Obsessive/Compulsive Disorder? Brand-name recognition?"

"All I asked was a civil question: Which tribe are you from?" Dov said. He sounded petulant and no longer cared about whether or not "tribe" was the politically correct term of the moment.

"Yes, and I have chosen not to answer. Is this the only reason you came here to see me? I don't think so. You're here because of what I do, not who I am; where I'm going with my business, not where I came from. And what difference would it make to you if I did tell you my tribe? Would you have any idea of what that meant, besides having a label to slap on my forehead?"

"Hey! I happen to have a great deal of respect for—"

"—'you people'?" Sam chuckled. "Which aspect of 'you people' am I for you? The Noble Savage? Hmm, probably not: much too dated. The Proud Rebel against the White Military-Industrial Complex Oppressors? Nope: too guns 'n' granola. Thank God you're not a woman! You'd be casting me in every white woman/red man romance novel you ever read: *Blazing Breechclouts, Tender is the Tepee, Whoopee Warrior* and all the rest." He laughed again, louder. "I'd only disappoint you. I never work out, I couldn't find my abs on a bet, and I look like a real dumbass in a skimpy loincloth."

"Look, what I'm *trying* to say—" Dov made another effort to be heard, but Sam had his own agenda in high gear and was not about to be stopped.

"No, wait, let me guess! It's more fun this way." Sam picked up a piece of toast and waved it around as he spoke. "You once actually went and *got a whole book* about Native American cultures so you know lots and lots about what makes each nation special. Or else you've only got one or two tidbits you can toss off to impress me with how *informed* and *aware* you are. So if I tell you I'm Hopi you'll say, Right. Kachina dolls. Cool. Zuni? Yeah. All those little stone fetish animals. Cute *and* ecologically sensitive. Makes a nice gift for the folks back home and doesn't take up much room in the suitcase. Or Navajo? That's the motherlode: blankets, silver and turquoise jewelry, sheep, and maybe, if you actually *read* that book of yours instead of just looking at the pretty pictures, you'll remember the Code Talkers from World War II. But I'm not holding my breath."

"I wish you would," Dov snarled. "It's the only way I'll get a chance to say anything in my own defense."

"Oh, you don't have to *defend* yourself to me." Sam took a big bite of buttered toast and beat it senseless with his horrible teeth. "Maybe I'm right about you, maybe I'm wrong. Maybe you really do know more than a couple of sound bites' worth about us injuns, *keemo sabee*. I don't care. It's not worth my time to find out, and it wouldn't give you any sort of leverage with me. So how about we stop trying to become each other's best buddies and just be businessmen? It's what I do best."

"Funny coincidence, that," Dov replied, giving Sam the gimlet eye. "So do I."

"Good." Sam polished off what was left of his toast and soft-boiled eggs, then slapped a twenty down on the tabletop and stood up. "Now we can go."

Dov followed him out to the parking lot, but he balked at getting into Sam's late-model Jeep. "Was that supposed to impress *me*?" he asked, one foot up on the passenger's side step-up.

"What?"

"Flashing that money. We both ordered the $1.99 breakfast special. Unless they charge one hell of a refill fee on the coffee in there, you just overtipped by a factor of five."

"Four," Sam corrected him. "And that's based on a

twenty percent tip which is not the norm in these parts. You think I did that to impress *you*?" His mouth twisted into a sneer.

Dov felt his face flush. "So why *did* you do it?"

"Tell you later. Maybe. If I feel like it. Now either get in or stay out there, eat my dust, and haul your sorry ass back to the airport. Me, I've got customers waiting and if I leave them on their own too long, there's always the danger that they'll wise up and go home."

"Customers? You mean the distribution network for the fetish animals and the dreamcatchers?" Dov had done his homework: Sam Turkey Feather was on the E. Godz, Inc. books as the Southwest's major mass producer of Native American merchandise with a "spiritual" subtext. "I thought you had enough sales reps to monitor that for you. How can we have an effective business meeting if you've got to futz around with a lot of piddling details that your subordinates should be handling?"

Sam looked at him as if he'd stuck a pair of chopsticks up his nose and started barking like a walrus.

"Kid, you ever get tired of chewing on that foot, you come to me and I'll spice it up with a little Earth Magic-brand salsa before you stick it back in your mouth. I've been running a successful organization since before you were born and dropped on your head, and that includes knowing how to get the most out of business meetings. You think I do a hands-on customer call when it's not completely necessary? Check the spreadsheets. That's not the way we drum up the big profits, no pun intended."

"What pun?"

"Whoa. You sure you're Edwina's boy? See, I said

'drum up the big profits,' and what I do is— Oh, the hell with it. That's what I wanted to show you right now, if you could maybe stop holding us up with a lot of stupid remarks and let us get started. So which is it, kid? You in or you out?

"In." Holding in his frustrated anger, Dov got into the Jeep. Sam didn't even wait for him to buckle up before flooring the accelerator and taking off.

Distances in the Indian territories of Arizona were best calculated using the same mind-set brought to understanding space travel. Folks from Back East who sighed like martyrs over having to face two-hour commutes each morning went into slack-jawed shock when confronting the southwestern concept of a "short" drive. Two hours on the road *might* get you out of the figurative parking lot. The day was young and the summer heat was still weeks away, but by the time they reached their destination, Dov was exhausted, sweltering, his eyes were full of grit, and he felt as though someone had run his kidneys through a blender with a handful of rocks thrown in to really get the job done.

As he climbed unsteadily out of the Jeep, Dov looked around. They had left the highway some time ago, heading over secondary roads and fifth-rate sheep tracks towards a distant prospect of tawny mountains, but the mountains still looked just as distant even though the highway itself was long gone.

*This isn't even the* middle *of nowhere*, Dov thought. *It's the suburbs.*

As for Sam, he'd jumped easily down from his seat and was now striding across the arid terrain, heading for a cluster of what looked like rawhide igloos. The brown humps in the distance reminded Dov of the coconut halves used in the old shell game at turn-of-the-century carnivals. Shills and sharpers knew that you didn't get a lot of milk out of a coconut, but you could use them to milk the suckers for plenty.

"Watch where you step," Sam called back to Dov.

"Snakes?" Dov cast nervous glances at the ground. Unlike Sam, he wasn't wearing boots; just designer running shoes.

"Nah; empties."

"Emp—?" That was all Dov had the chance to say before an ill-placed foot landed on a discarded bottle of high-priced mineral water. His legs shot out from under him and he landed on his rump.

"Ow! Get off me, you big hippo!" Ammi's muffled voice rang out loud and clear under the wide open sky. It should have reached Sam's ears as the yelp of a far-away coyote, thanks to the A.R.S.

It didn't.

Sam gave Dov a hand getting back to his feet, then said, "White man speak with surly butt."

"You heard that?" Dov was incredulous.

"Only part of me that doesn't work up to snuff's my teeth."

Slowly, almost shyly, Dov pulled the silver amulet out of his back pocket and held it up for Sam's inspection. The man stroked his chin and mused aloud: "You know, I could really use something like this." He tapped Ammi's nose lightly, making the amulet swing at the end of its chain. "How about it, friend?" he asked the amulet. "Ever thought of a career in show business?"

"What's in it for me, Turkey Plucker?" Ammi retorted.

"That's Turkey *Feather*," Sam said evenly.

"No, it's not." The amulet flashed a silver smirk. "I used to work for the boss lady, Edwina Godz herself, before she gave me to the kid, here. I was in on plenty of official correspondence, including all the paperwork that went through the office back in the days when you first joined the organization. Your real name is Sam Turkey *Plucker*, only you changed it to Turkey *Feather* on Edwina's advice, because it'd sound better for attracting the tourists."

"Is that true?" Dov gave Sam a questioning look.

Sam tossed his head back and laughed. "Yeah, Tex, he got me, all right. Pow, right between the eyes. Another one bites the dust. My true name's Turkey Plucker and when I met your mama I wasn't much more than that, except I was maybe starting to figure out that there was better money to be made plucking the tourists. Edwina and me, we were living together out here for a while—she said she wanted to be somewhere she could tap into the earth magic without hitting a telephone cable. Your mama, she was good for me, taught me to stop *looking* and start *seeing*, know what I mean? Seeing things like opportunities."

"You and my mother were—?" Dov couldn't believe it.

"Back when she was maybe eighteen, nineteen, around then. Why? Shocked? Scandalized? Grossed out? What?"

"Hey, I don't care if you and my mother slept together or not," Dov protested. "It's just that you don't look anywhere near old enough to have known her back then."

Sam picked up one of his black braids. "Hair dye. Better living through chemistry. And once my business got going I had more than enough cash to buy me my own private plastic surgeon, if I wanted, plus a carload of retin-A."

"Then why didn't you do anything about your teeth?"

Sam smiled extra wide on purpose. "Because my spirit guide Old Man Coyote told me that if I tried to make my mouth look as young as the rest of me, he'd make sure that all the words that came out of it were young too. Young and foolish. Gotta listen to your spirit guide, kid. Bad medicine if you don't pay heed."

Dov grabbed Ammi from Sam's hand. "If you're *quite* through yanking my chain?" he inquired frostily.

The older man clicked his tongue. "I can tell you're not gonna listen to me. Too bad. I expected more from Edwina's boy. Oh well, nothing to be done about it. Come on. I've kept the Seekers waiting long enough." He turned and started off for the cluster of brown domes again.

"Now just wait one minute!" Dov objected. "I think I'm entitled to know what's going on here."

"No, you're not," Sam said, never breaking stride. "Edwina always *saw*, always *listened*. Taught me to do the same. I'm not gonna *tell* you another word about who I am and what I do. You'll only hear the sounds my words make, but you won't *understand* a damn thing. If you're your mother's son, you'll catch on quick enough. If not, no charge."

"No charge? No charge for what?" Dov demanded, scampering after Sam.

By this time they were within a stone's throw of the brown domes. It was flat land, but tough going. The ground underfoot was thickly littered with at least two score of the same kind of bottle that Dov had slipped on before. Other detritis cluttered the earth: empty energy bar wrappers, used tissues and paper towels, toothpaste-stained twigs and one lonely, tapped-out tube of hemorrhoid cream. As Dov approached, he noted that the domes, which he had initially believed to be made out of hide, were actually cheap tents, their ripstop material painted to imitate leather. They were set up in a ring around a circle of cleared, beaten ground. All of the rubbish he'd been dodging was kept to the outer perimeter of the tent ring.

*Out of sight, out of mind,* he thought.

Sam strode into the very center of the ring and cupped his hands to his mouth. Throwing his head back, he let loose a series of yips and yowls that any self-respecting coyote might envy. Immediately the door flaps of the brown tents stirred and a chorus of random animal noises streamed out in response. Grunts and bellows, hisses and squawks, meows and chitterings and even a few pathetic squeaks broke the silence of the desert. Then, from inside one of the tents, someone began to beat rhythmically on a drum.

"*Gerald*! Stop that, you idiot!" a very strident female voice overwhelmed the menagerie and cut the drumming off cold. "You don't do that until *later*, when Master Turkey Feather calls us into the circle and tells us it's okay. Jesus, are you actively *trying* to embarrass me?"

"Sorry, Pookie," came the chastened murmur.

Sam gave Dov a look of intense amusement, then whisked his face clean of all trace of levity. Looking grave and stoic, he sat down crosslegged in the middle of the circle and began to sing. The melody was almost nonexistent, nasal and repetitive, but the words were in pure English, a summons for all Seekers to emerge into the Light of Truth and walk the Path of Dreams that would take the Truly Worthy to the very Heart and Soul of the Great Eagle's Egg of Life. (It wasn't often you could hear spoken words being capitalized but Sam made it so.)

One by one, the tent flaps lifted and the inhabitants crawled out into the sunlight, blinking like moles. There were ten of them, all told. Most walked upright, but one platinum blond woman chose to hop along on all fours like a bunny rabbit while one of the men kept his arms stretched out while he swooped in a looping pattern around the outside of the circle, like a little boy pretending to be a jet plane. All regarded Dov with suspicion and jealousy.

"Who *is* this?" one woman wanted to know. She looked like a Barbie doll that had been left out in a sandstorm. "I've been camping out here for *two whole days*, and I still haven't been contacted by my spirit guide, which I think is *all Mimsy's fault*, by the way, because she went and hogged the spirit of White Buffalo when it showed up, even though it was *obviously* supposed to be *mine*, and if this guy can just come waltzing in here and join up on the Vision Quest at the *last frickin' minute* like he was boarding the A train, for God's sake, then my aura is gonna be *entirely* thrown out of whack and I want a refund!"

"The great spirit guide White Buffalo says to tell you that Courtney speaks with forked tongue," another woman tranquilly told Sam. She was built on the same model as the first whiner—a toned, tanned, and tucked physique enhanced by strategic lumps and bumps of silicon, saline, and collagen. "The great spirit guide White Buffalo also says that if Courtney can't remember that my name is no longer Mimsy but Flower-in-the-Crannied-Wall, then it's no damn wonder she can't get a spirit guide of her own."

"Oh yeah? Well if you ask me, the only spirit guide that should've shown up to claim you is a double-dyed *bitch*," Courtney sniped. "You've got no right to White

Buffalo and no right to that name! If anyone should be Flower-in-the-Crannied-Wall, it's me!"

"How would you like my boot so far up your Crannied Wall that you sneeze shoelaces for a week?" Mimsy countered. Her self-satisfied serenity had blown away like a tumbleweed and she was ready to rumble. This was serious. The woman doing the bunny hop paused, the swooping man stood stock still, the other Seekers froze on point like a pack of bird dogs, eager to watch a good old-fashioned catfight. Only Sam looked worried.

*I'll bet,* Dov thought. *Now I see how he's been pulling in the serious money all these years. This is much bigger than the fetish bead market: made-to-order Vision Quests for the financially affluent and spiritually destitute. Sure, take them out into the desert, burn some herbs, chant your grocery list at them, have them thump on some drums, and make them go on a fast until they get their Vision. How long do you think these overgrown spoiled brats would go without food before they start seeing things? Or imagining that they do.*

*Only trouble is, this fight isn't imaginary, and if one of these two Minnehaha wannabes gets hurt, she'll hire Big Chief Sues-With-a-Vengeance and hold the company responsible.*

Dov had always had a keen nose for Brownie Point Earning opportunities. The only reason he'd managed to finish college was his ability to ingratiate himself with his professors while all the other suckers were burning brain cells by actually studying. He figured that if he could defuse the impending Mimsy-Courtney blowup, he'd be in good with Sam, which meant Sam's considerable financial clout would be backing him when it came time for the corporate showdown with Peez.

Sam could also provide Dov with another, perhaps stronger sort of influence: Having one of Edwina's old lover's on his side could only help Dov's chances for persuading her to give him the company. It was a win-win situation, and both of the winners were Dov, just the way he liked it.

Eyes on the prize, Dov took action.

Amazing how fast he was able to slip out of his clothes and stand there naked under the startled eyes of Sam's little group of Seekers. The hardest part of his impromptu striptease was kicking free of his lace-up running shoes and yanking off the socks beneath, but he managed to do so and to make it look like part of a ceremonial dance step. Now, as bare as a lizard, he proceeded to leap and stomp and cavort all around the earth circle, raising his voice in the nearest thing he could remember to a genuine Indian chant. (Could he help it if it was the lyrics to an Israeli rain dance, left over from Edwina's days of full immersion in folk culture studies?)

As he completed his orbit, Dov was pleased to note that Mimsy and Courtney had dropped their feud in favor of gaping at him like a pair of beached halibut. *Objective number one achieved*, he thought gleefully. *Commence accomplishment attempt on objective number two.*

Flinging himself at Courtney's feet, despite the grit that scraped his bare knees raw, Dov bowed his head, raised his arms, and declared, "Hail, Woman-Who-Is-Worthy. I am he who is sent from the Great Spirit to bring you word that you have been chosen. From this day forth, your spirit guide shall be Great Goo-ga-li-moo-ga-li, the White Otter, and your tribal name shall be Lives-Long-and-Prospers."

"Yeah?" Courtney brightened. "Nifty!"

"No fair!" Mimsy wailed. "She didn't get a Vision! How come she gets a spirit guide and a name and everything like this? Like it's— it's— like it's some kinda *pizza delivery* or something? And how come she gets an otter for her spirit guide? Otters are *way* cuter than buffalo! *I* want the otter!"

"Behold!" Dov shouted, leaping to his feet. Naked as he was, there was plenty of beholding for the assembled Seekers to do. "Behold that your mighty shaman, Master Sam Turkey Feather, has used his powers to summon me from the realm of the Great Spirit through long hours of self-sacrifice, fasting, and chanting. He has placed me within this body so that your eyes may see me and so that I may walk among you and give you the spiritual gifts which all of you have earned. Verily, even those of you who have already been vouchsafed a Vision of your spirit guides shall have these same Visions confirmed and sanctified. So decrees the Great Spirit, for never in countless generations has he ever known a group as worthy of this special blessing as all of you!"

A chorus of approving murmurs ran through the group. Why wouldn't they approve? The Great Spirit had just confirmed their own inflated opinions of themselves. Dov took that opportunity to duck into one of the dome tents and leave it to Sam to handle the loose ends. Alone in the dark he smiled, more than satisfied with how well he'd handled the situation. He'd saved Sam's bacon and now Sam would have to give him his approval and backing. It was that simple.

The tent flap lifted.

"*You,*" Dov said as the Jeep jounced down the road heading back for the Blue Coyote Diner. He sounded as prickly as a giant saguaro cactus. "You, Sam Turkey Plucker, are one sneaky son of a bitch."

"Compliment accepted," Sam replied, grinning ear to ear. "Don't blame me. Did I make you take off all your clothing and declare yourself the Great Spirit's messenger boy?"

"No, but you're the one who told that nest of yuppie toad-lickers that the reason I'd appeared to them in the form of a naked man instead of an animal was because there was only *one way* for me to confer the Great Spirit's official tribal names on them."

"I didn't hear you complaining when you were *conferring* Courtney and Pookie and Heather and—"

"Yeah, but how about when you sent Gerald in to see me? Not only was I half dead from conferring Nicole—let me tell you, it's no wonder her spirit guide's a bunny rabbit!—but I do not swing that way."

"Neither does Gerald. Trust me, he was just as relieved as you when the Great Spirit beeped you to report back to headquarters ASAP, though I think Prescott was a little disappointed."

"Prescott? He the one doing the air show?"

Sam nodded. "I'll go back and give him his tribal name myself, with no *conferring,* thanks. Now if I could only remember what kind of bird he saw in his Vision, hawk or eagle."

"It couldn't have been a turkey buzzard?"

"Not if I want him to tell all his friends to come see me for all their gen-yoo-wine authentic Native American spiritual needs. How would it sound? 'Hey, man, it's the greatest thing: I just paid some old injun three thousand bucks to tell me that my spirit guide is a turkey buzzard! You should try it. Maybe he'll tell you that *your* spirit guide is a muskrat.' I don't think so. That kind of money changes hands, you give the customer eagles, hawks, bears, buffalo, wolves, like that, or you go back to the reservation."

"Glaminals," Dov mumbled.

"Say what?"

"Glaminals," he repeated. "The *glamorous* animals. The ones the customers can casually mention at cocktail parties and get all their friends staring at them enviously instead of rolling on the floor laughing. You know what I mean."

"You bet I do."

"So . . ." Dov tapped his chin. "Three thousand dollars a pop. Impressive."

Sam dismissed Dov's admiration. "That's a low-end package. No frills. My high-end Vision Quests go for up to five and a half K, all major credit cards accepted. Discounts for senior citizens, not that any of the buyers I attract would ever willingly admit to being over thirty-five, let alone fifty."

Dov whistled long and low. Now he really was impressed with Sam's setup. "Is that why you tossed me to the wolves? Afraid I was going to muscle in on your market share?"

"Kid, I couldn't let you steal all my thunder. What if you *had* been able to 'confer' all of them? They'd tell their friends and then everyone who came to me for a Vision Quest Weekend Package would be expecting the same treatment. I had to do something so they'd understand it was a one-time-only experience. I mean, have some mercy: I'm not as young as I used to be."

"Who is?"

Dov intended his flip response as a joke. Sam didn't take it that way.

"No one is," he said. "Least of all your mother. She and I— Well, it was a long time ago, but still, I'll never forget it, or her." He lapsed into a silence that did not permit interruption. The sun-washed miles rolled past outside the Jeep. In a while he spoke again: "You see me as just a hustler, don't you?"

"I see you as a businessman," Dov said calmly. He was picking up some odd vibes from this man and he wasn't sure what to make of them. It was true: He *did* think of Sam as little more than a snake-oil salesman, peddling Enlightenment to the terminally trendy, yet every instinct in him screamed that he was wrong, that this man held some of the true power within him.

*Mom would never have wasted her time with him if not,* he thought. *Even when she was still in her teens, she knew where to look for the real magic.*

"A businessman," Dov repeated, "who actually happens to be a shaman, too. A real one."

Sam nodded. He seemed pleased, though he didn't crack a smile. "Kid, I'd like to come with you, see your mama, put everything I've got into trying to heal her."

Dov fidgeted uneasily. "I— I appreciate the offer, Sam, but when I leave you, I'm heading for Los Angeles."

"Your mama's dying and you're heading in the *opposite* direction?" Sam's brow looked like a thunderhead. "And there I was, wishing that you were my son."

"It's business!" Dov said. He was surprised at his own tone of voice, pleading so abjectly for Sam's understanding and approval.

"What kind of business makes you put your family second? From there it's just one small step to forgetting you've got any family at all."

The words stung like scorpions. For an instant, Dov forgot that he was here to curry Sam's favor and gain his backing for the takeover. "Oh, like your family must be *so* proud of how your selling their culture by the pound to a bunch of yuppies?" he snapped.

"They're not," Sam replied, his voice cold. "Most of them no longer count me as kin. Some don't even count me as alive, but I'm both. Even if they pretend I'm not there, I still do what I can to stand by them. That twenty dollars I put down back there in the Blue Coyote? Our waitress is my great-niece. She doesn't speak my name, I don't try to make her, but I go there every day for breakfast and I always leave her plenty. I know she needs it."

Sam pulled the Jeep over to the side of the road and turned off the engine. He looked Dov right in the eyes and said: "When I was growing up, we couldn't afford a lot of things. Regular dental care was one of them. You see what my teeth look like? I could change that if I wanted, now, buy me a smile that would blind an army, but I don't. I leave it the way it is so I'll never forget where I came from, or how it made me who I am."

He got out of the Jeep and walked a little way into the roadside scrub. Dov followed him, not really understanding why he felt compelled to do so. When the shaman had gone far enough away from the car for his liking, he tilted his head back and began to chant. Dov listened, and something inside him stirred, something told him that this was not the same sort of flim-flam that Sam fed to his willing marks. This was the real thing. This came from the heart, from the soul, from the earth itself. Dov didn't know the words, but he could pick up the tune, and he did his best to hum along. He didn't feel stupid for trying.

When Sam finished his song, he looked at Dov. "Here," he said, reaching into the small leather pouch that hung from his belt. He pressed something into Dov's hand. "Charms to guard her. Send these to your mother, since you can't be bothered to bring them to her yourself. Tell her that Sam Turkey Plucker sang for her spirit and also sends her his promise that he will perform a healing ritual for her body."

"Sam, you know what the company means to Mom—" Dov began.

"Kid, if you're fishing for my endorsement to have you take over E. Godz, Inc., forget about it."

"You mean my sister already saw you?" Dov silently cursed Peez for a shifty-souled varmint.

"I mean I'm not saying yes or no to you or your sister or anyone until I have to. Your mother's still alive; don't be in such a rush to divvy up what's still hers."

"I didn't mean to—"

"Hey, spare me the speech about how you're really doing all this for her, okay?" Sam started back for the Jeep. "My people have a long history of white folks telling us how whatever they do to us, with us, at us, it's all for only the best reasons. You know what they say about the road to hell being paved with good intentions?" Dov nodded. "Well, look around you." Sam's gesture embraced the endless miles of glorified goat tracks crisscrossing his home turf. "Not a lot of paving done out here at all."

"Ahhhh, decent air conditioning at last!" Ammi rested on the armrest tray of Dov's seat and basked in the blessed coolness of the L.A.-bound jet's first-class cabin. "No offense, boss, but your pants pocket was starting to smell like a prairie dog's armpit."

Dov said nothing. He was gazing out the window, watching the blood red mountains slip away beneath them.

"Hello?" Ammi probed. "Earth to Dov! Please tell me you're not deciding to go off on one of those cockamamie Vision Quest scams yourself! I can come up with about twenty-seven better ways to drop five grand over a weekend, and I'm just jewelry."

"It's not always a scam," Dov said absently. "He can do the real thing, but that's not what the customers want. They'd throw a fit if you served them coffee that wasn't hand-picked, hand-roasted, hand-ground and hand-brewed, but when it comes to spiritual fulfillment, they want it instant or not at all."

"Whoa. Sounds like he got to you big time." Ammi clicked his nonexistent tongue.

"I think he did." Dov pressed his forehead against the window.

"So does that mean we're heading back? Going to visit Edwina, see how she's doing?"

"And give Peez a chance to snatch the company right out from under me?" Dov sat up straight and knocked back his glass of single malt. "No way."

# ⇒CHAPTER EIGHT⇐

PEEZ STARED OUT THE WINDOW of her hotel room at the prospect of downtown Seattle. To the north, in the distance, the unmistakable shape of the Space Needle towered over the many and varied attractions of the great metropolis on Puget Sound. Flowers bloomed in a riot of gay colors in the city parks, museums bided patiently as drowsing dragons over their treasure troves of art and artifact, and if you listened really, really hard, you could swear that you heard the strains of all the different kinds of music that the city nurtured and enjoyed. Had she taken the trouble to go up to the roof-top restaurant, her journey would have been rewarded by a view of Mount Rainier, so far away yet somehow seemingly so close.

Peez did not bother. She had other matters on her mind.

"It's raining," she said.

"Gee," Teddy Tumtum said, trying not to sound *too* sardonic and failing miserably. "It's raining. In Seattle. In the springtime. Color me shocked. My gracious goodness me, what *were* the odds? And this just in: It is somewhat dry in the Sahara Desert."

"There's no need for you to get sarcastic with me." Peez scowled at the small stuffed cynic.

"Someone better," Teddy Tumtum countered. "It's the only thing that ever seems to motivate you."

"How the hell is sarcasm a motivational tool?"

"Simple: You piddle around a task, not really doing anything about achieving it, I sneer that you'll never get it done because you haven't got what it takes, you get all hot to prove how wrong I am, and *that's* when you put your butt in gear and actually get the job done! It's been this way since you were in grade school, missy. I know; I was there, and what a long, boring trip it's been."

"That's not true!" Peez objected. "I'm a highly motivated self-starter."

"Buzzwords, *bah*! Then why have you been hanging out in this hotel room for the past twenty-four hours instead of going out there and making your next business call? Don't bother to answer, you'll only waste more time trying to come up with a lot of self-justifying blather. I'll *tell* you why: It's because Fiorella shot you down in flames and you're afraid that this next guy—whatzisname—is going to do the same. That'd mean two strikes on you, and you're totally convinced that your baby brother's been batting a thousand in the meantime."

To Teddy Tumtum's surprise, Peez didn't jump back at him to point out that Fiorella might have snubbed her, but Ray Rah and the Chicago mob had given her their wholehearted support. Instead she subsided into a hunched-over knot of glumness and muttered, "Yep. You're right, Teddy Tumtum. That's exactly why I've been putting off my next call. Sure, I told myself it was just because I was jet-lagged, but I couldn't even fool me with that one. Not when I've known how to do a Jet-lag Begone spell from the time I was twelve."

"What?" Teddy Tumtum's glass eyes almost bugged out of his head. "I must have a really big ball of loose stuffing in my ears. I could swear I just heard Peez Godz admitting defeat. That's not the girl *I* sleep with talking! So the witch-queen blew you off; so what? You've got those Egyptian guys on your side."

"Oh, please, *that* bunch of idiots?" Peez sighed. "That's not a religion, it's an extended frat party, a bunch of Baby Boomers trying to hold onto their youth with both hands and no holds barred on looking ridiculous. Why follow the Grateful Dead when you can mummify them?"

"*Now* who's being sarcastic?" Teddy Tumtum asked, folding his chubby arms.

"Doesn't it bother you, Teddy Tumtum?" Peez asked.

"Doesn't what bother me?"

"The fact that the Chicago group is about as spiritual as a sack full of tacos. At least Fiorella seems to believe that what she does is something more than just an excuse to wear funny costumes, get together with her old college pals, and party."

"Right, because she's got an excuse to wear *sexy* costumes, get together with a bunch of *new* people, and party."

"Oh, come on!" Peez exclaimed. "You know that's not true. She really does care about raising the power of the old earth magic. I can't vouch for her followers—

for some of them, it probably *is* just an excuse to let it all hang out—but for Fiorella— It's not like that for her. I can tell. For her it's about real power, and she didn't want to have anything to do with me. I'm not worthy."

"And Dov is?" Teddy Tumtum snorted, then melted into more of his stomach-churning baby-talk mode. "Duzzums Peezie-pie need a dweat big warm mooshy dollop of self-esteem, hmmmm? Izzums all droopy-woopy 'cause 'ums t'ink dat nasty ol' baby bruvver got the chops an' 'oo doesn't?"

Just as Peez felt drops of syrup crystallizing on her eyelashes from all the sweet talk, the bear did an instant presto-changeo from goopy guru to boot camp drill ser-geant and barked: "So ****ing *what* if he does, woman? He does not matter! Repeat: Dov Godz does *not* mat-ter, what he may or may not be doing does *not* count, as far as you are concerned he does *not* exist from this second until the glorious moment of triumph when your mama passes full and complete control of E. Godz, Inc. into your hands. Do you copy that, soldier?"

"Soldi—?"

"I said, *do you copy that*?!"

"Sir, yes sir!" Peez barked back.

"I can't heeeeearrrrr youuu!"

"*Sir, yes sir!*"

"Now you rise up, you get some coffee into your sorry gut, and you march yourself right out of this hotel room and off to your next battle. And that is a battle which you will *win*, is that clear?"

"But I—"

"I said, *is that clear*?"

"Sir, yes sir!"

"Good. Now move 'em out!"

Fully under Teddy Tumtum's control, Peez snapped to attention, slapped the bear to Right Shoulder Arms, and marched out of her hotel room on the double. Just as the door swung closed behind them, she shook off his charismatic spell long enough to say, "Coffee's not a bad idea. Know where I could get some?"

"You want to know where you can get coffee in *Seattle*?" The sound of a teddy bear plotzing from shock echoed through the hotel corridors.

Martin Agparak was not having a good workday. Because of the nature of his craft, he labored in a more-or-less open-air situation. The tools of his trade were sheltered from the weather in a series of watertight cupboards that were in turn mounted on the back wall of a large shed. The shed itself looked as if it had encountered a giant with a chainsaw who had sawed it neatly in half, right along the rooftree, leaving it with the same three-wall construction favored by dollhouses everywhere. Martin's actual workspace was outside the halved shed, a suitably huge open area roofed only by a tarp. It was just what he needed.

The problem in general was, when you worked out in the open like that, some people considered it to be a likewise open invitation to no-holds-barred kibitzing. They refused to understand that you *could* be distracted and that you did *not* want to listen to their ongoing stream of unwanted conversation.

The problem at the moment was that not all such clueless people were, well, *people*.

"So then she says to me, she says, 'Do you know where I could get some coffee around here?' and *I* say to her, I say—"

"Teddy Tumtum, shut up." Peez picked up the

garrulous bear and tossed him back over one shoulder. He landed in a big pile of sawdust.

Sawdust, like rain and coffee, was everywhere.

Martin Agparak watched the bear's trajectory and ultimate soft landing dispassionately. "Sounds like one of Edwina's creations," he remarked. "Same kinda pushy."

Peez felt her face color up. "That's not how I would describe it," she said.

"Sure. She's your mother." Martin leaned back against the trunk of what had once been a towering pine tree. When Peez had first come into the glorified lumberyard that served as his studio, he'd been in the process of removing the last of its bark. Her visit had forced him to put off beginning the real work. He wasn't too pleased by the interruption and he didn't mind showing his displeasure by being rude.

"If you find her style to be so abrasive, why have you signed on with E. Godz, Inc. in the first place?" Peez asked somewhat sharply.

Martin shrugged. He was a young man in top physical condition, and the Mariners singlet he wore to work in showed off his muscular arms to advantage. A simple shrug from him should have been poetry in motion, but his attitude reduced the poetry to a men's room wall limerick.

"Because I can use the contacts that membership gives me," he said. "You know the old saying about us Eskimos: We got thirty-seven words for snow but not one for networking."

Peez's brow creased. "I thought you called yourselves Inuit. I thought that Eskimo wasn't—"

"Was, wasn't, was again, who cares?" A pair of safety goggles was perched atop his head. Now he pulled them back down over his eyes and turned his back on Peez, the better to study the log before him. "That's the sort of thing that bothers the folks whose ancestors were actually native to this place; not me. As an Eskimo, I'm a *real* out-of-towner. I'd call myself Tinkerbell if it gave me a bigger market share."

He pulled a piece of chalk from the back pocket of his skin-tight jeans and made a few preliminary markings at one end of the log. Peez recognized the stylized face of Raven. Moving down the log, Martin Agparak sketched in quick succession the images of Bear, Wolf and Salmon, then paused for a moment at the bottom of the severed trunk, thought long and hard, then added the final face.

"What—?" Peez peered at the chalked lines, trying to recognize which spirit the young Inuit artist had chosen to invoke for his totem pole in the making. Try as she might, she couldn't figure the last one out at all. "What is that supposed to be?"

"Huh?" Having finished the drawing, Martin was now over at his workbench, selecting a chainsaw of the proper size with which to begin the actual carving. "Oh. I guess you don't have kids." He popped on a pair of soundproof earphones. "If you did, you wouldn't just recognize that one, you'd probably be trying to kick the crap out of it." He found the saw he wanted and revved it up. "Don't worry; it'll look *much* more familiar once I paint it purple."

Peez stood there dumbstruck, staring at the now-recognizable face that would be the base of Martin's totem pole. "Purple . . ." she repeated, locking eyes with that vapid, grinning, irrationally irritating icon of toddler TV. Martin ignored her and began to carve.

"Yow!" said a voice by her ankle. It was Teddy

Tumtum who had managed to pull himself out of the sawdust pile and across the floor to rejoin his mistress. "Am I seeing things? Do my glassy eyes behold that heinous purple blobosaurus on a *totem pole*? Naaahh, can't be. I must be hallucinating. I blame myself for chug-a-lugging that quadruple espresso before we came in here. Those lemon twists will get me every time."

Martin stopped his chainsaw. "What did you say?" Amazingly enough, he had heard Teddy Tumtum's words even through the earphones. Or perhaps it was not so amazing after all: Peez had lifted the A.R.S. on the little bear when she entered Agparak's open-air studio. As heir presumptive to the E. Godz, Inc. empire, Peez could tote Teddy Tumtum along as a bespelled Object of Great Power, but as a plain old ordinary-looking teddybear? No. Not if she wanted to maintain her credibility with her potential supporters as a serious contender for the corporate throne. Teddy Tumtum's ability to talk was the gift of magic, and as such, stronger than any sound-blocking device available to mere mortals.

"I said that anyone who'd put *that* thing on a totem pole is probably wanted by the FBI for a slew of lesser crimes against nature and humanity," Teddy Tumtum replied sweetly.

Martin set down the chainsaw and took off his earphones. "Look, I'm doing this job for a big computer company exec who *does* have children. If I showed you the down payment check, you'd choke on your own stuffing. How about taking a look around, seeing some of my other pieces before you get all bent about this one?"

He gestured at the small army of finished and half-finished totem poles standing guard at various points under the big tarp. The timeless features of Bear and

Whale, Wolf and Raven shared poles with the leering features of sports stars, politicians, pop idols, and other celebrities. One pole featured none of the old spirit animals. After Agparak had carved in all the members of one particularly testosterone-challenged boy band, there simply wasn't enough room.

"*This* is what you do?" Peez gasped. "But—but I thought your carvings were intended to raise the power!"

"I'd rather raise the rent. Hey, there's all kinds of beliefs in this world, all kinds of totems. Who are you to judge?"

"You mean we came all this way across the country to talk to a *sellout*?"

Agparak gave her a hard look. "No, you came to talk to me, the representative of one of E. Godz, Inc.'s most profitable subsidiaries. I happen to know that my contributions account for a major chunk of your yearly income, with unspecified significant growth potential predicted within the next fiscal year. Translation: I'm teaching my little brother how to use a chainsaw without cutting his foot off."

"Thank you," Peez said coldly. "The translation was not necessary. Neither were the financial buzzwords. I studied the reports: I know what you're worth to the company on paper."

"Same way I know what I'm really worth to you, right now." Martin Agparak had large, perfect teeth. When he smiled it was like facing a friendly grand piano. "Too bad about your ma, but that's the way it goes, sometimes. She was one sharp cookie. I guess you have to forgive a little pushiness if it gets the job done. So—" He tilted his safety goggles back up, then removed them entirely and twirled them around one finger by the elastic. "You want something from me, I want something from you, I'm on deadline with that totem pole and you probably have another plane to catch: Let's talk."

"Well, someone around here doesn't seem to need a chainsaw to cut to the chase," Teddy Tumtum commented. "Do we talk out here or do we go someplace where we don't have to breathe wood?"

"Hush, Teddy Tumtum," Peez said, picking the little bear up by the scruff of his neck and sticking him in the crook of her arm. "I can handle this myself." She turned to Agparak. "What he said." She indicated the bear. "We both want to talk, but I'm not going to do it out here."

"So where do you *want* to talk, angel?" Martin said with a lift of his upper lip.

"Gee, I don't know," Peez replied, deadpan. "Think we could find somewhere around here that serves coffee?"

Peez lay back among the pillows in Martin's bed and stared at the ceiling. "I blame the espresso," she announced.

"Espresso?" Teddy Tumtum leaned over the top of the headboard, a mischievous glint in his eyes. "From where I was standing it looked more like café au lai—"

"Shut up!"

"Why? You've got nothing to be ashamed of. You're a grown woman. You ran a medical history viewspell on him before you jumped into anything. You sounded as if you were having a good time. And perhaps most important, you never once made any puns about Agparak's personal totem pole. Good girl! Points to you for self-restraint, and help yourself to the biscotti. You earned it."

"But I've never done anything like that in my life!" Peez whined. "I'm a *virgin*, for Vesta's sake!"

"Um, not to point out the obvious, but not any more, you're not."

"I don't even *like* him! He's snide and opportunistic and mercenary and—!"

"You called?" Martin Agparak came back into the bedroom carrying a tray. It was laden with a pair of cappuccino cups large enough to drown kittens. He set the tray down on the night table, sat on the edge of the bed, and offered Peez a frothy cup. "Was it good for you, too?" he asked with a roguish look worthy of Teddy Tumtum.

Peez groaned and buried her head under the goose-down comforter.

Martin looked to Teddy Tumtum for aid and comfort. "What's her problem? I didn't think I was doing anything wrong, not pressuring her into it, not rushing things. *You* were there, *you* saw! It was creepy having you hanging off the back of the bed the whole time, watching us, but still, you *did* see what was going on. If she wasn't behaving like a consenting adult, she was doing a damn fine imitation. I thought she was enjoying it!"

"Trust me, she was," the bear said.

"So what's wrong now?"

"Well, I'm no mind reader, but I've been with her a long time, so I kind of understand the way she thinks." Teddy Tumtum motioned for Martin to lean closer, then shielded his mouth with one fluffy paw and whispered in the artist's ear, "I think she's afraid you'll think she only slept with you to get your support."

"I am not," Peez's muffled voice came from under the covers.

"Good, because it'll take a lot more than that to earn my backing," Martin said. He drank half his cappuccino in one gulp, then peeled the comforter off Peez. "I've got to admit, girl, you got my number: I *am* mercenary. That's what it takes to survive, these days. So I like to eat on a regular basis, so sue me. Man does not live by coffee alone, not even in Seattle. The future of E. Godz, Inc. is a part of *my* future; my economic future. The new head of the company can make or break that future for me. I'm not about to give my vote to one candidate over another just because she's good in bed."

"It's not just *your* future we're talking about here, you selfish— *What* did you say?" Peez stopped in mid-scold, letting the comforter drop unheeded.

"He said you were good in bed," Teddy Tumtum repeated in a stage whisper that might be heard throughout Martin's one-bedroom apartment. Peez grabbed him by one leg and threw him across the bedroom. He splatted against a poster for the previous year's Seattle International Film Festival.

"Hey! Why'd you do that?" Martin protested. He retrieved Teddy Tumtum and held him against his chest. "What'd he do to you?"

"Told her the truth about herself once too often," Teddy Tumtum replied in a melodramatically weak voice. He gave a few tubercular coughs, for added effect, then added: "That's a hanging offense with Ms. Peez Godz."

Peez glowered at the pair of them. "You're both unspeakable *brutes*!" she announced. Then she burst into tears.

The bespelled bear and the Inuit sculptor exchanged a look whose meaning transcended all borders of race, place, time, and even species. It contained the cornerstone truth of the Universal Male Language, which was, roughly translated into mere words: *I don't know what's the matter with her. Do you know what's the matter with her? I don't know, but I'm sure as hell not going to ask her. Asking always makes it worse, and she'll only complain that if we really cared about her, we wouldn't have to ask, we'd know. Okay, so in that case let's just wait it out. I mean, shoot, she can't cry forever, can she?*

And lo, within five minutes Peez had in fact stopped crying, thus proving that some truths really are eternal.

Martin gave her a tissue.

Peez wiped her eyes, blew her nose, and handed it back, then sheepishly asked, "Was I really good in bed, or were you just saying that?"

"Trust me." Martin smiled. "And for a first-timer, too!"

"I've read a lot."

"I wish you'd give the name of that library to some of my other girlfriends." When she flashed him a wounded look, he raised both hands and said, "Aw, come *on*. Don't tell me you think that—"

Peez turned her head away. "This is just the sort of heedless, reckless, careless thing my brother would do."

"Not with me, he wouldn't," Martin said.

"If it meant getting your backing, he would."

The sculptor grabbed her by both shoulders and made her look at him. "Peez, you're a smart woman, and no matter what the glossies say, brains really are better than beauty for getting you what you want, in the long run. So stop acting stupid, okay? I didn't sleep with you because I wanted preferential treatment with E. Godz, Inc. and you didn't sleep with me because you were hoping to turn me into one of your corporate allies. What I *do* want is someone who can help me get my carvings into the big-name, high-ticket art galleries back East. I'm not throwing my support behind either you *or* your

brother until I've seen proposals from both of you showing me you've got the plan *and* the power to get me what
I want. Clear?"

"Very." For a wonder, Peez found herself smiling and
she felt as if the weight of the world had been lifted
from her shoulders. Her head rang with happy thoughts,
though she couldn't tell whether she was getting the
most enjoyment out of the one exulting *He said I was
good in bed!* or the one that proclaimed *He said I wasn't
like my brother at all!*

Peez extended her hand to Martin and shook his
firmly. "I'll get that proposal to you ASAP, Mr. Agparak.
I'm sure you'll find that my plans for the future placement of your artwork will meet all your needs. Thank
you for doing business with E. Godz, Inc. We hope for
your repeat business soon."

"How about now?"

In the taxi on the way to the airport, Teddy Tumtum
stuck his head out of Peez's carry-on bag and remarked,
"Well, *that* little expedition gave a whole new meaning to *Another satisfied customer*!"

Peez tied her emergency underpants over his mouth
and jammed him head-down into the bag, then settled
back in her seat to think things over.

She wasn't quite sure how she felt about Martin's
refusal to make a commitment to her bid for company
leadership, but she knew she didn't feel *bad*. In fact,
she was surprised by how well she was taking it.

*He's a heavy hitter on the financial side, but look
where the money comes from!* she thought. *Maybe he
had some magic once. Now it's all about the bottom
line. He's a sellout, but a very good sellout, and he's
also a very,* very good—

She smiled, remembering. Then she thought about what Wilma would say and she smiled even wider. The Great Mother was very big on fertility, but there were some aspects of her worship where only a virgin would do. Up until a short while ago, Peez had been the New York office's Emergency Virgin. Now Wilma would have to put out an APB to get a new one on the payroll. Wilma hated it when she had to do Human Resources scutwork.

*She won't know whether to congratulate me or kill me. It'll be fun to find out.*

Fun . . . She startled herself with the realization that the word now held a whole new meaning for her. It was a surprising transformation, one that was almost—

*Gee*, Peez mused. *I guess Martin Agparak has some magic after all.*

# ⤜CHAPTER NINE⤛

THE PEOPLE WHO LIVE IN THE GREATER Los Angeles area take umbrage when outlanders think of them and their sun-kissed life-style solely in terms of media clichés. Dov Godz had been made aware of this fact on the first of his many non-business-related trips to the Left Coast, when he had casually remarked to his dining companion about how many impossibly perfect-looking people he'd seen since his arrival.

"Even more than in South Beach," he said. "I guess there must be something in the water, huh?"

He meant it as a joke. It was not taken as such. Indeed, he was promptly taught that he had said the Wrong Thing. He would never forget that lesson. He thought about it every time he returned, mostly because the earache he contracted from the ensuing lecture/rant never cleared up completely.

Now, watching the hazy landscape below come closer

as his plane made the final approach to L.A. International, the memory came drifting back as it always did. Once more he was seated at one of the best tables at Marozia's, the Pacific-Rim-Italian-Macrobiotic-Thai-Fusion restaurant *du moment,* listening to his ladyfriend Brytanni calmly explain to him how he had erred.

"Oh wow, I mean, like, what *is* it with you people from Back East?" she shrilled. (Having a native-born SoCal accent, her pronunciation made *Back East* sound like *Among the Lepers.*) She crossed her long, tan, lotion-sleeked legs, revealing a number of fascinating views easily ogled through the glass tabletop. Dov nearly choked on his brioche, but Brytanni was oblivious.

"You're all, so, like, *L.A. is all palm trees and smog and movies and Porsches and Rodeo Drive* and crap. It's all: *You're from L.A., you must be shallow.* As if! I mean, my friend Wyndsong is from Marin, if you want to talk about posers, and even *she's* smart enough to know that we are not all body-image-obsessed media slaves around here." She took another mouthful of imported Finnish mineral water and chewed it carefully, making every calorie count. "If we were that two-dimensional, would I have agreed to meet you now, right when they're announcing the winners of the Shimmies?"

"Uh, what's the Shimmies?" Dov had asked, wiping soggy brioche crumbs from his chin.

"Oh . . . mah . . . gawd!" Brytanni was so taken aback by his woeful ignorance that she slapped her forehead. Then, realizing the harm she might have inadvertently wrought to her skin's elasticity, she broke open a collagen capsule, slathered it over the assaulted area, used her cell phone to speed-dial her plastic surgeon for reassurance and to make a just-in-case maintenance appointment, and finally replied: "The Shimmies are *only* the numero uno premier award to recognize the achievements of spokesmodels in the cellulite reduction appliance field! I can't believe you didn't know that. And you call *us* shallow!"

Dov had apologized most sincerely for his lack of cultural awareness, but the damage was done: Brytanni was so upset that she actually *ate a piece of cheese* out of his chef's salad before rushing from the restaurant and driving off in a huff to see her guru. (There was no need to phone ahead for an appointment: Baba Yamama was also a registered psychic.)

She did call back later that evening to reassure him that Baba Yamama had said that Dov's ill-advised attitude towards all things Angelino did not stem from deliberate evil on his part, but rather was the product of improperly stored karmic leftovers from previous lives currently festering within the refrigerator of his soul. The guru advised an immediate therapeutic aura-fluffing for the unhappy man, preceded by a combination past-life regression/rebirth ritual.

"He said for me to tell you that you should come tomorrow at ten-fifteenish," she chirped happily. "That's when he'll have the amniotic hot tub all filled up and good to go. Oh, and also that I should remind you he doesn't take out-of-state checks, but all major credit cards are way cool. So! Want me to pick you up?"

Dov demurred. He told Brytanni that he couldn't possibly have his aura fluffed until he'd gotten his chakras aligned, and doing both in close succession was almost as big a no-no as going swimming less than half an hour after eating. Brytanni was assuaged and he kept his opinions about L.A. to himself for the rest of the trip.

He closed his eyes and wondered whatever had become of Brytanni. He had not sought out her company on subsequent trips to the City of Angels. First she'd sent him a totally unnecessary Dear Dov letter the week after he got back to Miami, informing him that it was all over between them since she'd gotten involved with a Pomo Indian shaman out in Claremont. Next he got an e-mail saying that the supposed shaman was really an Anthro student named Mitch who'd flunked out of Pomona College, but she was mending her broken spirituality under the supervision of Vigbor the Galactic Redeemer ("You'd totally like him. He's an alien from an interstellar civilization far more highly developed and advanced than our own, but not in that creepy sci-fi fanboy kinda way. < G > "). And when Vigbor's visa from Amsterdam ran out, she faxed Dov to tell him all about her latest soul-guide.

At least that was what he *assumed* was the message the fax contained. Did she ever contact him for any other reason save to chitter at him about her newest, shiniest, most improved path to enlightenment/salvation? Dov had lost interest. He shredded the fax unread. He knew it was from her without looking: Somewhere in her spiritual blunderings, Brytanni had acquired the unholy power to make her letters, her e-mails, and her faxes all smell like strawberry incense.

The plane made a smooth touchdown and Dov recovered his luggage almost the instant he stepped up to the baggage carousel.

*That's a good omen,* he thought. *Here's hoping it holds true. I don't have any use for another yes/no/maybe meeting like the one with Sam Turkey Feather, Plucker, whatever. Who knows what Peez is up to, or how far she's gone to grab the company?*

He dug into his pocket and pulled out the little clutch of healing charms that Sam had given him for Edwina. He felt a faint pang of guilt for not having taken the time to send them on their way to Poughkeepsie before he'd boarded the L.A. flight in Tucson, but he talked himself out of it in short order.

*I'll FedEx them from the hotel, and I'll slap a spell of Extreme Expedition on them too, just to make sure. She'll get them* yesterday. *Man, I hope Sam hasn't called her yet or anything. If she thinks I'm neglecting her, that's another point for Peez.* He frowned. *No, wait, it wouldn't be. Mom would understand. I'm not* neglect-ing *her, I'm* paying attention to the business. *Hell, that's what she always did. She can't complain. In fact, she'll probably be proud that I'm following in her footsteps! Game, set, and match to me.*

Pleased with himself, Dov stuck the charms back in his pocket and headed for the exit.

"Dov! Whooo, Doooviiieeee!"

Dov stood stock-still, clutching his suitcase with fin-gers that had gone suddenly ice cold. There, just under the sign directing deplaned passengers to all ground transportation, was Brytanni. She was holding a sign shaped like an old-fashioned sunburst, wavy yellow rays emanating from a disc painted with the bizarrely bene-volent cartoon visage of Ol' Sol himself. The curlicued calligraphy of the words BROTHER DOV GODZ made an outrageous moustache across the anthropomorphic sun's rosy upper lip.

"Wow, is this karma or what?" she squealed, link-ing her arm through his. "I mean, when the Reverend Everything told me that I had to go pick up a very important visitor at the airport, I was all, like, *Euw. Traffic. Exhaust fumes. Smelly people. Not enough moisturizer in the world to save my skin from that little slice of Hades, and boorrriiinng!* But then he was all, *Thou are the Chosen One, the only one among us who hast achievedeth third degree* fengsama, *and besides, the church Porsche is in the shop.* So of course after that I just *had* to go. Plus he said if I didn't he was going to send Brooke, and we're both up for the same facetime op to be a seat filler at the Emmys, and if you think I'm giving that fat-assed little bitch the chance to beef up *her* Elysians doing a good deed like this, then you don't know your li'l Brytanni at all." She gave his arm a python's squeeze and twinkled at him.

"Fengsama? Face-time op? Elysians? Where the blazes are we and why don't the natives speak English?" Ammi squawked from inside Dov's shirt.

"Baby, why is your pacemaker talking?" Brytanni asked, pooching out her lips in the way her drama coach had taught her to indicate Sincerest Sympathy.

"That's not a pacemaker, that's—" Dov cudgeled his brains for the right excuse to explain away the chatty amulet. "That's my portable aura monitor," he said. "It issues me periodic verbal bulletins about, uh, which cosmic subsections of my spirit need an emergency fluffing."

"Ooooh! Can I see?" Brytanni didn't wait for permission; she thrust her hand into Dov's bosom, pulling out Ammi and a pinch of chest hair for good measure. "Eeeee! This is, like, sooo *cute*! Where'd you get it? Tibet? Khatmandu? Sharper Image?"

"I could tell you, but that would mean I'd have to spend an additional fifty thousand life-cycles in the Seventh Hell of the Demon Pimlico," Dov replied gravely, disengaging Brytanni's greedy fingers from the amulet. (He let her keep the wisp of chest hair, though.) "Of course I'd be happy to tell you anyway, with no thought for my own spiritual health whatsoever, but then the Powers of Ultimate Judgment might hold *you* accountable as an accessory to my downfall. No telling what penalty you'd have to pay for that in the afterlife. But if you do insist on an answer—"

Brytanni made haste to aver that she cared too much about Dov's soul to pursue the matter. Dov's cavalier mention of the chance for a less-than-blissful afterlife had a radically sobering effect on her, and she withdrew into an unbreakable silence that a Trappist monk might admire. Not a word did she speak as she conducted him to her Masserati and drove away from the airport. Dov did his eager best to keep up the social amenities, though his only topic of conversation was his abiding fear of the Ever-Vengeful-and-Vigilant Demon Pimlico and his hellish consort the Demon Queen Belgravia.

He was elaborating on the keystone doctrine of his supposed faith ("Damned if you do, damned if you don't") when she pulled into the parking lot of a towering multi-spired building bright with chrome, glass, and neon lotus flowers. A two-story-high sign out front proclaimed it to be the Serene Temple of Unfailing Lifescores. She hit the brakes, leaped out of the car, and dashed into the building without a backward glance. Dov thought he heard her utter a strangled sob.

"DING!" Ammi announced. "Fifteen minute aura-fluffing penalty for unprovoked chain-yanking. Why did you have to make that poor kid believe you worship demons? Couldn't you have just told her you were a Republican? It'd sound like the same thing, to her."

"I never said I worshipped demons; I just told her I was scared witless of them," Dov said. "If you'd been paying attention instead of just hanging around, you might have noticed that I never told her what I *did* worship."

"Besides yourself?" Ammi said with a lift of one silver eyebrow.

"You make it sound like it's a bad thing." Dov straightened his shoulders. "There's nothing wrong with being the number one parishioner in the First Church of Me."

"I'm not going to fault you for having a healthy self-image—" Ammi began.

"Gah! Watch your mouth. Talking about how healthy my self-image is, is like the gateway drug to pure psychobabble. It can only lead to gratuitous aura-fluffing."

"Fine." The amulet was miffed. "I was trying to be nice, but forget about it. You're a conceited, smug, self-centered twit and if you don't wrench your shoulder from constantly patting yourself on the back, you'll snap your spine from trying to kiss your own a—"

"*Brother* Dov!" A warm, rich, resonant voice poured down the steps of the Serene Temple and crashed over Dov like a deluge of heated oil. "We've been waiting for you. Approach and be welcome, if that is your life goal of the moment."

Dov looked up a flight of cyclopean white marble stairs that had apparently been lifted wholesale from the set of *Intolerance*. At the top of the steps, wearing a blue silk tunic, a wreath of fresh gardenias, and a cape of hummingbird feathers, stood the Reverend Everything. He was a hale and hearty man in his fifties, with the honest face of an infomercial spokesperson and a body that spoke of intense, regular workouts with the best personal trainers money could buy. His black hair, artfully kissed with gray just at the temples, had the look that only came from being cut and tinted by one of L.A.'s premier stylists, for a sum (without tip) that could feed a family of four for a week as long as they didn't go to Spago's.

"Reverend Everything, it's good to be here," Dov said, putting on Smile #496, a superstrength experimental prototype he'd been holding in reserve for an occasion like this. The Reverend Everything had been in business at the same location, under the same management, for years longer than E. Godz, Inc. had been in business. The electronic records that Dov had studied en route from Arizona told him that it would take something more than his normal line of business-speak and charisma to make a man like this throw his congregation's considerable support behind Edwina's baby boy.

*Watch your step, Dov,* he told himself as he ascended the snow-white steps to shake Reverend Everything's beautifully manicured hand. *This guy's got the smarts to recognize a line of bullshit from ten miles away, in the dark. No pretty promises, no claims you can't substantiate on the spot, no IOUs, financial or spiritual. He'll see you and call you on them in a flash. When you're dealing with the truly successful phonies, the only way to win is to keep it real.*

"Ah, Brother Dov, so good of you to visit us," Reverend Everything said, shepherding Dov through the towering doors of the sanctuary. "What a pity that it has to be under these grievous circumstances. I still recall the day that your dear mother approached me about affiliating the United Mithraic Order with E. Godz, Inc. Why, it seems as if it were only yester—"

"Uh, excuse me?" Dov paused beneath a tapestry depicting the Reverend Everything, dressed as an Aztec emperor, slaying a hydra whose wings were clearly labeled DISUNION and NEGATIVITY. "The United what?"

"The United Mithraic Order," the Reverend Everything repeated affably enough. "That was what we called our congregation in those days. Ah, simple, humble beginnings! Not quite so simple once your dear mother provided us with the methods for channeling our collective zeal into tangible power, not to mention her invaluable advice in matters concerning what we need and need not pay the government."

He walked on, Dov by his side, until they reached another pair of doors, these adorned with quilted panels made from pieces of gold lamé, burgundy-hued crushed velvet, bronze-shot turquoise brocade, sea-green silk, kingfisher-blue moiré, and silver point-lace.

"Holy Seventh Avenue!" Ammi exclaimed. "I knew that Liberace was dead, but I never knew they skinned him for his hide!"

"And what might this be, Brother Dov?" Reverend Everything asked suavely, bending low to peer at the little amulet. "My, my. I had one just like this on the fax machine for the Blessed Keepers of the Holy Actualization—that was the name of our divine mission about two years ago. It was a gift from Edwina. Why do you carry it around with you?"

"Oh, he—it's a later model with more technological capabilities than simple fax interfacing," Dov said a little too quickly, a little too glibly.

"I see." Reverend Everything smiled and patted Dov on the shoulder. "There, there, son. We all get lonely at the top." He opened the doors with a dramatic flourish just as he added: "But we all find our ways to make do."

The full glory of the inmost sanctuary of the Serene

Temple of Unfailing Lifescores burst upon them with the impact of a Fourth of July fireworks extravaganza. Row after row of plexiglass pews filled the chamber, sparkling beneath the battery of complexion-flattering pink lights on high. A raised platform stood at the end of the white-carpeted aisle that looked about as long as a football field. Twin choirs of fresh-faced young men and women with flowered sarongs wrapped around their lissome bodies stood ranging all up and down the length of a pair of airy spiral staircases, the banisters draped with luxuriant vines. They burst into song as soon as their leader noted the Reverend's entrance. Exotic blossoms were everywhere, and Dov could have sworn he heard the soft calls of tropical birds and monkeys echoing through the sanctuary. Somewhere a steel drum band was playing a Shaker hymn.

Dov was surprised, but not by the splashy display itself. The last he'd heard, the Reverend Everything's church had been decorated to resemble the grand saloon of the Titanic, with authentic early-twentieth-century costumes available for rental by the congregation upon receipt of an "offering." What sort of costume you were issued certainly did *not* depend on the amount of your donation, but it was an amazing coincidence how readily the Reverend's friendly Mistresses of the Sanctified Wardrobe could discover that, if you were a parsimonious giver, the only costumes left in your size were suitable for steerage passengers. On the other hand, more open-handed donors inevitably took their seats dressed in period evening gowns and tuxedos, fully accessorized.

It really was astonishing how it always worked out that way.

"This isn't what I was expecting," Dov murmured to his host as they made their way up the aisle.

"Oh, I had a spiritual evolution about three weeks ago," Reverend Everything confided. "Rather than remind the faithful of how, while our lives may appear to be unsinkable luxury vessels designed to take us to our ultimate destination, there's always the unexpected spiritual iceberg, I realized that our lives are really more like the vast and powerful Aztec Empire. Are they not rich? Does not every person command *some* sort of power over his inferiors? And nevertheless, are we not vulnerable to losing everything at a moment's notice if we continue to live heedlessly?"

"So where does stuff like 'fengsama' and 'Elysians' fit into all this? Brytanni said—"

The Reverend Everything chuckled. "Oh, that Brytanni! Fengsama is a way-station to enlightenment on a path that we haven't used since last November. Elysians are a method of keeping track of your progress that is, as Brytanni herself might say, *so* last season. I do wish she'd try to keep up with the rest of the congregation, but she's rather a slow study. Still, a devoted follower is always a blessing."

They mounted the platform stairs together and Reverend Everything motioned for Dov to have a seat on a high-backed chair that had been painted to resemble a crouching jade idol. Dov drummed his fingers on the heads of the Feathered Serpent armrests and glanced at the choirs. There was nothing even stage-Aztec about their outfits. The choir director was still wearing a tuxedo, left over from the church's previous incarnation. The transformation was not perfect, yet as Dov looked out over the sea of eager faces cramming the crystal pews, he only saw joy, faith, and readiness to gulp down whatever words of wisdom their leader might toss their way.

They did not have long to wait. Reverend Everything took center stage and raised his arms, letting his hummingbird cape fall back. "My friends, success and serenity be with you!" he declared.

"Precious and productive be your passage!" the congregation responded.

"Hear the words that will guide you!"

"We hear and heed and hearken!"

"Now . . . who wants to *score?*"

Dov sat bolt upright. As soon as the Reverend Everything uttered those words, the aisle filled with the bodies of the faithful, and mighty admirable bodies they were. L.A. was famous for annually exceeding its production quota of Pretty People, but the Reverend Everything's temple seemed to have cornered the market on that commodity.

It was bumper-to-bumper time on the Silicone Highway, and those who had not come forward took up a rhythmic chant of "Score! Score! Score! Score!" seldom encountered outside of football arenas. This had all the earmarks of an impending orgy, and for the life of him, Dov could not remember whether or not he was wearing decent underwear. (It was clean, yes, but that was not the point. Some men went out and got embarrassing tattoos when they got drunk. Dov bought comic novelty underwear, the sort with witty mottos like *Warning: Heavy Equipment*, or pictures of happy gorillas with their paws disappearing inside the fly.)

His qualms were soon put to rest by his host. The Reverend Everything made a slashing movement with one finger across his throat and the mob fell into immediate, total silence. A thread of piped-in organ music sent up a soft, soothing rendition of the theme from

*Fame* in funeral dirge tempo to underscore the words he spoke.

"My dear, dear fellow star-wanderers, your response is wonderfully gratifying. To think that my teachings have yielded such luscious fruit! We are a product of universal love, and we are placed on this earth to seek, to learn, and perhaps to know the reason for that divine product placement. We are all One with the universe, but one is the loneliest number. One can only win us the game of life if life itself fails to score, and we all know, life scores bigtime. It is therefore our mission to discover what our own lifescore must be and then to get out there and make that point spread! To see so many of you here, come to report on your latest successes, makes me realize that in a way, I, too, have added to my lifescore through you. And you have thus added to your own lifescore through me."

He went on in the same vein for about the length of one Super Bowl commercial break before having the lined-up congregants come up onto the stage with him one by one to announce their lifescores for the week. They spoke of audition appointments granted, screen-plays written, producers "not completely disinterested" in their next project, even contracts signed. He had words of praise and encouragement for each of them, words which inevitably ended with: "And do you truly *value* what you have achieved through our spiritual partnership?"

Well, of course they did.

"Oh, how we all want to believe that! For it is only through our continued belief in you that the veils of Illusion are parted and your eyes can see clearly the ultimate lifescore that will bring you joy in this world and serenity in the next."

Well, of course they wanted to make sure that the whole congregation believed in them.

"If only there were some small way, some token gesture you could make here, now, today, before all of us, to show proof of your sincerity, that our belief in you might endure."

Well, of course there was.

Dov watched as each successful lifescorer passed from the Reverend Everything's hands into the waiting embrace of the Temple Maidens, a bevy of Palm Pilot-bearing beauties who took the happy congregant aside and duly recorded the "token gesture" of a funds transfer into the Reverend Everything's coffers. Even knowing that a healthy chunk of those funds would wind up in the hands of E. Godz, Inc., Dov still felt a touch of moral queasiness.

And yet . . .

And yet, despite the Reverend's flashy, trashy, soundbite showmanship, his line of spiritual gobblede-gook that was little more than a recycled, regurgitated, retread mishmosh of bargain basement Zen and yard sale Taoism, his scarily efficient methods for fleecing the flock, Dov still sensed a great emanation of magical power coming from the congregation.

*They* believe *this stuff!* he realized. *They actually believe in it, and true belief's one of the biggest sources of real power I know. Can I really fault the Reverend Everything for knowing his customers, giving them what they want, even what they* need? *Sure, most of them have the attention spans of kelp, but the Reverend's allowed for it, changing the packaging on the same old product as much as he has to, to hold onto his audience. He's sharp, they're happy, and E. Godz, Inc. shares the profits, but . . .*

*. . . but do we really need to get rich like this?*

*Do I need to become the head of the corporation by getting someone like him as a backer? Even if this whole thing didn't smell funny, would I want to owe anything to the Reverend Everything?*

The services were still in full swing when Dov crept up behind his host, murmured something about an emergency call on his pager, and slipped away.

# ≋ CHAPTER TEN ≋

ALWAYS ONE TO MAKE SURE his bridges were in good repair behind him, Dov made it a point to call Reverend Everything from a coffee shop in L.A. International Airport. It was a very cordial conversation. The Reverend was all kindness and understanding, and he quite agreed that it would be for the best if the two of them were to continue and conclude their business meeting another time, via teleconference. He assured Dov that he would have his entire congregation pray for Edwina's recovery or peaceful passing, depending on what the universe had in mind for her. This little chat left Dov with a warm and cozy feeling, although that might have had less to do with the Reverend Everything and more to do with the fact that he had accidentally slopped a little of his coffee down the front of his pants.

Dov was still blotting at his fly with a wad of paper

napkins when Ammi set up a frightful row from inside his shirt.

"*Now* what?" Dov demanded after pulling the obstreperous trinket out into the light.

"Oh, nothing much," Ammi drawled. "I was just wondering how *much* of your mind you lost, running out on the Reverend Everything the way you just did. You think that guy didn't see right through you and your little 'Mercy me to gracious, I simply *must* run, I left the cat on the stove!' ploy? You think he's a man who enjoys being dumped just because you got all schoolmarmy and—dare I say it?—*ethical* all of a sudden?"

"Dumped? For pity's sake, Ammi, you're exaggerating. He and I are just business associates, not lovers! Do you have to describe it like I broke off our engagement?"

"You did leave him waiting at the altar," the little ornament replied. "Besides, this is L.A.: Business *is* love, and love is business, at least in the media industries. When you left right in the middle of the Reverend Everything's lifescore spectacular, it was a slap in the face. Worse, it was a kick to the ego. You know how any performer feels about audience members who walk out while they're on stage? You hurt his feelings, except he's too much of a pro to show it."

"Come on, he was perfectly okay with my leaving. I told him it was an emergency."

"Why didn't you just tell him you had to wash your hair, or that you hoped the two of you could still be friends? Oh! Did you tell him 'It's not you, it's me?' Very important to say that. It's not an official breakup otherwise." Ammi batted his lashless eyelids and, in a bad imitation of Dov's voice, added: "Darling, it's not fair to keep you tied down like this. I think we should both see other religions."

"Hey, I don't care what you have to say, I don't think I alienated him at all. And so what if I did? I don't even know if I want his support."

"You'll want it plenty once your sister grabs it out from under you," Ammi said sagely. *"Pecunia non olet,* baby: Money does not stink, and neither does power, no matter how they're generated. I'll bet Peez doesn't even hold her nose while she's signing the Reverend Everything onto her side. *That's* when you'll be sorry, but by then it'll be too late and too bad."

Dov snorted. "Peez? Please! Even if she were going to try grabbing the Reverend Everything for herself, which I doubt she'd have the chops to do, one look at his set-up and she'd run shrieking for the hills. She takes faith *seriously,* my sister does. Any trace of show-manship makes her break out in a case of acute dis-approval. Once when we were kids Mom took us to a wedding in an Episcopal church and Peez couldn't stop complaining about how they were swinging the censers *much* too wildly, in a frivolous manner. If you think *my* ethics are holding me back, you ought to get a load of hers. The girl's still a virgin!"

"Not any more, she's not," said Ammi.

"Says you."

"No, says her."

"What?" Dov's logical mind insisted that the amu-let had to be lying. Ammi was annoyed with him for having failed to bag the Reverend Everything and this was payback. It *had* to be . . . didn't it? "When? To your face?"

Ammi smirked. "Where else? It's not like I've got a back for her to talk behind. Or a behind, for that matter."

"What I mean is, if it's true—and I don't believe *that* for an instant—then how did you find out?"

"Hey, who's the communications device here?" Ammi was enjoying this. "Information is my life."

"This is not the sort of thing that gets posted on the Internet. Wait. Let me rephrase that. This is not the sort of thing that *my sister Peez* would post on the Internet. Even if it were, you haven't had Internet access, or access to anything but my pocket lint, since we left Miami."

"And chest hair," Ammi prompted. "I've also had access to your chest hair, don't forget that. God knows, *I* never will."

"Will you leave my chest hair out of this and just answer the question?"

The amulet chuckled. "Elementary, my dear Dov. I was created to monitor communications. I sift hard information from idle chitchat, real news from spam. Do that long enough and it makes you sensitive to nuances, not just in information, but in people. No surprise: What are people besides information dumps with legs? Change is a nuance, and losing your virginity is one significant change. For a device of my sensitivity, your sister's altered sexual status came in loud and clear, like she'd walked up to you and hollered it in your ear."

"It must've been one hell of a first time if you could sense the change in her at this distance. She must be at least a couple of thousand miles away," Dov remarked.

"A couple of thousand miles? That's a laugh! Try feet, a couple of dozen at most." The amulet grinned. "Unless that isn't who I *know* it is. See there, over at that newsstand? Checking out the latest copy of *Cosmopolitan*?"

Dov whipped his head around to peer at the airport shop just across the way from the table where he'd been enjoying the unspilled portion of his cup of coffee. That is, he'd been *enjoying* it up until that very moment when he saw that Ammi was not joking: There was Peez, as big as life and twice as condescending.

She stood by one of the many magazine racks in the newsstand and was, as advertised, scanning an issue of *Cosmopolitan*. Dov realized that he'd caught a glimpse of her over there earlier, but that he had failed to recognize her at the time. There were a number of good reasons for this, the copy of *Cosmo* being number one. Five minutes ago, Dov would have bet his life that Peez would rather be caught in the middle of Fifth Avenue during New York City's Easter Parade, naked except for a pair of pink plush bunny ears, sooner than touch any magazine that tossed the word *orgasm* hither and yon like handfuls of confetti.

Another reason Dov had noted but not *seen* Peez was more basic: She'd changed her looks. Gone was the severe, serviceable hairstyle. Somewhere along the line she'd gotten a stylish cut and was wearing her hair loose, lightly curled and— Were those *highlights*?

"Son of a seamstress," he muttered. "She's actually got a *figure!*" It was true. The same impulse that had made Peez set her hair loose had also caused her to wear clothing that was shorter, tighter, and a lot more colorful. She didn't look like one of the Reverend Everything's Temple Maidens by any means, but her ample curves were more welcoming and less intimidating than those California-perfect bodies.

"Well? Aren't you going to go over there and say hi to your beloved sister?" Ammi teased.

"In a pig's eye," Dov said through tightly gritted teeth. "Damn it, she *is* here to bag the Reverend Everything. And looking like that, she just might do it!"

"Told you so, told you so," Ammi chanted in an obnoxious singsong. "Unless *you're* right—as if!—and she's still got too many scruples to deal with the First Church of Perpetual Gimmickry."

"You think there's a chance of that?" Dov sounded pathetic.

"How should I know? You're the one who thinks you can bank on your personal charms forever. The Reverend Everything's going to wait for you to call because you've got such a winning smile; is that how you see it? Ha! I'll bet you even have a whole wardrobe of smiles, one suitable for every occasion!"

Dov pressed his lips together and said nothing. Bad enough that Ammi was right; he didn't need to let the amulet *know* it had hit the mark.

Ammi didn't much care about scoring points off Dov. The little amulet would have made a very unsatisfactory member of the Reverend Everything's Serene Temple of Unfailing Lifescores. "You think you're the only one with charisma? All it means is a fancy Greek way of saying you believe in your own abilities. Show a little of that self-confidence to the world and before you know it, you've got a crowd clamoring for your company, hoping that if they stick close, some of that magic's going to rub off on them. The Reverend Everything knows all about charisma: He'd bottle it, if he could! Well, guess what? Now your sister's in on the secret, too."

"How? Just because she finally got la—?"

"No vulgarity, please." Ammi could sound like a Puritan when it suited. "The change in Peez's, ah, status, was only the catalyst. Deep down inside, she always knew she had what it took to get ahead in life. She just needed a little push."

"Now who's being vulgar?" Dov smirked.

"That would be you," the amulet replied. "*Some* people have the ability to think outside the box *and* out of the gutter. Obviously you are not one of those people. If I had shoulders, I'd shrug them, and if I had hands, I'd wash them of you. You're only being snide about Peez because now she's a real threat to you getting the company. You big baby. You brought this on yourself, you know."

"If I wanted a lecture, I'd go back to school," Dov growled. He dunked Ammi in his coffee cup for emphasis. A galaxy of tiny bubbles rose to the surface, bursting into sparkling pinpoints of magical power. The amulet couldn't drown, but it didn't care for being treated like a teabag. The bubbles were a warning to Dov: *Get me out of here before I send up a freakin' flare of magic! Or do you want your sister to know you're here?*

Dov did not want that at all. In fact, he was plotting on how best to use this unexpected, clandestine Peez-sighting to his advantage. Accordingly he jerked Ammi out of the coffee and dried the amulet off on a paper napkin. "Oops. My bad," he said, using a very disarming smile.

The amulet wasn't buying. "News flash, slick: Butter will not only melt in your mouth, it'll vaporize."

"Okay, okay, I'm sorry. Now let's get out of here before she notices us."

"Hey, don't waste time selling *me* on an escape plan. You're the one with the legs."

As quietly and unobtrusively as possible, Dov tucked Ammi back inside his shirtfront, gathered up his carry-on bag, and headed for the gate area to catch his next flight. The untrained eye would have seen nothing odd or disquieting about a well-dressed single traveler walking nonchalantly through L.A. International Airport, but the eye trained in the detection of magic and all of its attendant effluvia would have noticed a pale, minty mist floating off Dov's shoulders and drifting away in his wake like a foggy cape.

It was a spell that caused the victim thereof to become a human magnet for every bore on the planet. Total strangers would glance at the spell's target and feel the irrational compulsion to unburden themselves of the full details of their gall bladder operation, or their four children's latest achievements, or the absolutely darling trick that their cat Fluffy always did when he wanted to be fed. The spell's power to attract tedious, rambling, unstoppable chitchat was quadrupled when it detected that its victim was in an escape-proof situation, such as a moving vehicle of any kind. Silent but deadly, it wafted through the terminal corridor, blew into the newsstand, and settled itself lightly over Peez.

As for Peez . . .

"Is he gone yet?" Without looking up from her copy of *Cosmopolitan*, Peez nudged her own carry-on bag gently with the tip of one shoe.

"Yeah, he's outa here." Teddy Tumtum stuck his muzzle out of the bag. The little bear was just as unaware of Dov's parting "gift" to his sister as she was. "Him and that dumb amulet of his. What kind of a person talks to a communications device?"

"I'm going to pretend you didn't say that." Peez closed the magazine and took it over to the cashier. As she pocketed her change, she rubbed one of the quarters in a very *particular* way. It was one of those commemorative issue States quarters, specifically the Massachusetts coin. Its "heads" side still showed George Washington's profile, but "tails" was no longer the American eagle. Instead, in honor of one of that great state's most memorable historic events, it gleamed with a miniature representation of Paul Revere making his famous midnight ride.

Or so it did until Peez got her hands on it. Rubbing her thumb counterclockwise over the slightly raised design and muttering a few well-chosen words of power had the desired effect: A ghostly horse and rider rose up from the surface of the coin, leaving only smooth metal behind, and set off at a gallop after Dov. Peez chuckled.

"Just wait until they catch up to him, Teddy Tumtum," she said. "As soon as that horse rides right up his pants leg, he'll be hexed good and proper." She turned her back on the departing spell and headed for Baggage Claim.

"The Lost Luggage spell, I presume?" Teddy Tumtum sighed wearily as he swung along in her carryon. "That is *so* juvenile. So ineffective, too. Sure, he'll be annoyed the first time it happens, but he'll get over it. And by the second time, he'll catch on to the fact that someone jinxed him. Then he'll just invoke a counterspell. In the meanwhile, he's got credit cards and he's not afraid to use them. There's nothing in his check-in bag that can't be replaced by a quick shopping trip."

"A shopping trip that will steal precious time from his interviews with potential allies," Peez pointed out. She smiled.

"Why are you smiling like that?" Teddy Tumtum asked, looking suspicious. "I've never seen you smile *that* way. It's almost . . . Machiavellian. You're up to something more than a simple Lost Luggage spell. What is it?"

"Oh, nothing much." Peez said airily. "Just a two-for-the-price-of-one deal for my darling baby brother.

Not only will his check-in bag go wandering through the cosmos, but every time he comes up against any kind of security checkpoint in his travels, he's going to set it off like Krakatoa on a bad day."

"Why, you sly dog, you!" The bear was impressed. "I didn't think you had it in you."

"And he won't just set off mechanical screening devices," Peez went on, relishing Teddy Tumtum's admiration. "It works on humans, too. When he tells the person at the check-in counter that he packed his bags himself, they won't believe him. When he's asked to step out of the boarding line for a spot search of his carry-on bag, they'll examine it so closely they'll split the seams. *Strip-search* will become his middle name, and by the end of his trip he'll be announcing his engagement to a pair of latex gloves!" She cackled wildly.

"Oh, Peez." Teddy Tumtum sighed in bliss. "My little girl is growing up. You were never this ruthless when you were a virgin."

Peez blushed. "That has nothing to do with it," she said.

"Maybe yes, maybe no. Could be that you always had the *capacity* for sheer, cold-blooded skullduggery, but you've never really exploited your talent to the fullest until now." The bear wiped away a nonexistent tear. "I'm so very proud of you."

It was the strangest thing: While waiting for her suitcase to appear, Peez was accosted by a kindly little old man who decided that she looked *just* like his late sister, Beruria Jane, who had done missionary work in China and came back home to Ohio with the most fascinating collection of hand-carved ivory snuff bottles. There was one that looked like a dragon. Was she aware that the Chinese used an entirely different zodiac system than we did? They still had a dozen different signs, but instead of your fate depending on which *month* you were born, it all relied on a rotating twelve-*year* cycle. Each of the years was ruled by an animal, including the dragon, the horse, the ox, the rat, the monkey, the tiger, the snake, the dog, the rooster, the rabbit, the pig, and what was the twelfth one again?

She smiled and tried to be polite about it—he was such a dear, grandfatherly type—but he kept droning on and on and *on* about that elusive twelfth animal. Then he let her know that he had been born in the Year of the Rabbit, while Beruria Jane had been born in the Year of the Dragon. Naturally this led him to explain the characteristics of people born under those two signs, and which signs were compatible, and that his late wife had been born in the Year of the Horse. He had forgotten whether that made the two of them compatible or incompatible, but since she had been run over by a combine harvester on their fifth anniversary they really had not had much opportunity to discover whether or not they were compatible in the long run.

"And have you ever seen a combine harvester in action, my dear? Fascinating things, really. Even in spite of their tendency to run over a person's wife now and then, they are quite ingenious machines. It makes me proud to be an American, just thinking about them. Even if the Industrial Revolution didn't get started over here, we Yankees sure as shootin' knew how to make the most of it, I'll say. Although a body could come to believe that the Industrial Revolution has generated more problems than solutions, especially if you listen to the way Beruria Jane's boy, Kelvin, tells it. Not to speak ill of one's own nephew, but if that boy wasn't a born Bolshevik, then God didn't make little green apples, and I know for a fact that He did. Mighty tasty things, too, with enough sugar sprinkled on 'em. There's not enough sugar in this world to take away the taste of that Kelvin's sour attitude, though. Still, he's my dear, late sister Beruria Jane's only child, and children are a blessing. Too bad my darling Lucy Kathleen and I were never so blessed—did I tell you the peculiar way she died? It's not the sort of thing you hear tell of every day—but it was the Lord's will, and what's more—"

The man was still bemoaning the fact that he and his prematurely harvested wife had not had any children of their own—not even a Bolshevik to bless themselves with—when Peez croaked out a desperate, " 'Scuse me, please, but I really have to go to the bathroom *right now,*" and fled for her life.

Alone in the stall, she leaned her throbbing head against the cool metal wall and mumbled, "What did I do to deserve *that?*"

Meanwhile, Dov had just been asked to step into a side room and disrobe. He heard the snap of a latex glove being donned and shuddered. *What did I do to deserve this?* he wondered.

He was not alone. The spells that the warring siblings had unleashed upon each other were fired off in haste, impulsively, and without filing an Environmental Impact Statement beforehand. Innocent bystanders and passersby in the general vicinity when the spells were launched found themselves enduring weaker versions of the same ordeals assailing Dov and Peez. Never had so many suitcases taken off for parts unknown, never had so many bores and buttonholers decided that the total stranger who just happened to be seated next to them on the plane needed to know their life stories.

As for that part of Peez's spell causing security systems to go berserk, the less said, the better. Things were bad enough without vindictive magic mucking them up even further.

Fortunately for the continued smooth running of L.A. International, the fallout effect of the Godz siblings' spells had a very short half-life. Though the magic would continue to dog its original targets until they realized they'd been hexed and wiped it away with a counterspell, it did not continue to plague the truly innocent indefinitely. By the time Dov's Seattle-bound flight was airborne, most of it had dissipated, and by the time Peez arrived at the Serene Temple of Unfailing Lifescores, it had all vanished.

# ≷ CHAPTER ELEVEN ≷

"EXCUSE ME," PEEZ SAID, tapping the shoulder of the handsome young man who had picked her up at the airport. "I thought we were going to meet the Reverend Everything at the Serene Temple of Unfailing Lifescores."

"Yuh-huh," he replied with a smile as flashy as the world's largest cubic zirconia. They were standing in front of the very building which Dov had left less than a day before. The spires still glittered, the white stairs still gleamed, the neon lotus blossoms still winked on and off, and the parking lot still teemed with Porsches, Mercedes, Carmen Ghias, Alfa Romeos, and one lonesome Segway.

Only the name on the two-story sign in front had been changed to read SOULHAVEN RETREAT AND STARCHILD IMMERSIONARIUM.

"Well, I can read, you know," Peez said, tapping her

foot and pointing at the telltale sign. "And that does not say anything about serenity or temples or lifescores—whatever the heck those are."

"Yuh?" The pretty man tilted his head in a fetching manner and held that pose as if listening to the rapid-fire click-click-click of a distant camera shutter. Then at last he said, "Oh," and nodded, holding that pose for a few more imaginary headshots.

This was not a satisfactory answer for Peez. "Look, if you don't want to ask directions, I'll be glad to handle it. Better yet, never mind. I'll just give the Reverend Everything a call, tell him where I am, and he can tell us how to reach the Temple."

She suited the action to the words at once, feeling that life (and her allotted time in L.A.) was too short for her to await the mental processing that would elicit a confirming *yuh* from her handsome nougat-brained escort. The E. Godz, Inc. records provided the Reverend Everything's private cell phone number, and Peez was not afraid to use it.

"Hello, Reverend Everything? Peez Godz, here. I'm afraid that we've somehow managed to get lost on our way from the airport to the Serene Temple of Unfailing— Oh, really? . . . You don't say . . . Is that so? . . . Yuh-huh, yuh-huh, yuh-huh, I see. I think."

A look of consternation came over her face. She squinted at the two-story-high sign and nodded automatically, even though there was no way for the person on the other end of that phone call to see her doing so.

Then again, perhaps there was.

Peez looked away from the sign and up to the westernmost spire of the Retreat/Immersionarium. The Reverend Everything, a silvery cell phone in his hand, gazed down at her cheerfully and waved.

Shortly thereafter, Peez found herself touring the temporarily empty sanctuary. There had been some changes made, though she was not in a position to realize this. The pseudo-Aztec trappings and all the jungly glory of the building's previous incarnation had been swept away as if by magic. In place of the flowers, the vines, the fake jade throne, and the rest of the package there was now a towering, clear-sided tank where a pair of dolphins swam, splashed, and otherwise disported themselves.

"I am so very pleased to have you visit us, my dear Ms. Godz," the Reverend Everything said as he steered Peez around the wide, carpeted deck encircling the top of the dolphin tank. "I'm sure you're aware that your dear brother Dov was just here as well, though he had to depart rather precipitously. That was a shame. You see, while we were in the middle of our services, I was blessed to receive a revelation which told me that it was time to change the spiritual focus of my flock. Naturally I put my loyal followers to work upon making that vision a reality. Their labors are not yet complete, but we've managed to get things arranged well enough for us to celebrate our inaugural services within the hour. I do hope you won't have to rush off the way your brother did?"

"I, uh, really couldn't say," Peez replied, nervously eyeing the tank. She knew it was silly, but she couldn't quite shake the feeling that one misspoken word, rather than one misstep, could send her plunging into the depths.

The Reverend Everything smiled benevolently. In truth, he didn't seem capable of smiling any other way. While Dov had amassed a whole wardrobe of smiles, keeping one on tap for every possible eventuality, the

Reverend Everything had discovered that wondrous thing, the Little Black Dress smile, suitable for every occasion. It said, variously:

1. Everything is all right.
2. Everything *will be* all right.
3. You are Beautiful.
4. You are Smart.
5. You are Loved.
6. You are Special.
7. You may prove to be useful to me.
8. You are Nuts, but I think I can still find some profitable use for you.
9. I hear you.
10. I'm listening.
11. I am *really* listening.
12. I am listening to you the way no one else in this nasty old world has ever listened to you because I am the only one who recognizes your intrinsic worth, so you'd better get with my program because if you don't, I'll drop you like a bad habit and you'll have to go back to being an ordinary *zhlub* again.
13. I'm actually thinking about my tee-off time at the country club golf course, but you're going to look like a rude idiot if you try to challenge me for not listening to what you're saying because I am extremely good at faking an intelligent and insightful reply, so don't try it.
14. I'm actually staring at your cleavage, but this is another case where you'd better not try to challenge me on it because all I have to do is act shocked and hurt and then

you will look like a *conceited* idiot with severe personal problems that make you go around accusing a Man of God of all sorts of naughtiness that is obviously all in your twisted imagination. Don't try this either.

"My dear, I quite understand your reluctance to commit yourself," he said smoothly. "I respect your businesspersonhood. I sense that it's telling you to take as much or as little time as you feel we deserve. Your insightful wisdom is something we should all aspire to. You didn't get to be the head of the E. Godz New York City office on the basis of your family ties alone."

*I didn't?* Peez thought. *Like hell, I didn't! Oh, this guy is good at telling people what he thinks they want to hear! No spiritual movement ever went broke following* that *path. No wonder he's one of our top contributors.*

"Thank you," was all that she said.

It seemed to be enough for the Reverend. He turned that magical smile of his up a notch and escorted her to a seashell-shaped chair at the rear of the deck, a place Peez found herself thinking of as "center stage." Murmuring his excuses, he sidled over to a three-panel screen to one side of her seat, leaving her to take in the dubious beauties of the Retreat/Immersionarium without benefit of his commentary.

Peez seated herself beneath the garlands of green, blue and silver tinsel seaweed festooning her pearly throne. She gazed out at an unblocked vista of the sanctuary and saw that work was already well begun on decorating the walls and pews with similar marine-themed glitz. Enmeshed in the ersatz seaweed were scatterings of greenish-white plastic starfish. Peez glanced up at the electrical fixtures and spied the unmistakable presence of black lights among the ordinary bulbs and fluorescents.

*I'll bet dollars to dolphin treats that those starfish glow in the dark,* she thought.

"Ms. Godz?" Reverend Everything's mellifluous voice brought her sharply out of her speculations. "I'm not asking for any sort of a promise from you, but may I hope that you'll share our services? It would be an honor for me. This will be the first time since my transformational vision that our faithful will be sharing in the new path to being one with the universe."

"I suppose I could—" she began. The sight of him stopped her words cold on her lips.

"Is something wrong?"

*No,* she thought. *Nothing wrong at all. Not if you're used to seeing someone do a quick-change routine from Wall Street Formal to Atlantis Casual every blessed day!*

Broadway Merman, and no, she didn't mean Ethel: There was no other way to describe the Reverend Everything's new look. Somehow, in the short time Peez had been viewing the sanctuary's saltwater décor, he had stripped off his natty, cream-colored suit in favor of a multicolored, spangled fishtail that a bathhouse era Bette Midler would have rejected as too garish. His chest was bare, though he'd acquired a frosty green beard long enough to obscure most of it.

"Ohhh," he said, nodding in sympathy for Peez's abrupt silence. His foot-high diadem of shells and dried seahorses swayed gently. "I see what's bothering you. You've never attended one of my services before. I do this sort of thing all the time."

He used his crystal trident to retrieve the cast-off suit and held it out for her inspection. "It's a one-piece outfit with hidden Velcro closures. A lot like the sort of rental clothing they use for the dear departed in funeral homes, in cases where the family does not provide a, heh, going-away outfit; *much* easier to remove for reuse in that critical post-viewing, pre-burial time slot. Now, was that the only thing upsetting you?"

"Y-y-yes. That and—and—" She didn't know quite how to say it and still consider herself to be a lady, so she made vague motions at the Reverend's chest.

He looked down at himself in puzzlement, then chuckled. "Ah! It's the pasties, right?" He pointed at the pair of iridescent plastic squids covering his nipples, two islands in a Sargasso Sea of pepper-and-salt chest hair. Chuckling, he added, "I know they must seem a trifle over-the-top for some tastes, but I felt that as the spiritual leader of a large and loyal congregation, I owed it to the dignity of my calling to veil my vestigial mammaries from sight. It must be the quest for enlightenment, not the humble guide, that claims their attention. I would never want to distract my Seekers."

"Distract them? *Distract* them?!" Peez shrilled, rising to her feet. "You look like the illegitimate gay offspring of Poseidon and Cher and you're worried about distracting the congregation because you've got *naked nipples*?!"

Reverend Everything gaped at her. He wasn't the only one left stunned by her outburst. Peez herself gasped, clamped both hands over her mouth, and collapsed back into her chair, horrified at what she'd just done.

"I'm sorry," she whispered. "I didn't mean that. I didn't say that. Oh, I am so, so sorry."

Reverend Everything took a deep breath, tilted his head back so far that his shell crown fell off, and laughed until the tears ran down his cheeks. When at last he recovered himself enough to speak, he said, "Ms.

Godz, your innocence is like a breath of salt air from our own Mother Ocean's revivifying lips. Seen like this, outside of the context of our worship services, my garb must indeed look a trifle theatrical, but pageantry is often a part of religious rites. I assure you, when you see our rites *as a whole*, my chosen appearance will look perfectly natural."

"Of course it will," Peez muttered, still blushing.

And so it did.

—*for a freak show*, Peez thought. *No, that's too harsh. For a circus, then, or an aquacade, or whatever the hell this extravaganza is.* She took another pull at the loop-de-loop pink plastic straw protruding from her sacramental piña colada and took in the scene before her with a jaundiced eye.

Services were nearly over—the drinks had been distributed when Reverend Everything called his followers to partake in the "refreshment of the soul"—but plenty was still going on. It was standing room only in the dolphin tank, for one thing.

*No, not the tank; the Immersionarium*, Peez mentally corrected herself. *Where the suckers go to get a real soaking.*

Less than fifteen minutes ago she had sat back and listened while the Reverend Everything told the congregation that the way to become One with the Universe was to let your soul float free. Money was the ballast holding you down on the bottom of the great Cosmic Sea where the Crabs of Crotchetyness would nibble your toes and the Remoras of Remorse stood poised to suck the good karma out of you. The people groaned and made bubbling noises with their lips on hearing this.

Yet there was hope. Or, in the Reverend's own words,

"But wait! There's more!" He then called upon his lovely assistants to bring forth those worshipers who had given up the most ballast at the previous week's service. These finny handmaidens too were dressed like rejects from a Las Vegas-based road company of Hans Christian Andersen's *The Little Mermaid*. Their fishtails made walking up and down the aisles a chore, so they settled for announcing the names of the favored through microphones disguised as lobsters.

With joyous sounds last heard on episodes of *Flipper*, the chosen ones came forward, walking down the center aisle and up the steps to the deck surrounding the dolphin tank. One by one they were taken behind a dressing screen only to emerge shortly thereafter wearing swimsuits. Peez was impressed to see so many people mastering Reverend Everything's own talent for doing a quick change act until she noticed that the screen also concealed a picked team of additional assistants who could get the clothes off a body faster than a horny sixteen-year-old.

As soon as a worshiper emerged from behind the screen, he or she was escorted to the edge of the dolphin tank where the Reverend Everything was waiting, crystal trident in hand. He said a few words about there being a tide in the affairs of men, going with the flow, life as a river, the fount of all knowledge, sinners being pond scum, and brooking no arguments from any outsiders who decried the methods of the Soulhaven Retreat and Starchild Immersionarium because such drips were spiritual wet blankets.

Then he used his trident to swat the Seeker into the pool. The dolphins, aka Starchildren, swam around each new visitor happily, sometimes taking an interest, sometimes ignoring him completely. That was all right, though, because the Reverend's earlier preachings had made sure to point out that it was the Seeker's *soul* that the Starchildren would touch, and every person emerging from the tank insisted that he or she had been very touched indeed.

It was all deeply moving. In fact, it moved those members of the congregation who had not been chosen this week to renew their charitable zeal and fill the collection baskets to overflowing.

Afterwards, a fishnet curtain descended from on high, veiling the tank as the congregation made their exit while the organ played selections from Handel's *Water Music* over a tape recording of whale songs. These sounds mingled sweetly with the *squish, squish, squish* of improperly dried feet ruining costly Italian leather shoes. As the great doors of the sanctuary closed behind the departing Seekers, the Reverend Everything removed his shell tiara and fake beard. He ducked behind the dressing screen with a happy sigh whose meaning might have signified either satisfaction in a ministry well fulfilled or *Thank God* that's *over*!

Peez had her own convictions as to which one it was.

"That does it," she told the air. "I quit."

"What did you say?" Reverend Everything stuck his head out from behind the screen. He looked sincerely concerned.

"You heard me," Peez said. "I quit. This is not the right line of work for me. If the future of E. Godz, Inc. is going to depend on someone who's able to put up with watching this kind of hijinks with a big old Miss America smile on her face, I'm out. I'm leaving the field to my brother, Dov. Let *him* hitch a ride on the hurdy-gurdy, but I'm getting off now." She stood up and headed for the steps leading down from the tank deck.

The crystal trident drove into the wooden stair tread just an inch ahead of her poised foot. She jerked her head back to stare at the Reverend Everything, who had thrown the shining weapon with such extraordinary accuracy. Her expression was one of complete surprise seasoned with grudging admiration for such speed, panache, and marksmanship. He shrugged it all away.

"I used to work in the movies," he said.

"Really." This was old news to Peez, who had read up on the Reverend's background on the flight to L.A. Teddy Tumtum had provided plenty of additional insights for dealing with the man, all of which now seemed silly since Peez had decided to quit dealing with him and all of the other E. Godz subsidiaries on her list altogether.

"Yes, *really*," Reverend Everything said. "I know about quitting. I quit when they stopped having happy endings." He came forward and took her by the arm. "Come with me, please." It sounded like a courteous invitation, but the firmness of his grip on her wrist told her that it was more in the line of a command.

Peez was too weary to put up a fight. Why bother? As soon as she left this temple to theatricality, she was going back to the airport to catch the next flight to New York City. When she got back to the office, she'd tell Edwina about her decision to pull out of the race. Maybe she'd even go up to Poughkeepsie and deliver the news in person, then stay on to see if there was anything helpful she could do to ease her mother's last days on earth. Surely whatever she'd find to occupy herself would have to be more helpful than this ridiculous competition with Dov.

The Reverend Everything took her through a door leading from the tank deck to a behind-the-scenes hallway. Peez passed one office after another, all of them bustling with the noises of computers, fax machines, telephones, and cheerful people in the throes of reaching out to the spiritual Seeker. Or was that "sucker"?

There was a small elevator at the end of the hall which took them up to the topmost floor of the building. Here was the nerve center of the Reverend Everything's empire, his private office. Peez took it all in with the practiced eye of a woman who actually adored good interior decoration but who would sooner die than admit it lest she be tarred with the counterfeminist brush. Peez was smart and sensible: She knew it was possible to want equality between the sexes *and* monogrammed sheets (400 count Egyptian cotton, for preference) but she also knew that there were precious few people out there willing to accept that.

Reverend Everything settled into the tawny leather chair behind the burled oak desk and motioned for Peez to have a seat as well. The only furniture available for the purpose was a sofa of the same rich upholstery. When sat upon, it offered all the resistance and support of a toasted marshmallow. Peez found herself sinking deeper and deeper into the cushions. It was a pleasurable sensation, only marred by the revelation that she would need a winch to haul herself out of there should the need arise.

She also realized that this choice of furnishings gave the Reverend Everything a tacit psychological advantage over all his guests. He could get out of his chair with ease and, if he so chose, come over to the sofa/quicksand pit and *loom* over a captive audience. Peez didn't care for the idea of being helpless—she'd already experienced the reality of it too many times, in too many different situations, including but not limited to social, financial, and childhood. She began hauling herself towards the armrest, bent on seizing hold of it and hauling herself free of the cushiony morass.

Her exertions were not lost on the Reverend Everything. "My dear, aren't you comfortable?" he asked as if he really cared.

"Actually, I'm a little *too* comfortable," she said. She flashed him a charming smile. It packed nowhere near the power and versatility of his own toothy weapon of choice, but it was pretty good for a beginner. "I'd hate to doze off in the middle of our conversation, but who could blame me? This is *such* a lovely couch."

"Comfort is a wonderful thing, isn't it?" Reverend Everything winked at her. "But it can be a snare, too. That's one principle I learned a long time ago, back when I was just starting out. People need rituals. They give us a sense of continuity, security, and dependability in a world that often offers us none of the above. On the other hand, if you do the same thing in the same way for too long, it's more than likely you'll stop paying attention to the meaning behind what you're doing and just switch to autopilot. That's why I keep changing the format of worship services— to say nothing of the décor—for my followers. Is *that* what's bothering you? All the, well, *showmanship*, for want of a better word?"

"Oh, I can think of a much better word," Peez replied. "How about *phoniness*? Or *superficiality*? That's a good one! I can swallow a certain amount of snake oil, Reverend, but I think I've finally reached my limit. It was different when I was just doing long-distance administration work, pushing buttons, crunching numbers, filling out forms. Ever since I've hit the road and seen some of Mother's clients face to face, I've learned some hard truths that make it impossible for me to go on without getting disgusted with myself."

"As well as with us?" The Reverend Everything raised one ashy brow. "But what have you really seen of us, Ms. Godz? The flash, the spangles, the dolphins, yes, but what about the truth? Did you try to catch up to any of my congregation, to talk to them, to ask them about why they come *here* instead of some other house of worship?"

"That's pretty obvious," Peez said confidently. "You're the only one who gives them a show."

The Reverend Everything chuckled. "Remind me to take you on a tour of several churches I could name. No, Ms. Godz: If a show was all they wanted, they could get that elsewhere. For most of them, their *lives* are a show, their careers are all lighting tricks and special effects. What they come for here is something with a little more substance, something enduring, something that will last longer than their most recent hairstyle, or lift-and-tuck, or collagen injection, or producer's promise."

"Faith?" Peez still sounded dubious, but there was something about the Reverend Everything's tone and expression that was convincing. Either he really meant what he was saying or he was putting on a show so convincing that he'd even persuaded himself to believe it was true.

"If you like." He laid his hands on the desktop. "We spend our lives in the pursuit of what we call *solid* things, *practical* things: a big house, a fast car, a spouse who matches the drapes. We don't realize that these are the things we can lose most easily. The truth is, while some people say that keeping in touch with our spiritual side is frivolous, it's actually one of the most necessary things in our lives."

He stood up and came around the desk to loom over Peez where she slumped, engulfed in the sofa. Offering her a helping hand, he pulled her to her feet and said: "I provide the fulfillment of a human need, Ms. Godz. You might not appreciate the glitzy package it comes in, but the contents are solid. A bowl of soup, a plate of sushi, a granola bar, a slab of roast beef, a slice of smoked salmon rolled into the shape of a rose, all of these can satisfy a person's hunger. What does the outer semblance matter, as long as he is fed? Will you be the one to tell him that his choice must follow only one approved form? Would you rather have him go hungry?"

Peez shook her head. "No, of course not, but—"

"My dear, I am the chef, but E. Godz, Inc. is the catering service. Without you, my work would never be so simple nor so effective. Many Seekers would find themselves starving, unaware that they dwell in the midst of plenty. Your mother understood this. She didn't start E. Godz, Inc. just for the money. Mind you, she never complained about the money, but still . . .

"It would be easy for me to let you go, to allow you to back out of the competition for control of the company. But I see great things in you, great possibilities. If you don't believe in my way of bringing spiritual sustenance to my followers, that's fine, but the only valid reason for you to quit is if you don't believe in yourself." He clasped one of Peez's hands between both of his and pressed it to his heart. "Is that it, Ms. Godz? Is that going to be your . . . *final* answer?"

In the airport, waiting for the flight to Arizona, Teddy Tumtum said, "I know you don't think of the Reverend Everything as a big fake any more, but that doesn't make up for describing him as a"—the bear shuddered involuntarily—"game show host. Just because he chose to express himself that way doesn't mean—"

"It wasn't what he said," Peez replied. "It was the way he insisted that I accept some lovely parting gifts." She held up a large cardboard box, shook it gently, and asked, "So how *do* you use a Flashmatic Abscercizer anyway?"

"I don't know," said the bear, studying the fine print on the side of the box. "But it says that the hamster's not included."

# ⪢ CHAPTER TWELVE ⪡

IT WAS RAINING IN SEATTLE when Dov arrived.
Luckily he was able to find a place selling hot coffee
to take the chill off before he made his way to Martin Agparak's studio.

"Give me a small coffee, light and sweet," he told the
girl staffing the tiny kiosk on the corner of Martin's block.

"What kind?"

"Regular. I could use the caffeine." He shifted his
umbrella slightly and gave her one of his pocket-pack-
tissue smiles: clean, cheap, disposable, and plenty more
where that came from.

"Single, double, or triple?"

"What?"

"Caffeine. Or you want that espresso?" To his surprise, she did not pronounce it *"ex*-presso."

"Um, okay, sure, espresso, why not? Single," he
clarified.

"What kind?" she asked again.

"I told you, a single espresso, light and— Oh, wait, if it's espresso I don't want it light, but I still want it—"

"Beans. What kind of beans do you want? This is just a little stand so we don't have the selection you'd find in one of our shops. If it turns out that we don't stock your favorite, I'm sorry. Anyway, we *do* have Sumatran, Brazilian, Columbian, Nicaraguan, Costa Rican, Ecuadorean, Madagascar, Jamaican . . ."

Dov felt as if he were trapped on an endless voyage through the now-defunct Small World ride at DisneyWorld, only with all of the happy, prancing international puppets high on caffeine and armed to the eyebrows with coffee grinders. The girl was still rattling off the options when he cut in and said, "What would *you* recommend?"

"Oh, the Jamaican, definitely."

"Fine. I'll have that."

"What kind?"

"I *beg* your pardon?"

"From what part of the island? I mean, obviously you want the highlands, but do you prefer the northern, southern, eastern, or western face of the mountains?"

"Eep," said Dov. "Uh . . . you have anything from the middle? I don't like to play favorites."

Clearly this was not the choice of those in the know. The girl gave him a look as if he'd farted in church, but then remembered that she was a businesswoman, not an educator of woefully untrained taste buds. "What roasting process?" she asked.

"I don't care. Whatever they used on Joan of Arc. Look, all I wanted was a lousy cup of coffee, light and sweet, not the Spanish Inquisition!"

"Spanish roast process?" The girl frowned, then ducked down behind the counter. She popped up an instant later, like a gopher on springs, with a plastic scoop full of coffee beans. "Okay, but it kills the secondary bouquet. You sure? I mean, the customer is always right, but I don't want you to come back complaining to me when your soft palate doesn't get the full effect."

"Why don't we leave my soft palate to follow its own damn bliss and just *give me the freaking coffee*?!"

A strong hand fell on Dov's shoulder and spun him around, putting him face to smiling face with the very man he'd come to Seattle to see.

"Dov Godz?" Martin Agparak inquired casually. Dov could only nod. "Thought so. I got your message on my answering machine. I've been expecting you. Come into my studio and I'll give you that . . . *freaking* coffee."

Embarrassed, Dov let himself be led away like a little lamb. Behind him he heard the coffee kiosk girl calling, "If he still wants the Spanish-process Jamaican, Marty, make sure you use *distilled* water, not spring. It's the only thing that can save him!"

Rain pattered down on the tarps covering the workspace where Martin Agaparak created his customized totem poles. Dov sat on a stump that had been sculpted into the shape of Regis Philbin's head and sipped his coffee. Martin had very kindly given him a towel to blot up all the rainwater that his umbrella had failed to deflect, and now Dov wore it slung around his neck like a chubby ascot.

"I'll be with you just as soon as I put the finishing touches on this," the sculptor said, suiting up for work.

On went the goggles and the earphones, up came the chainsaw. Its full-throated, hungry roar was louder than Dov had expected. He shifted his seat to the head of Alex Trebek, over in the corner nearest the door back inside.

Agparak noticed the move. He turned off the chainsaw, took off the earphones and goggles, and said, "Sorry. I kind of forget how rough this can be on someone who's not used to it. I'll tell you what: How about we talk first, then I'll get back to work after you've gone, okay?"

Dov became suspicious. "You make it sound like you're going to give me the Uh-Huh treatment."

"What's that?"

"You know, pretend you'll listen to what I've got to say, nod your head, go 'Uh-huh, uh-huh, uh-huh' the whole time I'm talking so that if I'm dumb enough, I just *might* believe you're really paying attention, then get rid of me as soon you can do it without looking like a rude jerk."

"Uh-huh." Agparak nodded. Then he grinned. "Speaking of rude jerks, am I speaking with the president of the club right now? You ever listen to *yourself*, Godz? So far I've rescued you from that coffee girl before you had a total meltdown in front of her kiosk and she called the cops, I've given you a cup of coffee *without* the Caffeine Catechism, I've handed you a towel, and I've offered to put my work on hold so I could hear what you've come all this way to say to me. Gosh, how much ruder could *I* be?"

Dov hung his head. "Sorry," he mumbled. "I shouldn't've acted like that. That was jerky of me. I've been under a lot of pressure lately—not that that excuses my behavior or anything."

"Sure, I understand." The sculptor patted Dov on the back. "It can't be easy, worrying about your mother's health and all."

"Well, it's not as if there's anything I can do for her besides try to keep the company working at peak efficiency." Absentmindedly, Dov reached down and twiddled with Trebek's nostrils. "That's why I'm here, to see if you've got any requests or suggestions for change, any complaints about how we're handling your particular needs."

"You're from the government and you're here to help me?" Agparak had the talent to make a skeptical smirk look charming. "Like I told your sister, what I'm after is getting a foot in the door at the big Eastern art galleries, having my work seen by the people who matter. Well, seen *and* purchased. Anyone can be a starving artist; I'd rather be the artist who says, 'I'm starving; let's go grab a bite at La Côte Basque.' "

"You've become one of our top clients, Mr. Agparak," Dov said. "I think I've got the connections to get you just the sort of exposure you want for your art. Would you be kind enough to give me a little preview?"

"Of what?"

"Of the pieces you'll be exhibiting when I set up your New York City gallery début."

"Oh." Martin Agparak nodded, then said: "You're sitting on one of them."

Dov looked down at the head of Alex Trebek and withheld comment.

"That's just the one I did for practice," the sculptor went on. "The finished work will be a totem pole combining Trebek, Barker, Philbin, with—whatzisname, the guy from that old 1950s quiz show, the one where everyone got busted for cheating—anyway, with *him* for the base and Vanna White for the top figure. It's the last one I need to do for my ideal installation. I've already completed the totem poles of the NFL mascots, the fast food icons, and the sci-fi TV show heroes. That's another thing where I could use the company's help: Maybe *you* can get a hold of Shatner so he'll sign the release, because *I* sure as hell can't swing it."

Dov mulled over this information for a while, then finally laughed and said, "Oh, *I* get it. You do *funny* art! Like comic strips, only wood. Very smart, Agparak, very cutting edge, Rothko meets Ethan Allen."

He would have gone on to praise the sculptor's business savvy in greater detail, except he caught sight of the venomous stare Agparak was giving him.

"There is nothing 'funny' about a totem pole," Martin said. "Not unless you find yourself in the habit of going into St. Patrick's cathedral for laughs."

"Hey, I know all about totem poles," Dov protested, holding up both hands to ward off any accusations of religious insensitivity. "I have only the deepest respect for what the real ones signify, but if someone slapped a giant propeller beanie on top of St. Patrick's, you know you'd be right there beside me, laughing your ass off."

"The 'real' ones?" Agparak repeated. "What makes my totem poles less real than the ones you claim to respect? Because instead of carving Bear and Fox and Raven, I've used team mascots? Bear is an animal of great power who holds healing in his paws, but more people worship him when he holds a football. If I make a totem pole with the old images, they'll look at it and smile politely and say how quaint it is, how charming. It won't matter if I made it the week before: They'll still see it as a relic, a leftover, an artifact. But if I transform it, if I create it so that it shows them the things that they still worship, they'll be more likely to realize that it's not just a decorative religious fossil; it's a living, vital icon of spiritual significance."

Dov's brow creased in thought as he took in everything Agparak was saying. At last he asked, "You expect people to go into a gallery, see your work, and come away from it ready to worship *Regis Philbin*?"

It was Agaparak's turn to laugh. "I expect them to come away from my work thinking about their own spirituality. I've seen too many people who call themselves religious when they're really just the slaves of habit. They go through the same rituals their parents and grandparents did, but they never think about what the words or the actions of the rites mean; they never *feel* the spirit within them. Faith should be a part of life, something you actively *care* about, like catching your favorite game show every weeknight or rooting for your favorite team. Think of what so many people have lost, Mr. Godz, without anyone taking it away from them. Then think of what they *could* have, and how much it would enrich their lives if only they'd open their eyes and see."

Dov stood up and shook the sculptor's calloused hand solemnly. "You can count on my support, Mr. Agparak," he said. "Can I count on yours?"

Agparak didn't answer right away. "I did mention that your sister's already been here?" he asked.

There was something in the way he said it that set off a little alarm bell in Dov's mind. *Oh wow. This is the guy Peez slept with? Did she do it to cinch his support for her taking over the company? That skanky little—! Naaahhh. That's not her style. Still, I'll bet it didn't hurt her chances of winning him over to her side. And it sure as hell didn't do* her *any harm either.*

Dov applied a liberal coating of Smile #98.2 and said, "Mr. Agparak, I fully understand. You want to consider all your options before making a commitment. I can respect that. But more than that, after what you've told me about your art and its purpose, I really respect you. And I'm not just saying that to kiss up, either. I mean it. Whichever way you throw your influence, it's been an honor to meet you." He released his grip on the sculptor's hand and concluded: "So, would you mind calling me a taxi back to the airport?"

"Sure, no problem." Agparak looked genuinely pleased and flattered by what Dov had had to say. He whipped out a cell phone the size of a pack of bubble gum and put in the call, then said, "It's on the way. Want another cup of coffee while you wait?"

"Sure, thanks. Light and sweet."

"What kind?"

"You're kidding, right? I saw you just have the one can of Maxwell House in your cupboard, you populist rebel, you."

"Right, but I'm talking about the 'light and sweet' part. I'm a lousy host for not asking you before: cream, half-and-half, whole milk, one percent, two, skim, cow's milk, goat's, white sugar, brown, Demerara, granulated, lump, cube, saccharine, aspartame—?"

Dov's scream split Alex Trebek's head wide open.

# ≶ CHAPTER THIRTEEN ≶

"YOU TOLD THE REVEREND EVERYTHING *what?*"
Teddy Tumtum demanded, button eyes fairly bugging
out of his squishy fabric skull.

"I told him that I was thinking about quitting," Peez
replied in a calm voice. "You know: giving up on the
competition for backing, letting the chips fall where they
may as far as who gets to run the company after Mom—
I mean, who gets to run the company next. Why are
you acting like it's such a big deal?"

She had rented a car at the airport and was driving
to the prearranged meeting spot that Sam Turkey Feather
had proposed, deep in the heart of a Tucson shopping
mall. His choice of rendezvous had puzzled Peez, but
only for a little while. She no longer bothered herself
over the possible hidden agendas of everyone she
encountered. If Edwina could have known, she would

have been so proud of her little girl: Peez was finally learning to go with the flow.

Not so Teddy Tumtum. The only flow the little stuffed bear might conceivably go with was a river of blazing lava a mile wide, oozing its way down Mt. What-the-hell?! Peez had taken him out of the carry-on bag and strapped him into the passenger's seat beside her, hoping that the scenery would distract him. He hadn't been civil since the instant she'd told him about all that he'd missed during her visit to the Immersionarium.

"I knew it," the bear said, gazing up at the roof of the rental car as if it were about to split open so that the angels of mercy might reach in and snatch him away, ending his misery. "I knew this would happen if I closed my eyes for one second. I blame myself."

"Stop that; you sound like a stereotypical Jewish grandmother," Peez said gently. "Anyway, you *can't* close your eyes."

"But I *can* take a time-out," Teddy Tumtum argued. "Especially if some people I could mention pack me headfirst all the way at the very bottom of their carry-on bag, where old breath mints go to die, and leave me there, alone, in the dark. Oh, it's no better than you think I deserve, I'm sure. After all, what have I ever done for you? Just given you years and years of unconditional love and support and guidance is all! Helped you, counseled you, kept you from making an idiot of yourself more times than I can count on these threadbare old paws of mine. Look at these pads! Just look at them!" He stuck out his fuzzy arms and gave her an imploring look.

"What's wrong with them?" Peez asked the question even though she knew she'd regret it.

"Wrong? Nothing . . . *if you like rags*! When I was

first confected, these paws were *suede*! Now what are they? Tattered and frayed, worn down to *chiffon*, do you hear me? To *chiffon*! Would it kill you to pick up a needle and thread, give them a stitch here, a stitch there, maybe even appliqué a fresh set of pads onto them? But no. *That* you don't have time for. But for quitting, for giving up, for throwing in the goddam towel, for *that* you've got all the time in the world! For *that* you *make* time!"

Peez sighed. "Right now I'm tempted to ask directions to the Grand Canyon and drive us both over the edge," she said. "That's sure as hell where you're driving *me*. I don't know why you're carrying on like a crazy thing: I *said* I changed my mind. Or did you just stop listening to me at the point where you could start hollering your lint-filled head off for no good reason? Read my lips: I'm *not* going to quit the battle for the company directorship."

"Oh, puh-*lease*." Teddy Tumtum sneered better than a corps of trained sixteen-year-old mall rats. "So you're not quitting. Read my mouth stitches: Biiig deeal. You say you're back in the fight, but as what? A five-star general or some poor moop who got drafted when he wasn't looking?"

"What makes you think I won't give this everything I've got?"

"Don't try to fool me: I can tell. Who knows you, baby? You're still facing the fight of your financial life with that cutthroat baby brother of yours, and you're just gonna phone it in. And why? Because ittoo Peezie-pie went and gots her dewicate iwooshuns awww bwoke. Tsk, tsk, tsk. Po', po' ickle Peezie."

"I got my *what* broke?" Peez asked.

"Your illusions," the bear said, dropping the baby talk.

"So the Reverend Everything's all about show biz, and Ray Rah's gang is all par*tay* and pretending to be young, and Fiorella gave you the brush-off, and Agparak gave you— Okay, so maybe you did get something good out of that visit, but still, you're sniveling around because Edwina's top clients either don't want to know you or you don't want to know them. Why? Because you think they're phonies. So what? The checks don't bounce."

"Teddy Tumtum, it's not just about the money."

"What, do I look like I was stuffed yesterday? It is so too!"

Peez shook her head and fixed her eyes on the road. "There's no talking to you when you're like this," she said. "I give up."

"Yes, you're good at that," said Teddy Tumtum, smugly getting in the last word.

"Mr. Turkey Feather, I presume?" Peez said, extending her hand to the Native American spiritual leader. They had met, as previously arranged, outside The Gap. (To quote Sam, "These days it's the closest we can come to heading someone off at the pass.") "Or do you prefer Turkey Plucker?"

Sam's eyes opened a little wider in pleased surprise. "How did you know that?"

"I like to do my research," Peez replied. "I feel it's a courtesy to the client to know everything you can about him or her."

"Commendable. May I take your bag, Ms. Godz?"

"What bag?" Peez looked to left and right, puzzled. She'd left her carryon safely locked away in the rental car.

"The one with your chief research assistant packed inside," Sam said. "The bear?"

"How do you know about Teddy Tumtum?" Peez blurted.

The Native American laughed. "You're not the only one who does research. If we both make it a point to know as much about the other as possible, we can call it courtesy instead of espionage. And yes, I would prefer if you called me by Turkey Plucker, though if you really want to know what I'd like the most, just call me Sam."

"Only if you call me Peez." The pair of them exchanged smiles that were not in Dov's extensive repertoire.

Soon thereafter they were riding along the highway in Sam's truck. Teddy Tumtum, retrieved from the carry-on bag in the rental car trunk, was pressed against the windshield singing *Ninety-nine Bottles of Beer* at the top of his stockinette lungs.

"*You* were the one who insisted on bringing him," Peez said to Sam. "Happy about it *now*?"

"I can take it," Sam replied, his jaw set in grim determination. "I keep telling myself that after everything else my people have endured at the hands of the White Man, an obnoxious stuffed bear is no biggie."

"Is it working?"

"No. Right now I'm ranking him somewhere between broken treaties and smallpox-infected blankets."

"Hey, I resent that!" Teddy Tumtum interrupted his droning song to voice his objection, then groused: "Damn. Now I lost my place. I'll have to start all over from the beginning. Ninety-nine bottles of beer on the wall, ninety-nine bottles of— YEEE!"

Sam stopped the truck. "You really shouldn't have thrown him out the window, Peez."

"I know." Peez's head drooped in contrition. "But it just felt so *good*!"

It took her the better part of an hour to find the little bear again. After spending that much time out in the midday sun, the initial thrill of pitching him out the window was well and truly gone.

"*There* you are!" Peez panted when she finally laid hands on him once more. The little bear had been sprawled in the shade of a cactus plant. "Why didn't you say something to let me know where to find you? I tried invoking your homing hex, but it didn't work, for some reason." She gave him a suspicious look. "Did you disable it, Teddy Tumtum?"

"Oh, *I'm* sorry." Teddy Tumtum made an art of sarcastic payback. "I was under the impression that you *didn't* want to hear from me ever again. My goodness gracious me, wherever might I have gotten *that* idea? Oooh, could it have been something as trivial as *being flung out the window of a speeding truck*?!"

"Oh, calm down. You're stuffed. You bounce. The fall didn't hurt you."

"Maybe not my body." Teddy Tumtum sniveled and wiped invisible tears from his eyes. " 'Ooo went and bwoke my ickle heart. Bitch."

Peez laughed. "That's my Teddy Tumtum!" She gave him a hug and climbed back into Sam's truck.

"Found him?" Sam asked casually. "Way to go." He started up the truck again and drove on. Throughout the whole search-and-rescue operation, he had remained comfortably ensconced in the air-conditioned cab, letting Peez do all the work of finding the bear. Now it was time for a reckoning.

"Yes, I *found* him," Peez said angrily. "Not thanks to you, might I add."

"None expected. I wasn't the one who threw him out the window."

"Maybe not, but you've got to admit, you shared the benefit of it."

Sam shrugged. "I get a lot of that response from you city folk. First you do something I didn't ask for, maybe even something I never wanted, then you tell me I benefited from it so it's my duty to share the cost. But do you ever ask me if I think the results help me live my life more comfortably, or did they just help *you* advance *your* idea of how you think I'm *supposed* to be living?"

"Wow," said Teddy Tumtum. "That's an awful lot of resentment you're harboring just over tossing a teddy bear out of a truck."

"Friend, I've got resentment I've hardly used," Sam said. "The good news is, I don't think I'll ever bother using it. I've got better things to do."

"Like fleecing the woo-woos and wannabes of their wampum," the bear said. "We read the reports on your operation before we came here. Take one clutch of yuppies, stick 'em in the desert, hand them a rattle, a bottle of designer-label spring water, tell them that their true name is Squatting Iguana or Dances-With-Dot-Coms, and have them sign on the dotted line of any major credit card slip. Ka-*ching*! Money is the— YEEE!"

Peez looked accusingly at Sam. "Okay, this time *you* find him."

Sam pulled the truck over. "Sure you want him found?"

"Yes, I'm sure!"

"Find him, then."

"Hey, *you* were the one who—!"

Sam turned sharply and took Peez by the shoulders. "This isn't about finding that snide little scrap of fake fur. This is about finding something for yourself."

"A vision quest?" Peez smiled. "I don't think so. It's starting to get dark out there. Besides, do I look like a yuppie who wants to get spiritual enlightenment in just eight minutes a day?"

"Making fun of something you don't understand? I expected better of Edwina's daughter." Sam looked stern. "Don't be a fool, Peez. What I do isn't just about making a quick buck off gullible white-eyes. I could do that a lot faster and easier if I stuck to my fetish-bead business or started mass-producing medicine pouches. Do you even know why yuppies—people who've supposedly got everything money can buy—feel that they still need spirituality? After all, you can't take it to the bank, it won't help you get ahead in business, and it won't attract a trophy spouse."

Peez shook her head. "I don't know, but I do wonder. Truth is, when I started this whole journey of mine, it was all about just those kind of things: money, power, self-importance. Now . . ." She bit her lip, unsure of how to go on.

"Now it's different," Sam concluded for her, his voice gentle. "Now it's about something more, isn't it?"

This time she nodded. "I used to think that what E. Godz, Inc. had to offer was just like those mass-produced medicine pouches you mentioned. It was a business, pure and simple. Now that I've gotten out there and seen some of the people involved, I know it's more than that. Even the most showy, splashy, fake-looking ceremony can provide something that people really seem to *need*."

"It's hard these days, living in the cities," Sam said. "Hard to stay in touch with nature, with the changing of the seasons, the great cycles; hard to appreciate something like a harvest festival of thanksgiving when you buy your food in a supermarket. No matter how much we try to ignore the seasons and the cycles and the forces of nature, we're still a part of them. We're children, Peez, and a child who turns away from his mother before he's able to stand on his own isn't going to get very far. That's why so many people are looking to the religions that put them back in touch with the earth. All religions do, in their own way. But some people can't seem to find what they need in the faiths they were taught as children. For them, religious rites became something you did once a week or sometimes only once a year. People change their hairstyles more often than that. The important thing isn't *how* they rediscover their spiritual side, just as long as they *do* it."

"They do it, you help them, and E. Godz, Inc. helps you." Peez looked thoughtful. "I was thinking about stepping out of the competition for company leadership. I was upset by all the hucksterism I saw, but now I know it's only surface glitter. The heart of what we do is sincere. Mother didn't just set up a cash cow; she saw what people needed, and she created the most efficient way to serve that need. I know all that, now. I don't know if I'm the right person to take over the job."

"Maybe that's what you should be searching for," Sam said, leaning across her to open the door on her side of the cab. "While you're looking for the bear."

"Multitasking?" Peez gave him a shy smile and got out of the truck. "Just one thing: If I don't come back by daybreak, check to see if I took a meeting with a rattler, okay?" With that, she trudged off into the desert.

The first streaks of pink, purple and gold were lighting the horizon when she returned, holding Teddy Tumtum.

Her face was transformed with a deep serenity that Sam recognized at once.

"I see you found what you were looking for," he said softly.

Peez got into the cab without a word. Even Teddy Tumtum was silent. Sam started the truck and drove east. As they rolled down the road, he gave her a searching look. "You're all right? Cold? Want coffee? I know a place—"

"The airport, please," Peez said. Her eyes were fixed on something beyond the realm of ordinary sight. "I need to book an earlier flight to New Orleans." She turned to look at him. "It was there, Sam. It was there inside me all along. I just had to find the time and the silence before I could find the answer."

"Care to share it?"

"It's me, Sam. I'm the answer. My brother shouldn't be the head of E. Godz, Inc., but not because we don't get along or because I used to resent him or anything like that. The only reason he shouldn't guide E. Godz, Inc. is because I *should*. I know what the company is really about, and I've seen the best path for it to take." She blushed suddenly and added: "Wow, does that sound egotistical or what?"

"Depends." Sam regarded her with fatherly pride. "Why don't you ask the bear? He's usually got all the answers. Hey, you! Bear! How come you're so quiet all of a sudden? You have a vision, too?"

"No," Teddy Tumtum replied cautiously. "But I think I got a scorpion up my— YEEE!"

"I couldn't help it," Peez said apologetically as Sam stopped the truck for the third time. "I *hate* scorpions."

# ⋟CHAPTER FOURTEEN⋞

NO ONE WAS WAITING AT CHICAGO'S O'Hare Airport to meet Dov. That was annoying. The last he'd heard, he was supposed to be picked up at Baggage by someone named William Montrose who would be easily identifiable because he'd be holding up a sign with Dov's name on it.

There were plenty of people with signs waiting near Baggage, but not one of the signs said DOV GODZ or any variation thereof.

"I don't like the smell of this," Dov muttered down the front of his shirt.

"You should try the smell in here," Ammi replied. "Man, if you can't shower twice a day while you're traveling, would you at least *consider* shaving your chest? I know we've been through this before, but come *on*, man, it's a jungle in here! One where a whole lot of tigers have been wrestling in dead—"

"Shut up." Dov whipped out his cell phone and fired off a ring in the direction of the Temple of Seshat-by-the-Shore. He wrapped an insulating spell around it so that it would cause the phone on the receiving end of the call to ring at the decibel level of a Heavy Metal band. The selfsame spell would also make Dov's summons shoot straight through any call-waiting or call-screening devices like a bullet through butter.

The phone rang once and only once before someone answered. That was usually about all it took.

"Who in the blessed Afterlife *is* this?" a harried male voice boomed.

"Are you Ray Rah?" Dov barked.

"I am. Who are you and what did you do to my phone?"

"Why . . . don't . . . you . . . just . . . *guess?*" Dov said slowly, between gritted teeth. He was feeling more than a little testy and he had no qualms about letting it show.

"Oh!" A gasp of embarrassment filled the phone. Good. Dov wanted his neglectful host to suffer.

"Is that all you can say? I've been standing in this baggage claim area for an *hour,*" he lied.

"But the last we heard from you, your plane wasn't supposed to get in until now."

"Ever hear of someone taking an earlier flight? Or even of a flight getting in early?"

"Yes, but this is Chicago-O'Hare we're talking about and—"

"And even if I *did* come in at my original arrival time, which is *now,* so what? There's *still* no one here to meet me!" Dov was piling it on heavy and enjoying doing it. He had not had a good flight from Seattle. There was bad weather over the Rockies, the first-class cabin ran out of the Pinot Grigio he'd ordered and he'd

had to make do with Chardonnay, and the coffee they'd
served tasted so dreadfully . . . weak. He knew he
shouldn't have felt quite so homicidal over something
as ordinary as coffee, but this was a commonplace,
documented reaction among people who had spent more
than fifteen minutes in Seattle. Medical journals called
it "bean lag."

Perhaps it was unwise of him to take out his irrita-
bility on someone whose support he'd come here to
woo. Dov was aware that his snippy behavior might
alienate the leader of the Chicago group, but the possibility didn't faze him. He placed absolute trust in his
own charisma, sure that no matter how badly he antag-
onized someone, he had the power to convert any foe
into a friend by the judicious application of charm. It
might take a little time to undo this bit of preliminary
damage, but what was time to him? He had plenty to
spare.

Besides, if you made someone feel guilty and then
forgave them, even when they hadn't done anything
so bad in the first place, they became a little less likely
to take you for granted, a lot more likely to jump when
you said "frog." By Dov's calculations, Rah Ray should
be just about ready to offer an intense, humiliating
apology for leaving a top executive from E. Godz, Inc.
stranded at the airport in so barbarous a fashion. He
grinned at the phone and waited for the inevitable
groveling.

It did not come. Instead, to his shock, he heard a
hearty chuckle in his ear. "Oh, *I* see what happened.
I had Billy-hotep down to pick you up, only then we
all decided to do this lovely ceremony and I sent him
out for extra pomegranates. You can't have enough
pomegranates when you're trying to get Isis to pay

attention. You do know how important it is that the rites of Isis be properly performed, don't you, Mr. Godz?"

"Uh . . . I mean, yes; yes, of course I do. What do you take me for, an ignoramus?" Dov tried to lob the guilt back into Ray Rah's court, but the man wasn't even in the game.

"Of course you do! Doesn't everyone? I guess what happened is that I just got a little carried away and double-booked Billy-hotep. I mean, you can't be in two places at once until after you're dead, right? It happens. I'll tell you what: It's too late to send someone for you now. There's so much left to do before the ceremony if we're going to have everything ready in time, and I'm a little shorthanded. This happens whenever I schedule a holy rite for the same day as a Cubs game. Okay, so you nab a cab, get a receipt, and I'll reimburse you for it as soon as you get here. Unless you want to hold onto it yourself as a business expense, for taxes?"

Dov snapped his phone shut without another word and wished it were an old-fashioned desktop model of 1940's vintage. You just couldn't *slam* the receiver of a cell phone in a truly satisfying manner.

All the way to the Temple of Seshat-by-the-Shore, Dov's cabdriver labored under the impression that his fare was one of those oddballs who had to sing along to whatever music was playing in his portable CD player. That was the illusion conjured up by the ARS Dov had invoked to veil his angry conversation with Ammi.

"The nerve of that idiot! The bloody, unmitigated nerve, giving me the brush-off like that!"

"I thought that the only thing that could ever be

unmitigated was gall," the silver amulet remarked. "Gall and your chest hair."

"Does he even know who I *am*? Does he realize where he and his group will *be* when I take over the company?"

"Out in the cold?" Ammi offered helpfully. "Out in left field? Out on their butts? Out of time? Out of luck?"

"Try 'out of patience,' which is what I am with *you*, so don't push it."

"Hey, what's with the bruised ego?" The amulet clicked its nonexistent tongue. "All they did was forget to pick you up at the airport. You upset because no one gave you a big ol' gooey apology? That sort of thing never bothered you before. You'd just shrug it off. If it did bug you, you'd still act like everything was aces, file it away, and drag it out later on, when you could use it at the bargaining table. What's eating you all of a sudden?"

"I don't know, Ammi. I just don't know." He sounded just a little scared. "Maybe—maybe it's all that coffee I've been drinking. It's made me nervous, hypersensitive. You're right: This *isn't* like me."

"Coffee . . ." Ammi gave a deprecating snort. "Never touch the stuff if I can help it. I'm already awake 24/7."

"You lie. You slept through Seattle."

"I was *not* asleep," the amulet responded a trifle huffily. "I was simply taking some downtime to reconfigure my systems."

"What systems? You're an amulet, not a computer! A magically enhanced talisman!"

"Hey, spells need periodic upgrades too! And don't try changing the subject: You're acting weird, even for you. What gives?"

"I told you: *I don't know!*"

Dov's angry shout was loud enough to make the cab-
bie turn around and ask him not to do that again, unless
he really, *really* wanted to scare an honest driver into
making an unscheduled swerve into Lake Michigan.
Chastened, Dov didn't utter another word until they
reached their destination.

After paying the fare and obtaining a receipt for tax
purposes (Ray Rah had gotten that right, at least) Dov
went up to the great front door of the Temple of Seshat-
by-the-Shore and rang the bell. No one answered. He
rang again, longer, with the same lack of result. Only
when he switched to pummeling the wood with his fist
and it swung back under the first blow did he discover
that it had been unlocked, unlatched, and waiting for
a gentle push all along.

"No one at the airport, no one at the door . . ." He
was still muttering his way through a growing list of
grievances as he entered the house. The interior glo-
ries of the quasi-Egyptian temple made as striking an
impression on Dov as they had on his sister, though
in his case, admiration was severely tempered by
resentment.

"Where are they? Playing hide and seek? Stupid Ray
Rah. Stupid pomegranates. Stupid—*whoa!*" While searching for another human soul, Dov had failed to watch
where he was going, tripped over a monumental black
and white cat, and sprawled full length at the feet of
the image of Thoth. "Stupid cat!" he hollered, shaking a fist after the retreating animal.

"*Blasphemy!*"

A shadow fell over Dov. He turned his head and
looked up into the contorted face of a middle-aged
woman. She was swathed in a white gauze sheath, her

bare upper arms encircled by rich bracelets of gold and carnelian, her chest supporting a heavily beaded golden collar studded with turquoise scarabs. It was impossible to tell her original hair or eye color, for she wore a wig and had gotten a little overenthusiastic with green eyeshadow and thick lines of black kohl.

"I remember this movie," Ammi whispered, peeping out of Dov's shirt. "It's *The Revenge of the Mummy's Mary Kay Rep!* I love the part where she rings the doorbell and says, 'Ding-dong! Aten calling.' Get it? *Aten* calling? *Avon* calling? You old enough to remember back when Avon reps used to go around to ladies' houses and—? You know, like in *Edward Scissorhands?* Aw, *c'mon,* I know you're old enough to remember *Edward Scissorhands!*"

"Ammi," Dov whispered. "Shut up." He slapped on one of his most ingratiating smiles and turned up the Flirt-o-Meter to medium-high.

"Well, hel-*lo*, there. I'm sorry, I had to let myself in. I didn't think it would be a prob—"

"What have you done to the holy feline, Behold-all-the-moles-in-the-front-lawn-have-gone-to-Osiris?" The lady was not to be so easily won over.

"I'm afraid I tripped on him." Dov got to his feet slowly. The front of his traveling clothes had picked up an all-encompassing layer of cat hair, but he suppressed his annoyance and renewed his attack. "He's a beautiful animal. How did you ever get him to grow so fa—big and strong?"

The lady scowled. "Behold-all-the-moles-in-the-front-lawn-have-gone-to-Osiris is no mere *animal*. He is the holy creature of the Lady Bast. If I were you, I'd be praying that the goddess's attention was elsewhere when you called her precious one *fat*."

Since charm was scoring 0 for 0, Dov switched tactics to righteous indignation, which lesser souls might often mistake for good old-fashioned bullying. "And if I were you, I'd be praying that this so-called conversation didn't go any farther. Perhaps you don't know who I am? I'm Dov Godz from E. Godz, Inc. Heard of us? If not, have your leader Ray Rah bring you up to speed. E. Godz, Inc. is only the reason that this temple counts as a temple where being a temple counts for something *solid*, namely with the Internal Revenue Service!"

The woman smiled. It was a toothy grimace reminiscent of the sacred crocodiles who had once staffed the Nile-side temples in ancient Egypt and done their part for the ecology by devouring anyone the priests didn't like. The crocodiles became very devout and their descendants often bemoaned the modern world's comparative lack of religious zeal.

"A threat, Mr. Godz? You can't scare me; I have teenagers. You're not the head of E. Godz, Inc. yet, and if that day should come, I doubt you'll throw us to the wolves. We're far too valuable to you as a working subsidiary. You'd never do anything to dam the cash flow."

"You're a cynic, aren't you, Ms.—?"

"Call me Nenufer. And no, I'm not, but I think you must be. It's all about the money with you, isn't it? The money *and* the power. You like pretending to be everyone's best buddy, but only when you're hugging the knowledge that one word from you could turn everything upside down. It gives you a sick little thrill, playing the undercover mastermind. I'll bet you've got a tattoo on your butt that says *If They Only Knew*."

"How would *you* know what I am?" Dov shot back.

"Considering we just met, what, five minutes ago? Wait, let me guess: woman's intuition." He sneered.

"*Middle-aged* woman's intuition," an unruffled Nenufer replied. "It's like a superpower: modified X-ray vision. I can't see through a brick wall, but I've met plenty of your type before so I can certainly see right through *you*."

"Lady, you've got issues."

She laughed at him. "Nice use of a dismissive catchphrase; you'll get extra points for style. Sure, I've got issues. Who doesn't? I notice that you still haven't bothered to *apologize* for what you did to Behold-all-the-moles-in-the-front-lawn—"

"Apologize to whom? To the cat? You think he cares? You think he even *remembers*? He's got a brain the size of a walnut and most of the storage space is taken up with that ridiculous name you gave him!"

"To me," said Nenufer. "For having treated the things that I believe in as if they were all just part of a silly little game, something to keep an aging Baby Boomer busy. My generation gets into *such* mischief when we're not kept busy, don't we? Mischief like standing up for human rights, and speaking up for peace, and pretending the homeless aren't invisible, and seeing that women get treated like human beings, and giving the earth a fighting chance to dig out from under all the trash and sludge and poison that some people believe will just go away if we attend all the right cocktail parties and think happy thoughts."

"Look, lay off me," Dov snapped. "I don't like lectures, but this also happens to be one that I don't need. My mother's part of your precious generation, remember? Believe me, I know everything you've done—and not just the stuff you're proud of! If you want to assume

I look down on your beliefs, go ahead, but that won't make it true. One of the first things my mother did long before she set me up in the Miami office was teach me to respect every one of our clients. That was one lesson I took to heart, starting with respecting *her*. If you think I'm just in this for the money and the power, you might as well say that the same goes for my mother, because everything I know about running E. Godz, Inc. I learned from Edwina Godz herself!"

"Why, thank you, Mr. Godz." Like a brief summer cloudburst, Nenufer's dark scowl blew away as if it had never existed. Her face was transformed from Gorgon to Grace by a warm, affectionate smile. "That's all we were waiting to hear."

She turned on her heel, walked up to the statue of Isis, and clapped her hands four times. There was a great creaking of wood, a groaning of gears, and a squeal of moving parts as the statue of the goddess spread her arms wide. Fountains of blue and green sparks leaped from the gilded palms of her hands and the ceiling began to leak roses.

Before Dov's astonished eyes, the lights dimmed and a citrine glow suffused the great room. He smelled patchouli incense and heard many voices chanting sonorously, but he could not for the life of him figure out where they were coming from. When he looked for Nenufer, to ask her what was going on, he found her gone.

Now the gauze curtain at the far end of the room began to wave as if a small windstorm had darted into the house. With a clash of tinny bells, the fragile cloth was whipped aside and down the steps came Ray Rah, leading a procession of his followers—those who weren't watching the Cubs play, anyway.

They walked slowly, solemnly, in perfect order. Ray Rah himself was dressed to resemble the divine Osiris, ruler of the Afterlife. The thick layer of blue paint covering his face looked itchy—his nose and firmly closed mouth both twitched like mad—but despite his obvious agony he repressed any urge to break character and scratch. Behind him came two women dressed as the goddesses Isis and Nephthys. Musicians followed, playing small harps, drums, and the sistrum's jangling framework of bells. Next came those who carried burning bowls of incense, palm fronds to spread the fragrant smoke throughout the hall, and last of all a magnificently tall, regal woman wearing a gilded mask.

Dov drew in his breath sharply when he saw her painted face. It was Edwina.

Stumbling from the shock, he fell into line at the end of the procession and followed Ray Rah's congregation into a smaller room to one side of the hall of the gods' images. The walls were either stone or painted to look like stone. They were certainly painted to look as if they had been carved with low relief figures, in the style of the ancient Egyptian pharaonic tombs. Dov glanced to left and right and felt his heart begin to beat faster with dread.

The painted walls were covered with pictures of his mother.

As the rest of the procession circled the room, making reverential gestures at each of the pictures, Ray Rah dropped back from his place at the head of the line in order to speak with a trembling Dov.

"Please take your proper place, Mr. Godz," he said. "Ever since Horus first avenged his father Osiris' death, the firstborn son has been the most important participant in rites like these."

"But—but she's not dead yet!" Dov protested. "You're giving her a funeral and she's not dead!" Another, more terrible thought struck him: Could it be that while he was in transit, somewhere a computer had hiccupped and he'd missed out on a truly vital piece of news? "*Is* she?"

Ray Rah raised the ceremonial crook and flail aloft in a warding gesture. "May the gods forbid it! Of course not. We've been in touch with her on a daily basis ever since we heard about her illness."

"Oh." Dov lowered his eyes. *They've been in touch with her every day,* he thought. *And what have I been doing? Nothing. Just looking out for my own interests. I'm one hell of a son.* Suddenly he felt more ashamed of himself than when Sam Turkey Feather had called him on his lack of filial devotion.

"This isn't a funerary rite," Ray Rah went on. "Though I must admit that what attracted me to the ancient Egyptian practices was the emphasis on death. The trouble is, when you're at a cocktail party and someone asks you about your beliefs and you say something like, 'I belong to what's basically a death cult,' that kind of kills the conversation."

Dov couldn't disagree with that. "What is this if it's not a funeral?"

"It's our way of making peace with what must come. As much as we love Edwina, as much as we owe her, we knew that the day would come when we'd have to bid her farewell. That's how it is for all of us, isn't it? But in this country, death is an embarrassment. It's a wonder we can hear ourselves talk over the noise of several million people whistling past the graveyard. We worship youth and beauty not for their own sakes but because we tell ourselves that the young and the beautiful never die. We follow a thousand different health fads because we believe that there's some magic number of granola bars that will let you live forever, but only if you wash them down with the right kind of one hundred percent natural spring water while standing on the Sacred Treadmill. My generation's called the Baby Boomers for a reason: We *act* like babies when it comes to facing the inevitable. If we close our eyes, cover our ears, and hide under the blankets, Death won't be able to find us."

*The inevitable* . . . Dov thought. *My mother is going to die.* He had known it for days, he had been saddened by it, but for the first time he truly *felt* it. Tears stung the corners of his eyes.

"The ancient Egyptians loved life just as much as we do," Ray Rah went on. "They loved all the physical joys and comforts of day-to-day living. That may be why they found a way to take it with them. But our way is not just about being buried in your red Thunderbird convertible: It's about knowing that someday you will *have* to be buried. We who follow the old ways know this, and trust me, knowing that today could be the last day of the rest of your life is *not* as scary as it seems."

"You get used to the idea," Dov said. "Is that it?"

Ray Rah nodded and smiled, cracking his blue face paint. "Exactly."

"And this ritual is to help you get used to the idea that Edwi—that Mom is going to die soon?"

Ray Rah nodded again. "To help us, but mostly to help you. We figured that it was the least we could do for you, since we've already pledged our support to your sister as the future head of E. Godz, Inc."

Dov was surprised that the news of Peez's victory

didn't affect him at all. He was preoccupied by thoughts of a more important loss. "Thank you," he managed to tell Ray Rah. "It's very kind of you. I wish I could stay longer, but— I'm sorry." His usual glibness deserted him.

*My mother is going to die. I'll never see her again, never hear her voice, never even be irritated by the way she treats me like I'm still a baby. My mother is going to—*

He wheeled around and ran out of the Temple of Seshat-by-the-Shore before any of them could see him cry. On the way out, he collided with a young man carrying two heavy shopping bags. Dov knocked him off his feet without a second thought as he ran on, sending forth a taxi-summoning spell like a flare. By the time he reached the street, a cab was waiting.

The young man he'd overrun sat in a puddle of bright red fruit while he watched Dov speed away. The front steps soon crowded with Ray Rah and the rest of the congregation. The young man looked from the departing cab to the mounds of smashed fruit to the group on the stairs and said, "I got the pomegranates. Did I miss anything?"

"Not much, Billy-hotep," said Meritaten. "C'mon in and have a beer."

# ⪢CHAPTER FIFTEEN⪡

"MY DEAR YOUNG WOMAN," Mr. Bones said with a winning smile. "Had I but known how beautiful you were, I would not have been so quick to promise my support to your brother." He raised Peez's hand to his lips and bestowed a delicate kiss.

"You flatter me, Mr. Bones," Peez replied. "But please, don't worry about whatever you've promised or to whom you promised it. I'm disappointed, of course, but it was your choice to make."

The two of them were standing in front of one of several New Orleans restaurants calling itself the Court of the Three Sisters. Peez had found him there by chance, in the course of a thorough search of the Vieux Carré, in much the same way that Dov had encountered the venerable voodoo priest. It was at least as effective a way of finding Mr. Bones as saying "Meet me in front of the Court of the Three Sisters" without specifying which one. There were several. Since every tourist who came to visit New Orleans was told by the folks back home that he or she simply *must* eat at the Court of the Three Sisters, could the local restauranteurs be blamed for trying to accommodate them?

"You are as gracious as you are beautiful," Mr. Bones said. He was wearing his full regalia, though his staff had been redecorated recently. Fresh ribbons had been added, and fresh bones. He glanced up at the restaurant's artfully painted sign. Teddy Tumtum was peering over the lip of Peez's carry-on bag and misinterpreted what was really just a casual action.

"Sheesh! What's it gonna take, someone dropping an anvil on your head?" he hissed at her. "Mark my words, you buy the old guy a decent meal and he'll forget all about any promises he made to your brother!"

Before the bear could add any further tidbits of counsel, Mr. Bones stuck his staff under Teddy Tumtum's fuzzy chin in the manner of Errol Flynn playing sword tricks and lifted the unruly toy out of the bag. Teddy Tumtum described a small midair arc that ended when Mr. Bones caught him in his free hand.

"What *is* it with you people?" Teddy Tumtum complained. "Is this National Bear-Tossing Week or what? If I'm gonna spend this much time in flight, at least give me a bag of peanuts!"

"*Petit ours*, I am not sure I like you," Mr. Bones said, smiling. "I am thinking that if this gracious lady feels the same way, I might offer to trade her my support for your fat little body. Perhaps you will become the first of a new style in voodoo dolls, *hein*?"

Teddy Tumtum let out a squeak of terror so piteous that Peez snatched him out of Mr. Bones' grasp and was already glaring daggers at the man before she realized that he was only joking. Embarrassed, she smiled shyly and said, "As you can see, *monsieur*, I do *not* feel the same way about Teddy Tumtum as you do. He's been with me a long, long time. Believe it or not, I love him."

"Ah, well! If it is *love* then there is certainly no accounting for it. I am willing to believe anything where love is involved."

"Then I hope you'll believe me when I say that even though you've pledged your support to my brother, you and I may still have business."

"Is that so?" Mr. Bones adjusted the angle of his top hat and looked interested. "What manner of business might that be?"

"The business of learning," Peez said.

"Learning? Do I look like a schoolteacher, *ma fille?*" Mr. Bones was enjoying this.

"No, but you do look like a guide."

"A guide, a guide . . ." The old man twiddled his fingers as if his staff were a flute. "And where do you propose I lead you, if I am in truth a guide? Which path do you need to follow? Where do you wish to go?"

Peez tucked Teddy Tumtum into her carryon and said, "Why don't I tell you that *after* lunch?"

In the back room of Au Roi Gris-Gris, Aurore served coffee. She was wearing the outfit she used to please the tourists, though instead of her tignon she had a telephone headset. While she filled the cups and passed Peez a tray of pastries, she carried on a spirited exchange with the person on the other end of the call, most likely a broker. A vocabulary that was pure *Wall Street Journal*ese coupled with fluent *Fortune* magazine rattled from Aurore's lips as she shuffled portfolios without spilling a drop of coffee or a crumb of cake. It was a relief to both Peez and Mr. Bones when she finally left them alone and peace returned.

"Well now," Mr. Bones said. "Now that we are fed and settled, will you tell me what you wish from me?"

Peez sipped her coffee. "I wish to learn about the path you've taken, Mr. Bones," she said. "I know what the company printouts say: You're a voodoo priest. But what does it *mean*?"

"What do you *think* it means?" was Mr. Bones' canny reply.

"You play drums, dance around a fire, and stick pins in dolls to hurt your enemies," Peez said coldly. "Oh wait, no, that's what *you* think *I* think it means. I came to you looking for answers, not a fencing match."

"Really? I thought you came here to court my backing for the takeover of E. Godz, Inc."

"I did, except you told me you've already given that to my brother. Before, that would have annoyed the hell out of me. I'd've brought every trick in the book to bear on you, trying to get you to change your mind. Now I know better. I'm not the only one in this world with freedom of choice. Even when the choice others make doesn't suit my own wishes, I've still got to respect their right to it."

"This all *sounds* very fine," Mr. Bones said, rubbing his chin.

"Oh, she means every word of it." Teddy Tumtum's voice echoed out of the carry-on bag. "Let me tell you, this girl's gone through some changes, and I've got the scorpion eggs in my butt to prove it! If she says that it's cool with her that you're backing Dov, you can believe it."

"Is it so?" Mr. Bones leaned forward in his chair and looked deeply into Peez's eyes. "Yes, yes, I see that it is," he said when at last he sat back again. "You are one who seeks true answers. My faith, my practices, would actually be something real to you, and not just a source of photographs or cheap souvenirs to take home to your friends."

"*What* friends?" Teddy Tumtum put in. Mr. Bones shot an ugly look into the carryon, but Peez just laughed.

"He's right, you know," she said. "I have business acquaintances, but no friends."

"Can you not have both?" Mr. Bones patted her hand. "You have asked me to tell you about what it is I do, the path I have chosen to follow. It is a path that begins deep in the Mother Country, in Africa. Black men stole black men and women in the tribal wars and brought them to the black and brown men from the lands of mosque and minaret. These slave traders in turn took them to the coast, put them into the hands of men who make their prayers in churches. At last, after long days and nights of suffering, these poor stolen souls crossed the ocean to this side of the world and were put up on the auction block for sale. They were stripped of their clothes, of their families, of their freedom, even of their names. What more could be taken from them?" He sagged in his chair, closed his eyes, and wearily said: "Only their gods."

"Oh, come off it!" Teddy Tumtum said, hauling himself to the top of the carry-on bag and holding onto one of the handles. "That's one thing no one can take from you."

"Is that what you think, *petit*?" Mr. Bones' smile was sad. "But you would: You have only fluff for brains. Soft words may make some people turn from one faith to another, but the sword and the whip and the fire work more quickly. When my ancestors came here and tried to hold on to the one thing that had not been ripped from their hands, they were told that worshipping our gods and our ancestors was ignorant, primitive, evil! They were punished for it—for the good of their eternal souls, they were told. That was how they came to learn that *your eternal soul* is only another way of saying *your owner's peace of mind.*"

"The slaveowners were *afraid* of their slaves?" This was news to Teddy Tumtum.

Mr. Bones nodded. "They told themselves that they had done us a great favor by bringing us to this land, feeding us, clothing us according to their ideas of decency. They were sincerely puzzled by our failure to be thankful for all these blessings. Our ingratitude was just one further proof of our savage nature, and no wise man trusts savages who whisper behind his back, keep secrets, perform obscure rites where blood is shed. The whispers may be about him, the secrets may be plots, the spilled blood may shortly be his own!"

"Whoa. Not *too* paranoid, huh?" The bear dropped over the side of the bag and tugged on Peez's skirt until she picked him up and put him in her lap where he could get a better view of Mr. Bones.

"I don't think it's paranoia if they really *are* out to get you," Peez said, absently stroking his fur. A few leftover grains of Arizona desert sand pattered to the floor. "It's just that the owners thought their slaves were out to get them for *no good reason*. They didn't think they'd done anything wrong. Since when is paying a fair price for farm equipment and domestic appliances a crime? That's how they saw it, anyhow."

"So this is different from all those times you thought the toaster was out to kill you because it wouldn't pop up the bread and then when you tried to get it out with a fork it—?"

"Shut up, Teddy Tumtum." Peez hated to be reminded of her losing war with all small kitchen appliances. To Mr. Bones she said: "Please go on."

"There is little more to say. The people wished to hold fast to the one thing that they thought could not be taken from them, the owners did their best to prove them wrong. Any vestiges of the old African ways were seen as sin, blasphemy, treason, danger to those in power. Any attempt the people made to worship as they chose were cruelly suppressed. In time the slaves all became good Christians and the owners sat back, content with a job well done. So many souls pulled out of the darkness of savagery, saved from Hell!" He shook his head. "They never knew."

"Never knew what?" Teddy Tumtum asked.

"Never knew that the old ways still lived on. Never knew that the people still worshipped the gods of their ancestors in the way of their ancestors. How simple it was to trick the slave owners! If you cannot pay homage to a goddess because Master will see and whip you for it, then kneel before the altar of a female saint and Master will leave you be, thinking you are a good little slave. And there were so very many saints from which to choose! So the people learned that they could keep their gods of field and forest, earth and water, iron and air, so long as they found the proper patron saint whose robes could hide them."

Teddy Tumtum whistled without benefit of pucker. "That is sooo *neat*. Stealth saints!"

"Quiet, heathen," Peez said fondly.

"Well, *chère*, have you learned enough?" Mr. Bones asked her. "Are you satisfied?"

"There's more to what you practice than a history lesson, isn't there?" Peez said.

"Oh, you might say that. There are the rites and the spells and the names of all the spirits, good and bad, to be learned. But surely you do not need to know so much?"

"If all I'd wanted was a nodding acquaintance with the path you follow, I'd have bought a guidebook. Mr. Bones, my mother is dying." Her voice caught when she said that. "She's leaving me and I never took the time to learn anything about her when I had the chance. Most of what I know is that creating E. Godz, Inc. wasn't just a moneymaking scheme for her. She cared about the old ways, the faiths with their roots in the earth. She explored them, studied them, became one with them, understood why now, more than ever, they're necessary to us all."

"I cannot give you back your mother's life, *petite*," Mr. Bones said sadly.

"I know. But you *can* give me a start, a way to learn more about the things that matter to her. I have a lot to learn and I think that you'll make a very good teacher. May I stay here just a little longer to study with you?"

"Have you nowhere else to go? When your brother was here, he was in a hurry to be elsewhere. There were many other E. Godz, Inc. subsidiaries he had to visit, to gain their support for when he bid to take over the company. Is that no longer your desire? Do you not wish to give him, as they say, a run for the money?"

A half-smile touched her lips. "I thought I told you, Mr. Bones: It's no longer about the money. It's not about running anywhere. Oh, I still want to take over E. Godz, Inc., but only because I believe I can bring something more to the job than a lot of number-crunching and paper-pushing. Besides, I think I may have seen as many of our subsidiaries as necessary already. Well? May I stay? Will you teach me?"

Mr. Bones stood up and shook his staff to the four quarters of the compass. The bones clicked and clattered loudly. Aurore came bustling back into the room. "Prepare the upper chamber, *ma belle*," he told her. "We will have a guest. No: We will have family."

# ⋛CHAPTER SIXTEEN⋚

THE FULL BEAUTY OF A NEW ENGLAND springtime was upon Salem, Massachusetts, when Dov came driving into town. The purpose of his visit, like Peez's before him, was to seek out the self-proclaimed witch-queen Fiorella and secure her backing for the corporate take-over. Given the number of dues-paying followers she commanded, her approval was key to determining the final outcome of the great brother/sister competition. Securing it should have been a matter of the utmost urgency, but one would never know it by watching Dov in action. Instead of seeking out Fiorella immediately, he headed for his bed-and-breakfast lodgings, telling himself that it would be best to check in before he did anything else.

"Got to get organized," he muttered to himself as he steered the snappy red convertible through the city streets. "Got to get my ducks in a row."

"Now you're into ducks?" Ammi piped up. "Dov, Dov, Dov, you have *got* to start dating women."

Dov paid no mind to the amulet's sally. Ever since leaving Chicago he had been more than usually quiet and self-contained. Normally he viewed all airplane flights as golden opportunities for applied schmoozing. It was like getting an unexpected present: Either his seatmate would turn out to be someone attractive he could court (and, in some cases, seduce), someone with business or social connections he could exploit later on, or someone unbearable on whom he could practice the art of diplomatically telling a creep to bugger off. You could never get too much practice doing that!

This time, on the flight from Chicago to Boston, he had kept himself to himself, burying his nose in a book and behaving as if his seatmate—a highly attractive redhead—were invisible. When her perfume insinuated itself past his first line of defense, he clapped on a sleep mask and forced himself to nap, even though the flight was over too quickly for such a short rest to do anything but leave him logy and cranky.

His original plans had not included staying overnight in Salem, but he thought it would be wise to be in top form when he finally spoke with the witch-queen. For that he needed a base of operations, a way station where he could shake off his travel fatigue while he smartened up his appearance, his mental acuity, and his attitude. Despite the last-minute nature of his lodging quest, he managed to secure a charming suite in one of the better places in town. The innkeeper took real pride in showing off her lovingly decorated home-turned-hostel, particularly the working fireplace in Dov's room.

"You're very lucky that it's not the high tourist season yet," she told him. "We're booked months in advance for that time of year. You wouldn't be able to get a room here for love or money then. I'm not bragging; I'm just giving you fair warning, in case you want to come back some time."

"Maybe I will," said Dov, who knew he would not. As soon as she left, he flopped down on the bed and stared up at the spiderweb-lace canopy. He intended to do no more than stretch his drive-cramped legs, organize his thoughts, unpack his things, and maybe catch a quick shower before giving Fiorella a call to let her know he'd arrived and wanted to see her tomorrow. Then he'd make reservations for lunch at the best place Salem had to offer, give her the time of her little life, pour on the charm along with the champagne, and have her support all wrapped up like a fortune cookie before dessert.

Instead he fell fast asleep.

It was dark by the time he woke up, nine o'clock by the bedside clock. His dreams had not been pleasant ones.

In sleep, he wandered across an endless plain that shifted from sand to scarp to soil underfoot. He was trying to catch up with something or someone that was moving away from him in the distance, but he didn't know what or who it might be, only that it was essential for him to overtake it. There was no sky. The curve of space above his head was filled with masks: the garish pasteboard faces of Mardi Gras, the enameled gold funerary masks of ancient Egypt, the carved wood images of Bear and Raven and Wolf, all these and more. They leered down at Dov as he ran, and they laughed at him. The one that laughed the loudest was a silver mask with the perfect features of a Greek god: Ammi.

He ran faster, trying to escape the faces, and suddenly

found himself climbing a sand dune that had not been there before. The higher he climbed, the steeper it grew, until he was on hands and knees, crawling and clawing and kicking in a desperate attempt to reach the crest. At last he made it to the summit and gazed down at what awaited him on the other side.

*There you are, Dov,* said his sister. She waved at him from the shade of a willow tree. *What took you so long? We've been waiting for you.*

The willow grew beside a brook, the brook threaded its way between grassy green banks and sweet, cool meadows starred with tender flowers. The wasteland was less than a memory. Dov stumbled down into the lovely valley where Peez had spread a picnic on the grass. She was dressed like a refugee from a Jane Austen novel, but that wasn't the oddest thing about her: She was smiling. She was smiling at *him.* As soon as he came within reach she threw her arms around his neck and gave him a sisterly kiss of welcome.

She was actually happy to see him!

*This is definitely a dream,* thought Dov.

The dream-Peez shepherded him over to the picnic blanket and sat him down, putting a glass of iced tea in one of his hands and a plate full of his favorite finger-foods in the other. She began to talk with him about his travels, listening sympathetically to all that he had to say, telling him about her own adventures in return. Her dream-self confirmed that yes, she *had* slept with Martin Agparak and weren't his new-style totem poles the strangest things Dov had ever seen? Then she made a surprisingly naughty pun in which the word "pole" figured prominently (as well as the word "prominent"), setting the two of them off into gales of laughter.

*Wow, I'm actually having a good time talking with my sister,* Dov thought. *This really* must *be a dream!*

As they continued to eat and drink and talk, he noticed something: Peez was growing younger. Before his eyes, the years flowed off her face and body while she chattered on, oblivious. He was frightened, wondering what this meant, what he could do to stop it, whether she would continue growing younger and younger indefinitely until she became toddler, infant, newborn, fetus, embryo, and then vanished altogether. He reached out as if to halt the process and saw that his own hand had grown smaller, softer, a child's hand.

Seeing him reach out to her that way, his sister jumped up happily, grabbed him by the wrist, and hauled him after her, dashing off into the meadow. In the logicless way of dreams, the grassy field transformed itself into an idyllic playground, with slides and swings and seesaws and toys strewn everywhere. The siblings ran like young fawns, spun around until they got dizzy and fell over, climbed everything in sight, played leapfrog and hopscotch and can't-catch-me, hung upside down by their knees from anything that could bear their weight. Peez's fancy dress went inside-out over her head and Dov teased her mercilessly about the color of her underpants. She dropped to the earth and when she stood up again, a water balloon had materialized in her hand. He was soaked to the skin before he could say another word. The two of them fell over laughing again.

*Hello, kids, keeping busy?*

The two of them looked up into Edwina's face. She was smiling down at them from the great height of adulthood. She was not only older than they were, and smarter, and taller, but in the dream she had become a veritable giantess. She bent over and scooped the two of them into the palm of her enormous hand, lifting them high into the sky so fast that Dov's cheeks burned in the rushing wind of their passage. Terrified and exhilarated, Dov and Peez clung to Edwina's fingers the way a drowning man clings to a floating log. The beautiful valley, the trees, the stream, the playground, even the clouds lay far below them. For an instant Dov wondered what would happen if he let go of his mother's hand and tried to fly.

*Don't be stupid*, Edwina said, reading his mind the way all mothers can. *You're much too young to fly. You'll only fall.*

And then: *You don't see your sister trying anything as dumb as that, do you?*

Her words made Dov angry, but he didn't dare let Edwina know that he was mad at her. She might let him drop through her fingers and then where would he be? Instead he glared at Peez.

*Hey! What did* I *do?* Peez implored him.

*Like* you *don't know!* Dov sneered at her, and felt tainted inside for having said that, and for not having the courage to tell Edwina straight out that *she* was the object of his hostility. For some reason, knowing that he'd *never* find the courage to confront his mother, he became even angrier at his sister and decided to make her sorry.

But how?

A glitter of gold caught his eye. Something besides the sun was shining in the sky. He looked up and saw that in Edwina's other hand she held an old-fashioned weighing device, a pair of glittering pans swinging from a balance like the Scales of Justice. The giantess brought the scales level with the hand that held her children and gave them an encouraging look.

*All aboard*, she said. *We might as well get this started.*

*No!* Peez shouted, throwing her arms around Dov. *We won't! You can't make us!*

*Oh, please.* Edwina rolled her eyes over the silly notions of children. *You know very well that I can. Anyhow, what's wrong with a little healthy competition?*

*I wonder if "healthy" is the right word for this?* Dov thought.

*Stop it!* Peez said, hugging her baby brother more closely to her. *Leave us alone! We were having fun before you came along and spoiled it.*

*"Came along"?* The giantess was amused. *You silly nit, can't you see that I've been here all the time? Who do you think gave you this wonderful place without even asking if you deserved it? Who's got the power to take it all away from you in the blink of an eye? You're a very bad little girl, Peez. I don't see your brother behaving like that. He's smiling!*

Dov was puzzled. He knew the giantess was lying: He *wasn't* smiling, and yet . . . maybe he'd better do as she said. He slapped on Smile #1, the simple, sunny basic model on which his entire subsequent repertoire of artificially cheery grimaces was built. Peez saw him do it and looked betrayed.

*Dov is a* good *child. One point for Dov,* said the giantess.

Peez turned angrily on her brother. *Why are you helping* her? she demanded.

Dov tried to explain. Edwina was just so *big*, so *powerful*. She had the unassailable ability to control everything in their lives; didn't Peez see that? Wasn't it better to win her over rather than fight her? They were so small that they'd only lose.

He tried, but he couldn't find the words, so instead

he created Smile #2 and tried to use it to win his sister's understanding. He needed it badly, that and her continued support and protection. She was stronger than he was, and smarter too, and he loved—

*I love* her? *I love* Peez?

Dov was so shocked by this realization that the smile dropped right off his face and over the edge of Edwina's huge hand. Down and down he watched it fall until it struck the ground and shattered. He clapped his hands to where his mouth had been and felt only smooth, featureless skin. A scream rose from the bottom of his soul but could not escape. It echoed inside his head, thudding against the inside of his skull, wildly searching for a way out and finding none.

Through the panic and the pain, he heard his mother's voice: *Just see how good your baby brother is being, how nice and quiet. Quiet equals obedient. Why can't you be more like him? He's not angry all the time; he's* cheerful. *No wonder he has friends and you don't! And you never will until you become exactly like he is.*

Just before his head exploded, he heard Edwina say: *Two points for Dov.*

The idyllic meadow of his dream world vanished. In its place was only a land of swirling mists and shadows. Dov could see nothing, but he could hear the sound of chains creaking and knew they were the ones attached to the titanic set of scales in his mother's hand. They groaned and clanked somewhere out of sight. Though the noise they made was almost deafening, somehow he could still make out a different sound as well, a softer sound, the sound of someone else's footsteps besides his own. He couldn't explain why he knew that they belonged to Peez, but he did. That too was part of the dream's insane logic.

He wished that his eyes were as clever as his ears so that he might catch sight of his sister. She didn't sound as if she were far away. He realized that he missed her, that he wouldn't mind the darkness so much if only he could make his way through it with her beside him. Together they could form a plan, find a way to help one another escape this terrible place, if only—!

But that was impossible. That wasn't playing by the rules of the competition. Edwina wouldn't like that. He didn't dare do anything that Edwina wouldn't like. He walked on alone, and in the metallic complaints of the unseen chains he heard the twin pans of Edwina's golden balances rising and falling as she watched over him and Peez, always adding or subtracting those precious points that she awarded to her children.

*It doesn't really matter*, Dov thought as he slogged his way through the darkness. *Just a little longer and she won't be able to do that to us any more. Soon she'll be dead.*

As soon as he thought them, the words knocked him off his feet. He was sitting in a puddle of slimy, ice-cold water, alone with those words: *Soon she'll be dead.*

*And then . . . what?*

*What will I have left? Playing her game, fighting with my sister because I was too scared to fight with my mother, scoring points off Peez because I thought it was the best way to keep Edwina on my side, that's all my life's become! That's all it is!*

The thought no sooner formed itself than Dov felt the puddle beneath him ooze a little higher until it was a pool, then a pond, then a lake whose bottom and borders spread farther and farther away from him as his head sank beneath the clammy water. He splashed wildly, trying to stay afloat, but could not remember how to swim. The waters rushed into his chest and darkness followed. The giantess had taken her revenge.

And as he sank deeper into the black lake, all he could hear above the sound of the rushing waters was Ammi's persistent, penetrating voice insisting: *You know none of this would've happened if you'd only shaved your chest hair!*

Dov woke up in a wash of sweat almost as cold as the drowning lake of his dreams. He lurched into the bathroom, tearing off his clothes as he went, and threw himself into a hot shower. That made him feel a little better.

He came out of the shower and wiped steam from the mirror with a towel so that he could see his reflection. He looked awful, rumpled and haggard enough to be a shoo-in for the role of Willie Loman in *Death of a Salesman*.

"Work," he said aloud. "I've got to get to work. Salem is the last stop I've got to make. All I need to do is get this Fiorella woman's support and I bet I can swing the rest of the fence-sitters. Then I can go back to Miami and not have to think about Edw— I mean, I'll bet that there's a ton of stuff back in the Miami office that needs my attention. I've been letting things slide too damn much, being on the road like this. Whether or not I get control of the company, I've still got an obligation to the accounts that we handle directly in Miami. I don't care how much is at stake, I am *not* going to let the home team down!"

"Rah, rah, rah," said Ammi, deadpan. "And might I add, boola-boola."

Dov was in no mood for sass. He jerked the amulet's chain so hard that he snapped the clasp, then he flung it out the bathroom door, vaguely hoping it would land on the bed so that he wouldn't have to hunt for it on hands and knees when he wanted to find it again.

He toweled himself off, picked his damp clothes off the bathroom floor, unpacked his things, got dressed and groomed to his own satisfaction, and only then checked on the amulet's whereabouts. He wasn't very surprised when he didn't find it on the bed; he knew his luck. A cursory survey of the bedroom floor likewise produced nothing.

"Come out, come out, wherever you are," he called, trying to put a little interest into his voice. He was too emotionally exhausted by his dreams to work up any enthusiasm for locating the sarcastic bit of jewelry in a hurry.

"Come on, Ammi, give me a hint," he said. "I've decided that I'm going to hunt up Fiorella tonight after all. I know it's almost ten o'clock, but that's not going to be too late to phone a witch-queen. If she says it's okay to come see her, I'm going. I can go with you or without you, your choice. So how about it? Are you in or are you going to sulk and miss all the fun?"

Silence answered him.

"Fine. Be that way. I don't have time for this. Catch you later." He walked out of the bedroom without further ceremony.

Once out on the nighted streets of Salem, he took out his cell phone and called Fiorella's home number. It rang for a long time without answer or answering machine. He was about to give up and go back inside to locate Ammi (and see if the little amulet had an alternate contact number for the witch-queen) when there was a click and a woman's voice, very low and sweet, saying: "Ye Cat and Cauldron, why not drop by for a spell? We now feature special evening hours the better to serve all your arcane needs. This is Fiorella speaking; may I help you?"

Dov introduced himself and secured a very warm invitation to come to the witch-queen's book shop as soon as possible. ("How very fortunate you are, Mr. Godz, that I have a call-forwarding spell put on my home phone. Just as good as a pager and much less annoying.") He found a parking spot right in front of Ye Cat and Cauldron, but didn't attribute it to either luck or magic. After all, the hour was fairly late, tourist season was not yet in full swing, and most of the good folk of Salem were home waiting for Letterman to come on.

A light burned inside the bookshop; several, in fact. Actually, the place was lit up like Christmas at Macy's and the crowds within were almost as thick. As soon as Dov opened the door and stepped inside, he found himself up to his eyebrows in women. They came in as many shapes and colors as that candy gel used to make chewy fish, worms, teddy bears, sharks, spiders, and the whole Noah's ark of tooth-rotting fauna. Tall, short, fat, thin, meek, bold, laughing, grim, their skin, eyes, and hair of every color found in nature or made possible through chemistry, cosmetics, and contact lenses, they surged and swarmed around the bookshelves, wicker shopping baskets on their arms piled high with purchases.

Dov felt his heart begin to beat faster with fear. It wasn't that he was afraid of being trampled or shoved. He certainly wasn't scared of women *per se*. What had him spooked was the way that every single one of the ladies present acted as if he weren't there. Their glances either bounced off him entirely or went right through him, seeing nothing where he stood. The phenomenon wasn't caused by active hostility on their part or even common rudeness. The room pulsed with magical power, more than Dov had ever felt centered in one spot before. They were the source of the power and its victims, for it was the power itself that possessed them and made them unable to recognize that Dov existed.

It was very disconcerting. He didn't know what to do. He thought about calling out Fiorella's name, but stopped short of doing it. What if the power caged within this room had also rendered him inaudible? What if it were only a matter of time before he dissolved clear out of reality and ended up . . . where?

"Mr. Godz?" A shapely green-eyed blonde materialized at Dov's side and took him by the hand. "I'm Fiorella; so pleased to meet you."

He tried to smile at her, but he was still fast in the thrall of unreasoning fear. She gave him a sympathetic look. "Oh dear," she said. "You poor darling, have we really got the power turned on *that* high? I'm so sorry. Come with me; it's better in the storeroom."

Dov allowed himself to be led like a little child on a shopping expedition with Mommy. "You mustn't feel bad," she told him. "This happens a lot on nights when we offer extended hours for shopping."

"Is it a . . . woman's magic thing?" Dov asked, his voice hoarse and fragile.

Fiorella showed her dimples. "Perhaps it is. Most of my female customers spend their worldly days being treated a little better than furniture. The people around them at home or at work or in the social whirl never seem to *see* them unless they absolutely must. Sometimes it's because they aren't pretty enough, or young enough, or wearing the right clothes, or holding down the right sort of job. They're the mothers with small children who get shoved aside by the people who think anything outside of an office isn't *real* work. They're the women who accomplish great things but who only turn visible when someone wants to ask them when they're going to get married and have kids. They're the ladies who wear size 18 dresses who can't get a sales-clerk to notice that they want to buy the lipstick that the size 2 model is wearing. They were once the eleven-year-old girls who wanted to play Spin-the-Particle-Accelerator instead of Spin-the-Bottle. They make most men and some women *nervous*. And do you know what else? They don't *like* being invisible. That's why they come here, seeking magic, trying to learn how to be *seen* again. Meanwhile, as long as there are enough of them banded together in one place, they automatically invoke the power to treat others the way they've been treated themselves. They can't help it."

While she spoke, Fiorella simultaneously conducted Dov through the thick of the females thronging her store, behind the main display counter, and out via a bead-hung doorway. The farther they went from the open-to-the-public part of Ye Cat and Cauldron, the better he felt, so he made no objection when she took him straight through the little parlor where she'd entertained Peez. A door at the far end of the Lilith Lair opened onto a narrow flight of stone steps that went down into the earth. A gust of warm air from below blew over his face and dried the beads of nervous sweat from his brow as he and Fiorella descended, a breeze that smelled of Oriental spices.

The steps ended in a room that was empty except for a wide green velvet divan, a marble-topped table bearing a crystal decanter and two silver goblets, and a pair of wooden chairs so straight-backed and uncomfortable-looking that they would have pleased even the critical eye of a Puritan elder. The walls were covered with *trompe l'oeil* paper printed to resemble the shelves of a well-stocked library.

"I thought you said you were taking me to a storeroom," Dov said, looking around uncertainly.

"This is it." Fiorella reached out and tapped the spine of the book closest to her. Its outline shimmered and an actual book popped out of the wall like toast from a toaster. The witch-queen passed it to Dov so that he could examine its solidity. The blank spot its removal had left in the wallpaper was already refilled by a fresh volume. "A little magic prevents a lot of storage problems, which can be the making or breaking of a small book business," she explained. "Plus it cuts down on the need for reserves against returns."

"Fascinating." Dov riffled through the pages, then handed the book to her again. She put it back in its original site. The replacement volume very agreeably sank into the wall to accommodate its twin's return.

"I was so glad to hear from you tonight," Fiorella said, waving him into one of the wooden chairs. "I've been looking forward to our meeting ever since your sister stopped by."

"How was she?" Dov blurted. The question surprised him. It just wasn't the sort of thing he'd expect himself to say. An inquiry as to whether or not Peez had secured Fiorella's backing for the company takeover, maybe; a query about any deals Peez might have offered the witch-queen so that he might, in turn, better them, perhaps. But a simple question about her health and well-being? A *sincere* one, no less? Astounding.

Because it *was* sincere; Dov couldn't deny that. He

actually cared enough about Peez to ask after her! This
was something new for him. How had it happened?

*And why* shouldn't *it happen?* he thought fiercely,
as though someone had challenged his right to feel con-
cern for her. *She's my* sister, *dammit! We're* family! *Why
the hell* shouldn't *I want to know how she is?*

"Just fine," Fiorella replied, sitting opposite Dov and
filling the goblets. "A trifle disappointed that I couldn't
bring myself to give her my unqualified support, but
otherwise well. You see, I like to hear both sides of
most things before I make up my mind. That's why
I'm so glad that you've finally come to see me. I'd like
to choose between you and your sister for the directorship of E. Godz, Inc., after Edwina—"

Dov burst into tears.

He was still shaking with sobs as he felt Fiorella move
nearer and put her arms around him. She stroked his
hair and whispered soft words of comfort, helped him
to his feet, led him to the green velvet divan and lay
down beside him, cradling him to her. He cried and
cried until all of his tears were gone. Then he closed
his eyes tight, took a deep breath, blew it out force-
fully, and thrust himself out of Fiorella's embrace.

"I am *such* an idiot," he said, sitting on the edge
of the divan with his head in his hands.

"Probably," Fiorella said, being amenable. "But would
you mind specifying what brought on *that* little bout
of personal evaluation?"

"Very funny. I've got a friend you should meet: He's
jewelry, but the two of you would get along fine in
spite of that. The two of you, working together, should
be able to get my ego whittled down to sand-grain size
without breaking a sweat."

"Jewelry doesn't sweat. Do you mean you're a fool

for crying, or for crying in front of me?" The witch-queen remained comfortably stretched out on the divan like a modern day Cleopatra. "Put your mind at ease, Mr. Godz: Men have been allowed to cry in public since the '90s, and not just over football games. Or are you afraid your outburst will make me think less of you as the potential head of E. Godz, Inc.? *Au contraire*, it's a blessing to find a CEO who's got human emotions. Why do you think we call it *sympathetic* magic?"

Dov sat up a little straighter, feeling the old self-confidence trickling back into his bones. "Really?" he asked.

Fiorella nodded. "Considering all the stress you're under, I'd be repulsed if you didn't show a little emotion. Mr. Godz, what I do within the spiritual path I've chosen—what all of us who follow such paths do—is to seek *connection*. If I wanted a leader who was cold and detached from everything except the dictates of his own ego—" She sighed. "Never mind. I hate discussing politics."

"It has been a rough time for me," Dov admitted. "I've spent most of it, ever since I heard about the report from Mother's doctor, trying not to think about what's coming. It all seems so . . . *strange* to me."

"You're not the only one," Fiorella said. "I must say, when I first heard about poor Edwina's condition, I was shocked."

"Of course you were. You and she have been more than business associates, right? When a friend tells you her doctor's only given her a short time to live—"

"Oh, it wasn't that so much as— Well, yes, it *was* that, but what struck me as even more shocking was that Edwina not only went to a common M.D., but that she actually *believed* what he told her. In all the years that I've known your mother, I can count the times she's seen mainstream medicos on the fingers of one hand. Frankly, I think she's only gone to see them *that* many times for tax purposes."

"Tax purposes?" Dov's right eyebrow lifted.

"Tax purposes, insurance purposes, something like that. You know, like when you want to take out a new policy and it calls for a physical? Most insurance companies won't accept forms that are signed by herbalists, no matters how reputable. Edwina just doesn't trust ordinary doctors; says their diagnoses are a crapshoot and they're too closed-minded to accept alternative methods of healing. I'd have thought that if one of them told her she was about to die, she'd laugh in his face and—" Abruptly, the witch-queen stopped talking. She stared at Dov closely. "Mr. Godz?" she inquired apprehensively. "Mr. Godz, is something wrong?"

"No," said Dov, his voice pitched to that soft, scary level that meant he'd had a very telling revelation. "Nothing's wrong at all. In fact, everything you've just told me is so very, very *right* that I was a fool not to notice it before now."

He stood up and bowed his head slightly to the witch-queen. "It's been a pleasure, but I have to go. Now. Will you excuse me? I'll see myself out."

Fiorella swung her legs off the divan and reached out a staying hand, "Wait!" she cried. "At least let me escort you back through the store. All that power—"

"Unnecessary," Dov replied as he stalked out. "Now I'll be able to stand it. Power and I are old friends. You might even say we're family."

# ⋛ CHAPTER SEVENTEEN ⋚

MIDNIGHT IN SALEM, MASSACHUSETTS.

The witching hour found Dov Godz slumped in his rental car in front of Ye Cat and Cauldron engaged in high wizardry of the most puissant order, namely using his palmtop to hack into the records of the M.D. who had supposedly pronounced his mother's death sentence. First he used his own tech skills, enhanced by every drop of magic at his command, to force a passage into Edwina's personal financial records, found evidence of payment rendered for a recent physical examination (for insurance purposes, as he had surmised), and obtained the examining physician's name from that.

Accessing the doctor's records was relatively simple.

Locating a copy of the report that the M.D. had e-mailed to the insurance company was child's play.

Discovering that, in the doctor's professional opinion,

Edwina Godz would live to see ninety, was a kick in the head.

Deciding that maybe Edwina would not live to see ninety more seconds of life if *he* had anything to say about it, was merely the vindictive desire of a moment, cast aside almost as soon as brought to mind. Funny how relief at knowing that his mother wasn't at death's doorstep after all was so quickly replaced by the urge to send her there, special delivery.

Maybe he couldn't kill her, but he sure as hell was going to make her pay for what she'd done to him.

"And Peez, too," he muttered at the glowing screen of his palmtop. "Damn it, Edwina, what the hell were you thinking, putting us through this? Especially Peez. She's always been more concerned about you than I ever was. She gets hurt too much, too easily, and you knew it! Or you should have known it, if you'd paid half a lick of attention to either of us. Why did you do it, Edwina? Nothing good on TV?" He snapped the palmtop shut, started up the car, and drove back to his bed-and-breakfast, thinking dark thoughts all the way.

The front door was locked and deadbolted when he got there. House rules clearly posted in his room indicated that all guests should either plan on being back by midnight or being elsewhere until six the next morning. Dov never was one for conforming to other people's plans. He stroked one fingertip over both locks and they yielded to him soundlessly.

As he climbed the stairs and opened the door to his bedroom he was still immersed in thoughts of vague payback plots to invoke against his mother. He was so distracted that at first he took the scene awaiting him— right in the middle of his bed, no less—for an illusion.

Ammi the amulet, Dov's faithful companion through-out his recent travels, was propped up on a lace-covered throw pillow, its silver eyes fixed on the wavering apparition of a teddy bear that floated in the air just above the headboard. Bear and amulet were in the middle of a very animated conversation:

"So then I says to her, I says, 'Peezie-pie, I jes' wuuvs New Owleenz all to eensy-beansy pieces, yes I does, but oo isn't doing um's job by camping out in this swamp like a brain-dead bullfrog!'" The ghostly bear looked angry and disgusted. "I says, 'You better get cracking, get back in the saddle, back on the road, or else your brother's going to beat you to the punch and steal the company out from under your nose!' And you know what *she* says to that?"

"No," Ammi replied. "But if you've got an ounce of mercy in your stuffing, you'll tell me without resort-ing to that dumbass baby-talk!"

"Hey, it keeps her happy, let's her believe you can hold onto your childhood forever." The bear grinned. "Like Edwina says, play 'em right and children are easy to lead anywhere you want them to go."

"Easy for *her*, maybe." Ammi snorted.

"Preach on," said the bear, in total agreement with the amulet. "I don't know what's been happening, but the more Peez travels, the harder it gets for me to guide her the way I want her to go. I sure could use Edwina's help on this, but whenever I try to get some feedback she says I should stick to giving her my latest surveillance report."

"Tell me about it. I've been giving her the lowdown on what her precious sonny boy's been up to, right on schedule, but when I ask her for maybe a *little* help with getting him to cooperate with some of my plans, she clams up."

"Plans?"

"Two words: chest hair. I've been trying to get him to shave it off for ages."

"That's *barbaric*!" the bear exclaimed, crossing his paws protectively over his own furry chest. "No wonder Edwina wouldn't—"

"Wouldn't what?" Dov asked, his voice dangerously free of all emotion as he stepped into the bedroom.

"Oops. Busted," said the phantom bear. "Tough luck, Ammi. At least my half of the operation's still safe. Ta-ta!" The apparition vanished just as Dov's fist closed over the little amulet.

"All right," Dov told Ammi. "Start talking."

"I don't have any idea what you mean," Ammi replied, trying to act innocent and failing spectacularly.

"Sure you don't. And I won't have any idea how you managed to get flushed down the toilet. Maybe the thought of spending the rest of your unnatural born days with sewage doesn't scare you. Maybe you figure that Edwina will rescue her faithful little spy. Maybe you've got some kind of homing device inside you and maybe you don't, but it all comes down to this: Are you feeling *lucky*, punk?"

"Aaaaiieee!" Ammi shrilled so loudly that it was even odds whether or not he'd wake up everyone in the B&B. "Not that! Anything but that! I'll tell you everything I know, only please, I beg you, I implore you, I cast myself upon your mercy and plead with you: *Stop with the bad Clint Eastwood imitations!* There's only so much that mortal silver can stand!"

Dov scowled. He thought he did a very *good* Clint Eastwood. "Fine," he said, biting off the word short. "Deal. Talk."

"There's not a whole lot for me to say that you don't

already know," Ammi began. "Edwina contacted Teddy Tumtum and me on the q.t., asking us to keep closer tabs on you and Peez than—"

"*Closer* tabs on us?" Dov cut in. "How long *have* you been spying on us?"

"How long has Peez had that blabbermouth bear?"

"Almost forever. But what about me, then? You've been part of my office equipment from the first, but that leaves some pretty big stretches of my life unaccounted for. I expected more thorough work from Edwina when it comes to domestic espionage."

"Then don't sweat it 'cause she didn't let you down. Your sister clings to that bear, so he was the logical place to lodge a listening post. You, on the other hand, haven't got any one thing that's special to you, so Edwina simply scattered dozens of information-gathering devices throughout your life. It would've been too complicated to do that once you hit the road, though, so she tapped me to take charge."

"And you talked your way into my confidence. Very neat, Ammi; very smooth. I ought to flush you for that, at the very least."

"Aw, come on, Dov, you know you don't mean it," the little amulet wheedled. "I admit that it was just a job to me at first, but the longer I traveled with you, the more I got to know you and like you. I know that I'm only a trinket and I'm not supposed to have feelings for anything or anyone, but when it comes to you, I do."

"Nice try. If I made a habit of believing in the impossible, you might have a fighting chance of fooling me some more."

"Hey, I just know what I feel! Don't ask me to explain why or how it happened. I'm *magic*, dammit! I've got enchantment oozing out of my pores! Okay, so I don't *have* pores, but maybe some of the spells Edwina laid on me became such an ingrown part of my essence that they screwed me up bad enough to have feelings, whether I want them or not. I *do* like you, Dov, and I'm honestly sorry about spying on you, but that's the work I was wrought for. And if you think that flushing me down the toilet will make you feel better about the whole thing, then go ahead and flush me with my blessings!"

Dov pursed his lips, thinking over the amulet's impassioned words. At last he said: "Nah. Why bother? You'll just clog up the pipes." He fastened Ammi back around his neck and added: "You can stay, but there's going to be a few conditions."

"Like what?" the amulet asked, suspicious.

"First, you let me slap a truth spell on you; a *destruction-level* truth spell."

"Uhhh." Resting on a tuft of Dov's chest hair, the little amulet vibrated with anxiety. Truth spells were not used to coerce or compel someone to tell the truth. Their actual purpose was to make it very, very *unpleasant* for the person thus bespelled should he choose to lie. Given the power of such enchantments, they required the full cooperation and consent of the recipient, something along the lines of *You knew the job was dangerous when you took it.*

A destruction-level truth spell spoke for itself as far as the consequences of telling a lie while subject to its power. It was, to say the least, a major commitment on the part of the recipient.

Ammi took a deep breath, blew it out, and finally said: "Okay. But put a time limit on it, all right? I don't mind swearing to tell you the truth, the whole truth, and nothing but the truth or else ka*blammo,* but not forever. I can't take the pressure."

"How would seventy-two hours suit you?"

"That's all?" The perfect silver brows drew together. "What's the catch?"

"Nothing. And I don't need a destruction-level truth spell on me to tell you this: Within seventy-two hours, Edwina will have no further use for you or Teddy Tumtum or any other device to spy on me *or* my sister ever again!"

# ⇒ CHAPTER EIGHTEEN ⇐

WHITE CLOUDS BILLOWED OUT in all directions from the open-air patio beneath the awnings of the Café du Monde in New Orleans. Passers-by exchanged nervous glances and sniffed the air, convinced that where there was so much smoke there had to be a fire of Hollywood disaster-movie proportions.

Then they sniffed the air a second time and drooled. Nothing was burning. The only scents on the early morning breeze were of heaping platters of freshly puffed-up beignets and oceans of chicory-laced coffee. Those white clouds weren't smoke; they were sugar.

Under the awning, at a table with a clear view of the sidewalk (under less cloudy conditions) Dov Godz sat at the epicenter of the sugar blast, leaned over, and offered his sister the use of his handkerchief.

"If I'd known you were going to react like *that*, I'd have phoned you," he said. His face, his hands, his

255

hair and the front of his clothes were all covered with a thorough dusting of powdered sugar. It had rolled over him like a tidal wave when he'd told Peez the truth about Edwina's condition and his sister had responded by shouting, *"WHAT?!"* right across the plate of beignets that their waitress was just setting down between them.

Unfortunately, at the time, the waitress was also balancing a tray laden with many more beignet platters, intended for other tables. Peez's unexpected outburst took the poor woman by surprise. She gave a little yelp of dismay and tossed her tray into the air. When it hit the floor, powdered sugar reared up like the stem of a mushroom cloud and spread everywhere. (Thus the appearance of a four-alarm fire at the Café du Monde when it was really only a multiple beignet pileup on the interstate.)

"How did you *expect* me to react?" Peez countered, wiping her face with Dov's handkerchief. She too wore a light dusting of powdered sugar, though nowhere near so much as her brother. "First you show up on my doorstep—"

"You don't have a doorstep."

"All right, on the threshold of my hotel room, then. My first thought was that Mom had died and you wanted to break the news to me gently, in person."

"Which would have been very kind of me to do," Dov remarked. "Even if it wouldn't be the sort of thing you'd expect from me."

"Why wouldn't I?" Peez was genuinely puzzled.

"Well, it's been years and years since we've seen each other. I assumed it was your choice because you, uh, weren't all that fond of my company. Most people don't tend to hold high opinions of the folks they avoid."

"Dov, we've been avoiding *each other*." Peez reached

out to pat her brother's hand. "We've both been stubborn and we've both been stupid. I've finally come to
realize that. I'm not very proud of the person I was.
You want to know what I *really* think of you?"

Dov pulled back just a hair and asked, "Is this going
to hurt?"

"I think you're someone who is more than capable
of kindness." It wasn't a lot, as tributes go, but it was
sincere.

*Just as well,* Dov thought. *If she'd started gushing
over me, I wouldn't have trusted her for a Miami minute.*

"You do?" he said.

"Of course I do! You know, Dov, I remember a lot
more about our childhood than I used to. I've *chosen* to remember it, and about time, too! While I've
been on the road, I've picked up a few new ways
of looking at things. I used to do my best to forget
all your positive traits because that might mean I'd
have to admit that the problems in *my* life weren't
all *your* fault."

"Same here." Dov scratched his head sheepishly. A
miniature white cloud detached itself from his scalp and
rained sweetened dandruff onto his shoulders. "That's
the good thing about having a rival: You've always got
someone to saddle with the blame for just about everything."

Peez nodded. She ran one finger around the rim of
her coffee mug, chasing away tiny drifts of fallen sugar,
and said: "When Mom first set this whole charade in
motion, I wanted to beat you out of the company leadership because I thought we were enemies. Later on,
I wasn't certain if I wanted the job myself, but I didn't
want you to have it because I thought you didn't appreciate what E. Godz, Inc. was really all about. I never

once thought to find you, to see if my assumptions about you were right or wrong."

"Same here twice," Dov said. "Well? Were you as wrong about me as I was about you?"

"Very wrong," she said. "Very wrong and very ashamed. We're family, Dov. Not enemies, not rivals, not strangers: *family*. We've had our differences—all families do—but we've made the mistake of letting them get out of hand."

"We had help," Dov said bitterly, recalling his dream. "Edwina. Maybe things never would have gotten so bad between us if she hadn't been playing games with us all those years."

"She's still playing games, according to what you just told me," Peez said. "Nasty, cruel games: telling us she's going to die soon, setting us up against each other *again*, making us compete for a business empire that she never had any intentions of giving up!"

"Oh, she's going to give it up, all right." Dov smiled while he drank his coffee.

"When? Years from now? Decades? You told me the doctor's report pegged her for dying at ninety, if then."

"How does tomorrow suit you?" Dov asked.

"Dov! You can't mean it."

"Can't mean—? Oh, I don't mean *kill* her. That would be bad corporate PR. What I've got in mind is this: Since she sent us out individually to gather enough support from the E. Godz, Inc. client base for one of us to take over the company after she's gone, we combine that support and use it to take over the company right now."

"Mmm. Tempting, tempting." Peez drummed her fingertips on the powdery white tabletop. "We'll have to plan this out carefully. If she's not sick, she's more than a match for the two of us. She's been in the magic game a whole lot longer than we have, remember."

"Yeah, but she's got one big weakness: She thinks that we're still a pair of snot-nosed little kids who'd never *dream* of challenging Mommy. She may have more experience than us, but we've got surprise on our side."

"Surprise and power." Peez licked her lips, though it was impossible to tell whether she did so because she could almost taste their ultimate victory over Edwina or because she could actually taste more of that blasted, omnipresent confectioner's sugar. "You *do* know how to tap into the client reserves?"

"Ummm . . . maybe?" Dov flashed a smile at his sister, one that did not belong to his professional repertoire. It was the smile he'd always worn back in their earliest days together, a helpless little puppy-dog of a smile that simply said how much he needed his big sister to look out for him when he wasn't sure he had what it took to look out for himself.

Peez smiled back. "You don't have a clue, do you?" she said without malice. "Every person or group with the ability to raise the earth-power is like a storage battery. The tapping spell is like a set of jumper cables. The only difference is you can't invoke it unless you have the implicit consent of the storage battery to divert *its* power to *your* purposes. It's an easy spell; you'll get it on the first try. And then I'll want you to teach me some of yours."

"My pleasure."

"So, who have you got?"

"Got?"

"For batteries. You've been out there in the field same as me, courting the company's most important clients, trying to get them to promise their collective support to you as the potential head of E. Godz, Inc. Anyone who's given you his word has fulfilled the condition of implicit consent that the tapping spell requires. I know you've got Mr. Bones on your side already because he told me so."

"Same way I know that you've got Ray Rah and the Chicago group behind *you*," Dov said. "Who else?"

"Uhhh." Peez mouth twitched just a tad. "No one," she said in a small voice.

"No one?"

"Some of the people I saw wouldn't give me their support, and the others, well, I wasn't so sure that I *wanted* theirs. I never imagined I'd need their power to fight Mom or I wouldn't have been so picky." She shrugged. "Too late for regrets. What about the other groups backing *you*? Besides Mr. Bones, I mean."

"Uhhh."

Peez clapped her hands over her eyes. "Oh, Dov," she groaned.

"Hey, it's not my fault that Sam Turkey Feather wouldn't give me an answer while Mom's still alive! Can you blame him? And that guy out in L.A., the Reverend Everything—"

"Say no more. I felt the same way you did about him, at first, but he's not just a big phony out to skin the suckers."

"He's not?" Dov was reluctant to believe her. "Well, I wish I'd known that while I was out there. I might've swallowed my scruples and given him the hard sell."

"You did what you thought was right," Peez said. "We both did. Isn't it nice to know that even when we weren't getting along, neither one of us hated the other enough to want the company *no matter what*?"

"I guess so. But that still doesn't leave us with a lot of firepower to use on Mom." Dov drained his coffee mug. "What about that guy in Seattle? The sculptor?"

Peez turned so radish-red that the waitress hurried up unbidden with a glass of ice water. Peez took a big gulp, regained her self-control, and said: "He— Martin— He wasn't ready to make a commitment. A *business* commitment. What about Fiorella in Salem? She blew me off, so did she throw her support behind you?"

"To tell you the truth, Sis, we never got around to discussing that. As soon as she made me see what Mom was really up to, I forgot about everything else."

"In other words, we've got *bupkis*, or a reasonable facsimile thereof." Peez sighed, blowing sugar into new patterns on the table and her brother.

"Does this mean we just quit?" Dov asked. "After all she's put us through, we do nothing?"

"What can we do? Tell her we're wise to her and we won't play her little games any more? She'll just laugh and put her mind to creating new games."

Dov shook his head. "No," he said. "I'm not going to give up so easily. Like I said before, we still have one thing on our side that she can't counter. We'll just have to lay plans that rely more on surprise than power."

"Dov, I don't know about this. There's only so much that surprise can do."

Dov clasped Peez's hands firmly. "Peez, what's the worst that can happen? We make our move on Edwina and we fail. What's she going to do to us then? Kill us? I don't think so. Punish us? How? By sending us to our rooms with no supper?"

"She could throw us out of the company."

"Right. And that's the answer to my first question.

Throwing us out of the company is the absolutely worst thing she can do to us. Know what? That's not so bad."

"It's not?" A glimmer of hope showed in Peez's eyes.

"Sis, if *I* say it's not bad, you better listen," Dov said, radiating confidence. "This is your baby brother talking, remember? The kid voted most likely to end up cleaning windshields or running for Congress? Without the company, what kind of a career can I hope for? I could fudge my resumé from here to next January and it *still* wouldn't get me a job bussing tables at McDonald's. If I can risk the wrath of Edwina, you certainly can."

"I don't know." Peez looked away. "I don't exactly have a whole lot of highly marketable job skills either."

"Are you kidding me? You're brilliant, you're beautiful, you were born to organize, and you've got an inborn talent for management that most people would *kill* for!"

His words made her stare at him as if he'd just been dropped out of the belly of an alien mothership. "That's what you think of me?" she asked.

"Every word, good as gold." He crossed his heart with two fingers and held them up in a Boy Scout salute, though the closest he'd ever come to the Scouts was an ill-considered summertime flirtation with khaki shorts. "I saw how you were running the New York office. Granted, I was watching you because I was hoping to catch you screwing up, but I never could. *That's* how good you are." He sounded proud of her.

Peez stood up, leaned across the table, and planted a kiss on Dov's forehead before sitting back down. "Dov, if you can come up with a plan that can surprise Edwina half as much as you just surprised me, I'll be right behind you all the way. Got any ideas?"

"You know I do. But let's go get cleaned up a little first. I think we're starting to attract bees." He pushed his chair away from the table and snapped his fingers to summon the waitress. "Check, please!"

She had just returned with his credit card when Peez's cell phone rang. "Ugh! I thought I had that thing turned off," she said as she answered it. "I hate people who turn a restaurant into the world's biggest phone booth. I'll make this quick. Hello?"

"Hewwo, oo' mean ol' Peezie-pie," a quavery little voice assailed her ear. "Why oo' goes away an' weaves um's Teddy Tumtum all by um's self? What has Peezie-pie's naughty brovver Dov been saying 'bout Teddy Tumtum? Oo' much too smart to beweev all the lies he gonna tell oo'. Lots an' lots an' lots of lies, lies, *lies*! Oo' comin' back soon, 'cause oo' doesn't wanna lose um's onwy fwend inna whole wide world, isn't dat wight? Teddy Tumtum misses his ickle Peezie-pie, yes he does!"

"How *dare* you call me like this?" Peez snapped. "You're a fine one to talk about lies! I told you, it's all over between us. You *used* me! You pretended to love me, you led me to love you, and then you *betrayed* me! Maybe you think you can sweet talk your way back into my heart, play me for a fool again. Ha! I'd like to see you try, if only so I could have the satisfaction of telling you to go to hell all over again! All those years together meant nothing to you. All that time I thought you were devoted to me when you were really *hers*. Well, no more; she can have you. Get off my phone and get out of my life because we are *through*!"

Like her brother before her, Peez regretted that you couldn't slam the receiver of a cell phone, so she did the next best thing, throwing it to the ground and stamping down on it so viciously that it shattered.

Throughout the Café du Monde, every woman and a fair number of the men present broke into spontaneous applause as she stormed out, with Dov hurrying after, trailing little puffs of sugar as they ran.

# ⋛ CHAPTER NINETEEN ⋚

"THE WAY TO A MAN'S HEART is through his stomach, but the way to Mom's heart is through the Internet," said Dov. He hunched over his laptop keyboard, his eyes alight with a zealot's wild devotion. From time to time he moved over to type in a few characters on Peez's laptop, which was set up right next to his own, attached by a tangled maze of wires, all of them glowing with the magic that the siblings had effectively used to double their electronic arsenal.

"How's it coming?" asked Peez from a short distance away. She sounded doubtful and with good cause:

The two of them had discussed potential strategies for hours on end, most of the way from New Orleans to Poughkeepsie, via airport limo and plane and train and taxi. They set aside all thought of using a rental car solely because they did not want the distraction of hands-on driving to eat into precious plotting time. They proposed and disposed and discarded unworkable portions of one scenario only to tack the useful leftovers onto the body of an altogether different scheme. They guzzled obscene amounts of coffee to keep themselves sharp, and the more coffee they drank, the more inspired every aspect of their conspiracy sounded.

But even the most potent of caffeine buzzes has a finite trajectory. By the time they actually set foot within the Poughkeepsie city limits, it was difficult to tell for sure whether their master plan was really as foolproof as it sounded, or if it only seemed foolproof because their brains were starting to turn into piles of played-out espresso grounds. Peez had come down off her mocha-java high just in time to realize this, and it was not the sort of epiphany that gave you confidence in the future.

"It's coming just fine," Dov called back to her. "The link's holding. We may not have as much magical power as she's got, but by taking our magic *plus* the stuff we're pulling in through the tapping spell and slaving the whole thing to our Net access, there won't be a firewall in existence that can keep us out of Edwina's system! It's just going to take a little time."

"You're sure she won't be able to tell we're doing this until we're ready to make our move?"

"Relax, Sis. We are golden. Say she does catch wise that someone's ferreting around in her system, the only way she can intervene is by locating the source. That would be child's play for her: Just slip a tracking spell into the wires. She can't do that to us the way I've got this set up. No wires, no way to trace the connection."

"No wires, no electrical feed for the laptops," Peez said. "I've never tried anything like this before. What happens if we power down in the middle of it?"

"We won't," Dov reassured her. "Not as long as we've got good, solid battery backup. Not as long as you keep feeding our batteries."

"Yeah, but what happens when I run out of peanuts?"

As if to answer her question, a large gray squirrel not six inches away from Peez's feet sat up on its haunches and set off a long stream of loud, chittering complaints. Peez threw him another peanut and thought that this was one hell of a way to harness the earth-power.

It did look somewhat bizarre to the untrained eye. It even looked bizarre by the standards of some of E. Godz, Inc.'s more eccentric (pronounced "woo-woo") clients. Of course anything looks bizarre when it involves squirrels.

A nineteenth-century French painter might have made a pretty picture of the siblings' command center for Operation Bad Mommy, titling it *Le Takeover Hostile Sur l'Herbe*. While Dov delved deeply into Edwina's data-banks, Peez sat on the grass under the outspread branches of a venerable sycamore tree on the campus of Vassar College, a giant economy-sized bag of pea-nuts in her lap. Every so often she tossed a handful to the coterie of about twenty squirrels surrounding her, making sure to keep them from losing interest and scam-pering away. The squirrels' plump bodies pulsed with waves of energy which was being siphoned away along threadlike conduits all leading to Dov's tandem laptops, giving him all the power he needed.

"By the time you run out of peanuts, we'll be done," he told his sister. "Then we'll go pay a little call on Edwina."

"I hope you're right," Peez said. "And I hope the crea-tures will be satisfied with what I gave them. I don't like the way that big bull squirrel's looking at me. I think he might be plotting something. Did we *have* to use squirrels? Even back in New York City, they gave me the creeps. They're always *watching*."

"Squirrels are nature's most compact and efficient gatherers of the earth-power," Dov said, sounding almost as dull as a tenured professor. "Have you ever seen how fast they can move? Pure energy. They press their little bodies right up against tree trunks for better power absorption, and they've perfected the method for extracting the potential energy of a full-grown oak, maple, pine, whatever kind of tree from the seeds, nuts, and acorns they ingest. You call them rodents: I call them fuzzy plutonium! And this place seems to have an infinite supply of the little buggers."

"If you say so," Peez said. She continued to dole out peanuts. The squirrels, much like a gaggle of junior faculty members, put up with any kind of public humiliation if it meant that they got to stick close to a source of free food.

At last Dov hit one final keystroke, slapped both laptops shut simultaneously, flopped over onto his back and triumphantly announced: "Finished!"

"What did you do?" Peez asked.

"Oh, nothing much." He rolled onto his stomach and sat up again. "I just isolated all of her assets, monetary as well as supernatural. She's down to the spare change level on all fronts. She may have more experience than we do when it comes to magic, but a fat lot of good that'll do her when she can't reach the stuff she needs to *power* her spells."

"Like owning a Mercedes but only having enough money to buy a teaspoonful of gas?" Peez liked the idea.

"Bingo." Dov tapped the tip of his nose. He stood

up and offered Peez his hand. "Give the furry-tailed rats the rest of the peanuts and let's go pay a call on dear, *dear* Mamma."

Giggling, Peez tossed the remaining peanuts to the squirrels before allowing Dov to help her up. As they walked off, Dov flipped open his cell phone to call for a taxi. He was so engrossed in the call that he didn't notice the big male squirrel sitting right in his path until he almost trod on him. The two of them exchanged peevish stares.

"Shoo!" Dov commanded. "Scat! Get out of the way!"

"That's him," Peez exclaimed, pointing wildly at the beast. "That's the one that was *looking* at me before! He *wants* something; I can tell."

"What he *wants* is a kick in the rump for bothering my sister," Dov said grimly. "And I'm the guy to give it to him." He drew back his right leg, ready to suit the action to the word.

"How are you feeling, Mr. Godz?" the doctor asked brightly.

"Better. I think." Dov moved cautiously on the examination table, but not cautiously enough. Sharp pains shot all up and down the length of his right side where the squirrel had ducked inside his trousers and run races around Dov's leg before finally scooting out and away.

"You're just lucky that the scratches were superficial and that you didn't get bitten," the doctor went on. "Of course even without a bite there's still the chance of rabies infection if—"

"*Rabies?*" Dov was panic-stricken. "But that's just from bites. That rotten little bastard didn't *bite* me."

"True, but if the squirrel was rabid and some of his

saliva got into your system via those scratches . . . Would you happen to know if that happened?"

"You want me to figure out if the bloody damn squirrel that ran up my pants was *drooling* at the time?"

"Well, failing that knowledge, and since we don't have the squirrel itself to examine, I would suggest that you have the inoculations."

"Shots? You want me to have rabies shots? No. No way. I know all about them and they *hurt!*"

"They don't hurt as much as they used to," the doctor said primly. "But rabies still kills."

"Doctor, let me talk to my brother," Peez said. "I think I can persuade him to take the shots. May we have a moment alone?"

The doctor shrugged. He was busy. "Have them page me when you're ready," he said, leaving the examination room.

"I am *not* having rabies shots!" Dov declared, clutching his leg. It was almost completely swathed in bandages where the doctor had tended to the squirrel scratches. Pulling his pants back on over all that gauze would be an adventure.

"Shush; you don't need them." Peez laid her hand on Dov's leg and closed her eyes. She began to hum and murmur, swaying back and forth gently. Dov felt a warm, pleasant sensation creeping over his leg, as if he were slowly immersing it in a tropical sea. Peez stopped humming and opened her eyes. "It's okay," she said. "The squirrel wasn't rabid."

"How do you know?"

"A little something I picked up in my travels. Part of it's stuff I learned out in Arizona, part's drawn from things Mr. Bones taught me, but it all boils down to being able to read the body so you can heal it.

Your body says it's definitely *not* harboring any rabies virus, the scratches will be gone in a few days, and for the love of heaven, *stop* eating all that damn pastrami."

"Thanks, Sis." Dov got off the examining table and started getting dressed. "We've lost enough time over that blasted squirrel. Let's get out of here, grab a cab to Edwina's and *do* this thing." He stopped wrestling with his trousers when he heard Peez laughing. "And what is so funny?"

"Remember right before that squirrel ran up your pants leg when I said he *wanted* something only I didn't know what?" she said, still snickering. "Well, now I do know what he was after: *bigger nuts*. Bwahahaha!"

Dov made a face. "I think I liked you better when you were a virgin."

The taxi dropped them off outside the gates to Edwina's house. Dov and Peez gazed at the building they hadn't seen in years. After they'd left home, their return trips had gone from compulsory holiday get-togethers bristling with hostility and ill will to grudging individual social calls. In time they'd given up coming at all, except when Edwina sent for them to discuss business matters. Soon even those visits stopped and all such meetings were held via e-mail, fax or phone.

"I never saw the point of coming back here," Dov said. "This never felt like *home*."

"What did?" Peez said.

"Nowhere." He looked at her. "Nowhere so far. Maybe that's going to change, too. Peez, have you ever seen Miami? It's a neat place. I think you'd like it, and I know a lot of people down there who'd help me show you a good time. How about Thanksgiving? Or before that, if you've got the time."

"I'd like that, Dov." Peez smiled. "But if you came up to New York for Thanksgiving we could see the Macy's parade together. My office has a great view of the route. Oh! And you absolutely have to come up for Christmas! Everyone loves the city lights, whether or not they celebrate the holiday. I have a duplex; you can stay with me."

"I'll tell you what: Why don't we take care of Mom first, then we can decide who's bringing the mince pie, okay?"

There was no problem gaining access to the grounds. Dov's explorations in cyberspace revealed that Edwina did not maintain the kind of security system you could buy through normal channels. When you had magic, who needed burglar alarms? Why defend your grounds when all the stuff worth stealing was inside the house?

The house itself was another story. Dov and Peez both sensed the all-enshrouding presence of warding spells. These were set on "Low," intended to be more deterrent than destructive. If a trespasser couldn't take the hint, there would be stronger stuff awaiting him inside.

Dov deferred to Peez, letting his big sister disarm the wards while he called up a counterspell to create the illusion that the wards hadn't been touched at all. Peez cleverly snagged a couple of scraps from the warding spells before discarding the rest. She slipped them over herself and her brother so that they could enter the house undetected. It was like tearing a camouflage tarp off a tank and using it to mask your own presence. The same wards that discouraged intruders by making them feel as though they were trying to penetrate doors and windows snugly clogged with yard-thick layers of rubber cement also had the power to make surveillance spells rebound.

Once thus concealed from view, there was no reason that Dov and Peez had to play ninja. They waltzed right into the house by the front door, their only precaution being to waltz as quietly as possible. Now all they had to do was locate their mother and spring their surprise.

*Where do you think she is?* Dov mouthed silently at Peez.

*What?* She mouthed back.

This time he exaggerated his lip movements: *I said, where do you think she is? In the bedroom?*

*Did you say the bathroom?*

*Right, right! Pretending to be dying.*

Peez nodded. *No harm in trying,* she agreed, starting to climb the staircase to the upper floors.

Dov followed. He had just set foot on the first step when suddenly, as if from nowhere, a small, round, bushy-tailed shape darted out of the shadows and planted itself right in his path. Beady eyes glittered balefully, teeth like tiny chisels clashed together, and Dov found himself staring into the fuzzy face of doom.

He couldn't help it: He screamed.

Peez whirled around just in time to be the first human being on the face of the planet to hear a squirrel laugh.

"There you are, children," said Edwina. A double crash underscored her appearance. She had thrust aside the sleeve doors of the front parlor (the actual parlor, not the one that was her incognito office) with a dramatic gesture like Samson pushing down the pillars of the Philistines' temple. The thick panels flew aside on their well-oiled brass rollers, making a thunderous noise that was quite impressive.

The squirrel bounded down the stairs and scurried up Edwina's skirt, hopped onto her arm, and clambered onto her shoulder. When she reached up to scratch his belly, he closed his eyes in delight and showed the world that squirrels do know how to purr.

"Ah, Mister Nibbles, what would I ever do without you?" Edwina mused aloud. "Good job." Returning her attention to her children, she added: "Come into the parlor, please. We've been waiting for you."

"And *we* have been waiting for *you!*" Dov declaimed, his cheeks still hot with embarrassment. "It's all over, Mom! Your days of deceit are at an end."

"Of course they are, dear," Edwina said placidly, still petting Mister Nibbles. "Shall we have a nice cup of tea to celebrate, now that you've finally arrived? I knew Mister Nibbles would manage to detain you for a time, but I didn't think you'd be *this* late. Either you took your sweet time treating Dov's leg or else my baby boy still runs to the ER over any little scratch." She turned her back on them and ambled into the parlor.

Dov and Peez exchanged a look that was half bewilderment, half apprehension. "I guess we've learned a valuable lesson here," Peez muttered. "Caffeine is no substitute for genius. She knew we were coming. She knew enough to sic a spy squirrel on us and hold us up so she could make tea! She probably stockpiled enough magic from her own batteries to counter any spells we could throw at her before you even accessed her accounts. Not a lot of punch left to a surprise attack once you take the surprise part away."

"Don't be silly, Peez darling," Edwina called from the parlor. "I was *very* surprised. Really, I was. Now come in here before all the scones are gone. I've got your favorite flavor: orange-cranberry."

Reluctantly, suspiciously, Dov and Peez entered the parlor just in time to see Edwina in a tug-of-war over the last orange-cranberry scone with Teddy Tumtum. Mister Nibbles was chittering angrily at the bear, who was seated on the sofa within easy grabbing distance of a large platter of scones, muffins, and assorted tea cakes.

"I might have known," Peez said bitterly, seating herself in a high-backed chair as far from Teddy Tumtum as possible.

"You and me both," said Dov, taking the chair closest to his sister. He had just caught sight of the glint of silver. Peez's treacherous teddy bear was wearing Ammi around his furry neck.

"Give me back that scone, Teddy Tumtum," Edwina said. "It's not as if you're actually able to eat it. You've just been tearing them to pieces and getting the crumbs all over my nice, clean house."

"And my nice, clean head," Ammi added.

"I don't care." The bear was sulky. "This way *she* can't have 'em either."

"Now you're just being needlessly vindictive," Edwina chided him. She let him keep the scone while she filled two teacups from the steaming pot and passed them around. "What next, dare I ask? Tying her shoelaces together? Lighting bags of dog poop on her front steps? Freezing her power assets through the Internet?"

She looked meaningfully at her children.

"You were right, Peez," Dov said.

"Once I found out that the two of you were together at last, I suspected you'd try something. I wasn't sure what, but thanks to some inside information and advice"—Edwina lavished a grateful look on Teddy Tumtum and Ammi—"I was able to narrow down your possible points of attack."

"And you didn't try to stop us?" Peez asked. "You didn't make any . . . withdrawals before Dov secured your system?"

"I suppose I should have, but I was just so fascinated, watching you and your brother at work together, that I lost track of time. Silly me."

"So that means that we—that we still control your magic?" The cup and saucer in Dov's hands were clattering wildly.

"Well of course you do, dear. And I wouldn't have it any other way." Edwina sipped her tea. "I suppose I owe you an apology," she went on. "Or not. I admit that I deceived you, telling you that I was at death's door when in reality I haven't even begun to ask for directions to his house."

"You don't think we deserve an apology for putting us through that?" Peez could hardly believe what she was hearing. Inside she was a turmoil of conflicting emotions which coalesced into the long, piteous *cri de coeur* that escaped her lips: "*Mooommm!* That's not *fay-yerrr!*"

"I didn't want fairness; I wanted results. And I got them." Edwina gazed at her children and smiled. "I also want to retire, travel, visit old friends, make new ones, and enjoy every last day of the rest of my life. I couldn't very well do that when the two of you were still at each other's throats, now, could I? Well, I suppose I *could* have, if I didn't mind watching the business I put together from nothing get torn to pieces before my eyes like—like—" Her gaze wandered the room as if searching for an appropriate image and at last fell on Teddy Tumtum. "—like a common orange-cranberry scone!" she concluded.

"So this was all just a ploy to get us to make

peace?" Dov asked, marveling at his mother's bald-faced effrontery.

"You make that sound like a bad thing," Edwina replied, feeding bits of corn muffin to Mister Nibbles. "But I don't think that's the only thing you got out of your travels, is it?"

The Godz siblings thought this over.

"I can't speak for Dov," Peez said, "but I learned more about who our clients are and what they believe than when they were just a list of names and numbers in the company databank."

"Me, too," Dov said. "I guess it's better for every-one this way, huh? For Peez and me, for the clients, for the company . . ."

"And for me," Edwina concluded. She gave Mister Nibbles the last crumb of corn muffin and stood up. "You may not believe me, but I love both of you more than words can say. You're my children, and I've raised you the best way I knew how. I made mistakes—I have yet to meet a parent who didn't—but I think that by and large you turned out beautifully. You just needed a few finishing touches."

"You may love us as much as you claim," Peez said, "but you love the company more. You said it yourself: The only reason you cared about getting Dov and me to reconcile was so that we didn't destroy your pre-cious E. Godz, Inc. after you were gone."

"Oh, Peez, do you really think that?" Edwina looked genuinely sad. "All this time you've spent learning about the different ways we seek the power of the earth-magic, and you've never once thought about how the earth herself treats her children? Sometimes she's kind, some-times harsh, sometimes she makes all of us cry out that she's unfair, but always, *always* she provides for us and does her best to scatter her gifts with a generous, even hand among all her children. If we can't see that, it's *because* we're children, and children never see things the way their parents do until they become parents themselves." Then she gave her daughter a very suggestive wink and added: "But that's something you'll find out soon enough, my darling."

"Find . . . out . . . soon . . . *what*?" Peez quavered.

"What it's like to be a mother." Edwina chucked Peez under the chin and added: "Close your mouth, dear, you're gaping like a halibut, and there's something highly disturbing about a pregnant halibut."

"Pregnant? Peez! I'm going to be an uncle!" Dov exclaimed. "Cool! Mom, are you sure?"

"When you're in tune with the earth-powers, you become sensitive to lots of things," a complacent Edwina told him. "My intuition is infallible in these matters, and much classier than going tinkle on a chemically treated stick."

"*Mooommm*!" Dov moaned in agonies of mortification.

"But I—but he—but Martin—" Peez sputtered. "For the love of Margaret Sanger, *we only did it once*!"

"I doubt that, dear," Edwina said, stooping to give her daughter a quick kiss on the forehead. "But in any case, once is all it takes. Now I'm going to leave the company to both of you and blow this pop stand as soon as humanly possible, but I promise I'll be back in time to help you with the birthing. You'll want to ask Fiorella for some anti-morning sickness spells right away, and get Mr. Bones to confect a little something to ease the pain of labor—although you might like to try having the Reverend Everything supervise an underwater birthing experience with those cute little dolphins of his. Oh, and we *must* ask the Seshat-by-the-Shore congregation to work up a horoscope for the child, and get Sam Turkey Feather to chant the proper blessings, and we have to invite Martin Agparak, for obvious reasons, and—"

"Don't worry, Sis," Dov said, putting his arm around her while Edwina chattered on. "You'll be a great mother."

"A Great Mother?" Peez echoed. She sighed and sank back in her chair, resigned. "Wait until I tell Wilma."